To Pauline,
- a fellow reader;
hope you enjoy it

Killed By Common Sense

Julia Vryheid

Yours
Julia Vryheid

AmErica House
Baltimore

First printing

ISBN: 1-58851-903-1
PUBLISHED BY AMERICA HOUSE BOOK PUBLISHERS
www.publishamerica.com
Baltimore

Printed in the United States of America

In memory of
James Owen Malcolm

For my parents
Hans and Betty Vryheid

With special thanks to Nathan Malcolm and my writing group Suzanne McElcheran, Yolande Hirdaramani and Peggy Lampotang

Günther (m.) German: from an old Germanic personal name composed of the elements *gund* strife + *heri, hari* army, warrior. According to Germanic legend, as recounted in the *Nibelungenlied*, Günther was the name of a king of Burgundy, brother-in-law of the warrior hero Siegfried. Siegfried obtains the beautiful Brunhild as wife for Günther, but the outcome is tragedy and destruction: Brunhild contrives Siegfried's death; Siegfried's widow, Kriemhild, Günther's sister, takes her revenge by destroying Günther, Brunhild, and all their house. This grisly story was taken up by Richard Wagner and adapted for his opera *Gotterdammerung* (1876).

This name has long been popular in German-speaking countries, in spite of the tragic story with which it is associated. On a more historical level, its currency in the Middle Ages probably owed something to the Blessed Günther (955-1045), a Bavarian monk, who was a cousin of St Stephens of Hungary.

Siegfried (m.) German: from an old Germanic personal name composed of the elements *sige* victory + *frid, fred* peace. This was a relatively common given name in the Middle Ages, but its modern use dates from latter part of the 19th century and reflects the revival of interest in Germanic legend, culminating in Wagner's operatic treatment in his *Ring* cycle.

Chapter 1

Morning, Tuesday, October 7th

Beatrix (Bea) Prancer arrived for work early. Turning on her computer, it beeped and flashed a password prompt. The office was almost silent; the only noise was the breathing whir of the computer fan which sounded much like an air conditioner in a hospital morgue.

Bea looked, with mild irritation, at the tiny square-red message light flashing on her telephone. If the psychometric test for dementia was remembering a password or PIN number, then she would fail the competency exam. She pulled out her address book where under "S" for secrets, she had written the various code words and PIN numbers necessary to function in the faceless world of computers.

After logging in, Bea decided to make coffee before checking her e-mail. To get to the coffee room, she walked down a pale salmon coloured hallway past the owner's office. Fred Waddle had interviewed her three weeks ago and had offered her a job on the spot. He was an effusive portly man with a beard like the bristles of a cheap square paintbrush. Her first impression: a nice man who liked his work and liked talking about it.

She glanced sideways into his office to say good morning as she walked past but instead did a double take. There stretched out under the round oak table; exposed, naked lay Fred. He looked pink. On his outstretched palm lay a stubby Crown Royal bottle. She pulled his door partially shut and scurried back to her cubicle.

“Damn, now what am I going to do. I never did like looking at naked people, especially fat, drunken men. Don't say fat, say chubby, obese, rotund,” Bea muttered to herself. “Maybe that's his exercise suit." No, because she had glimpsed, over his protruding stomach, his dark-brown pubic hair.

A few minutes later, Bea heard the front door open. She knew it was Maggie Nichelton, by the sound of her chunky heels, energetically bouncing down the hallway. Maggie peeked around Bea's cubicle just for a second to smile and to wave good morning. As she continued, down the hallway, she shouted behind her. "Hi, Bea. I need a coffee. Is it made? Isn't Fred in yet? His door is closed. I'm starving."

Five minutes later with a coffee cup in hand, Maggie returned and after sighing a dramatic tired sigh, she said, "Like, Bea. Where is Fred? He doesn't usually shut his door this early, unless he's meeting one of his special clients or if him and Niels want to talk about secret investments. Hey look, my horoscope says - be prepared for a dramatic surprise that could bring you financial security. Yea, right! I'll probably find a quarter on the sidewalk. I'm so tired. Do you think that I should take some vitamin C with echinacea? Maybe I'm getting the flu that can turn into strep throat or even pneumonia. I hope Fred comes in soon with the donuts. I need something or I'll be hypoglycaemic."

Young female lethargism or that genderless disease - morning melancholy always made Bea smile. She knew from experience that it was best to look a touch concerned, tilt her head to the side and nod in faint but not absolute agreement.

Maggie Nichelton was Fred's stepdaughter from a long since dissolved marriage. 'Fred,' Maggie had told Bea, 'has very, very bad taste in women and very, very good taste in employees such as herself, the payroll clerk/receptionist for the agency.' She was responsible for paying approximately one-hundred and fifty temporary office and warehouse workers every week and ensuring that each employer who phoned was handled with care.

Maggie asked again. "Where the h-e-l-l is Fred? I'm hungry."

"I think he's sleeping in the office," Bea looked down at her coffee cup. She turned toward her computer hoping that the girl would drift away.

"Sleeping in his office. I think not. He just, like, loves his beautiful house too, too much. Like, I hear the front door opening. See you later, it's payday and the temps want their mola." Maggie hummed as she clunked back to her desk in the reception area.

The other two employment representatives, Niels Wolfe and Daniella (Danni) Thompson, arrived, at the agency, on the dot of nine o'clock. Immediately, without saying good morning, they headed straight for the coffee. Bea also heard them talking about how unusual it was that the boss' door was closed. Niels had been cordial and helpful since she had started working there. Maybe she should tell him that Fred was zonked out under the table in his office. She wasn't yet comfortable enough to bluntly ask anyone if her new boss was an alcoholic.

Sitting behind the hollow tweed cubicle barrier, Bea could hear the comings and goings in the hallway because her office was halfway between Fred's office and the reception area. Beside her cubicle were two interview rooms and across the hall were Danni's and Niels' offices.

On paydays, the temporary workers popped into the back offices to talk to their respective representatives. If they had been working for the agency for awhile, they helped themselves to the coffee and the goodies that Fred brought in every Tuesday morning. There were usually boxes of donuts or danishes. When he was in a really good mood, two foot long slabs of black forest or carrot cake would appear on the table in the file room.

Being new, Bea had only one visitor, an older clerical worker, Mrs Fundy. She sat with her shoulders hunched forward and whispered at an audibility level louder than a saxophone. "I really need to speak to you, in private, about my last assignment."

“Sure, where were you working?” asked Bea. But before she had closed her mouth, the woman burst out.

“The job is over and it was dreadful. Dreadful! Please I really need a clean two-week assignment. I can't stand these one and two day jobs. Do you know what that crummy company did to me?”

Bea shook her head in the negative. Mrs Fundy responded by lifting her fist into the air. She then pointed her index finger at the ceiling but her purse dropped off her lap onto the floor. Out fell a bottle of spray cleaner, two bars of used-up yellow soap, a soiled tea towel and a damp wash cloth. She continued talking as she picked up her belongings.

“One! They gave me an old chair. Two! They gave me an office, in an old building, covered in ant and cockroach droppings.” Her fist went back up into the air and her middle finger joined the index finger pointed at Bea's nose.

“Three! The office was cold and air conditioned me nicely. Thank you very much. At least it wasn't 30 degrees below zero outside.” Ring finger opened angrily. “Four! I only stayed because it was a two-day assignment but the agency should know that the owner is filthy. He doesn't wash his floors every night. He's too cheap.” Both hands were simultaneously opening and closing expressing distress as she spoke. “I didn't want to let poor Fred and the agency down, so please, please next assignment, find me something clean and decent.”

Bea nodded and said, “Let me see what's available. It sounds like you had a pretty rough time.” She turned to her computer and found Mrs. Fundy a two-week assignment inputting invoices with plumbing contractor. The phone rang just as Bea finished writing up the job order which included location, hours of work, hourly wage and supervisor's name. She handed Mrs. Fundy the slip of paper and spoke into the phone with relief. “Hello.”

"Please, please take this call. Fred still isn't in. Do you think he had a car accident?" asked Maggie, on the other end of the phone.

"No, I'm positive that he didn't have a car accident. Who's on the line?" asked Bea.

"The cops, a Detective Bottleman. He's really pissed off because someone didn't show up for work this morning at exactly nine hundred hours," said Maggie.

"Please tell him that I'll call him back in a few minutes. That'll give me time to find the file." Bea listened to Maggie as she searched the database for the words - *police* and *Bottleman*.

"I already tried to take a message but I'll try again. I'm going to give him your name and tell him you'll call back right away."

After searching the database three time, Bea gave up, she couldn't find a job order for the Metro Police or any police station in the Greater Toronto Area. Fred must have filled the job request on his own without processing it through the system. She called the police station with trepidation for she loathed sounding incompetent. "Sgt. Bottler, hello, this is Bea Prancer. I work with Fred Waddle."

"It is Detective-Sergeant Bottleman, not Bottler. Where's the computer guy? He should have been here at nine o'clock sharp. In one short month the phone company is adding a new area code to the city and we have to have the software tested and loaded this week. Where's Fred?" bellowed the irked policeman.

"I'm sorry. He's in a meeting. Could you please tell me the name of the person you were expecting this morning?" asked Bea.

"The name! Don't you people know `o you were sending over here? Someone called Tom Clarke. Go get Fred out of his meeting. Tell him the police wish to speak to him." The detective's Scottish accent became more pronounced as he tried to control his temper.

"Okay, why don't I do that and call you back," said Bea politely as she twisted and untwisted a lock of her dark auburn hair around and around her finger.

“I don't want you to call back, lassie. I'll hold,” said the irate Detective-Sergeant Kyle Bottleman. His impatience flowed through the phone line like irritation in a lineup at a women’s washroom when the final bell, for curtain call, is rung.

“Fine. Thank you. Let me put you on hold and I'll find him.” Bea didn't push the hold button hard enough so he heard her mutter, “I don't want to get him.”

“Mrs. Prancer, I don’t care what you want, go find him,” boomed the voice as it moved away from her ear.

“Are you still there? Sorry, I thought I'd put you on hold,” stuttered Bea, jabbing the square button again.

She walked to Fred's office door, knocked softly once and called, “Mr. Waddle, telephone.” She knocked again this time harder and increased the volume of her voice. “Fred, the police are on the phone.”

No answer so she slid the door open a crack. He was still laying under the table but now the room smelled like an infirmary. She darted into the room, dropped on her knees and felt the side of his neck with the back of her fingers. Next she placed her cheek a millimetre above his nostrils and her palm on his chest. When she stood up a sharp shriek erupted out of her throat and without looking around she ran back to the telephone in her cubicle.

“Detective Bottleman. He's dead. I know he’s dead. You should come here right away,” said Bea, in what seemed to her a soft controlled voice.

“Mrs. Prancer, tell me who's dead?”

“Fred Waddle is laying under the table in his office. I thought he was drunk. But he's dead. He smells dead. I think you should send someone here right away, please, right away.”

While listening to the detective's instructions, she looked up to see five people crowding around the doorway of her cubicle. Niels listened for a second, then ran to Fred's office. Danni followed him a few moments later. Two temps, who had been walking down the hallway, looked at each other with exaggerated open eyes and faces that said, 'let's get outta here fast.' Curiosity, however, compelled them to take a darting detour to Fred's door to check out the accident site which was closer and more convenient than one seen on a highway.

When Bea hung up, Maggie said, "What happe..."

"Fred died in his office. I'm really sorry, Maggie. The police told me to make sure no one touches anything. I better go do that." She hurried when she heard Niels and Danni standing outside the office arguing about whether or not to cover him up.

"Well, at least shut the door if we have to leave him laying there exposed. It's disrespectful. When did you become such a prick?" Danni asked Niels. Her hands were fists and the veins on the back of her hands were starting to bulge with stress.

Bea interrupted before Niels could answer back. "The police and an ambulance are on the way. Don't touch anything. They said we should wait for them and not go into the room."

Peering over Niels' shoulder, Maggie gasped when she saw her stepfather in his final position. Fred's arms were neatly laid across his chest and his chubby legs were crossed at the ankles. His face was turned toward the window and his eyes stared into the wooden desk. Beside him was the whisky bottle and a wooden-handle serrated knife sprinkled with what looked like icing sugar.

"Danni's right. We have to cover him up. It's very, very disrespectful. Anyway, Bea, how did you know he was really dead? Did you check?" asked Maggie.

"Yes, I checked his pulse and breathing. I'm sorry, Maggie, but he's really gone. The police said we aren't to touch anything, nothing, not even the computers."

"We heard you the first time telling us not to touch anything. Maybe we should go sit in the lobby and wait for them," said Danni.

Suddenly, Maggie shoved everyone aside, scurried into the office, grabbed the rye whisky bottle and threw it like a basketball into the wastepaper basket. The liquor bottle hit the bottom with a metallic clunk vibrating the garbage can. Niels and Bea rushed into the room, each grasping one of Maggie's arms. She looked at them in disgust. “I'm not five years old, you know. I just didn't want anyone thinking he was a drunk when he wasn't.”

Pulling the door halfway closed behind her, she started to weep and ran down the hallway presumably to the ladies' room. Danni turned on the heels of her pumps and marched back to her office. Niels looked at Bea and said, “Well, too bad the liquor bottle is empty or else we could have had a drink. Let's go sit in the lobby and wait for the cops or better yet you go and I'll bring us a couple of hot coffees.”

“Yea, thanks, that would be great. Maybe I'll go answer the phones at the front. They must be ringing off the hook. It will give me something to do before the police come,” said Bea.

“So you didn't realize he was dead when you first arrived this morning?” asked Niels.

“I don't know. I just shut the door. The room didn't smell like death, either. Now it reminds me of the morgue.”

“A morgue. You've been to a morgue? Really,” said Niels, in response to Bea's nodding head. “Anyway, didn't you notice the knife?”

“The knife. No, I don't remember the knife until I took his pulse. I thought he was drunk.” Bea started to laugh but instead tears flowed. Niels patted her on the shoulder, turned to leave and muttered the word, coffee.

A few minutes later, the ambulance attendants rushed down the hallway. They checked the body for less than a second then they stood on guard outside the death room.

>>>>>

“The recently deceased obviously do not receive a quick response from the police,” said Bea, looking at her watch. She and Maggie were sitting in the lobby drinking their second cup of coffee when two large men, neither attired in traditional blue, walked in the agency’s front doors.

“Is one of you, Bea Prancer?” asked the older one. He was dressed in grey trousers, Spiderman tie and a burgundy shirt with a corduroy black blazer.

Bea jumped up from the couch, and said, “That's me.”

“I'm Detective-Sergeant Kyle Bottleman. You were speaking to me on the phone. Why don’t you show me where Fred is and Detective Sanderson will speak to the rest of the staff.” Bea followed Kyle down the hallway. If she had stood on her tiptoes, she would have seen dark freckles scattered on the shiny spot shaped like a full moon on the top of the detective's head. The partially bald head rested on a thick neck, broad shoulders and a six-foot tall body.

He stood aside to let Bea pass in front of him.

“In here,” she said. “I saw him laying on the floor about 8:20 this morning but I shut the door. I didn't see the knife earlier either.”

“Did anyone else enter the room?” asked Kyle.

“No, only me when I checked to see if he was breathing and someone moved the liquor bottle after I phoned you.”

“Let me get this straight, stop me if I am wrong, Mrs Prancer. When you came to work this morning, the door was open and the deceased was laying under the table. You didn't see that knife.” The detective pointed to the utility knife. “Take a look. Was he laying in the same position? I know it's hard for you but take another good look.”

Bea looked around the room, shut her eyes to concentrate and an image came to her. “He's not laying in the same position. His arms were outstretched when I first saw him. The room didn't smell as if someone had just died. He looked kind of pink and he was holding a rye whisky bottle."

"I don't see a rye bottle. Where is the bottle?" asked Kyle.

"In the garbage can. One of the staff thought it was undignified for him to be seen holding a liquor bottle. That's the only thing she touched."

"Who is the *she*, who discarded the bottle into the trash?"

"She was his stepdaughter, Maggie, and she's upset. She did it on the spur of the moment because she didn't want anyone to think her stepdad was an alcoholic," explained Bea.

"Fine, spare me the justification, now we know who put their fingerprints on the bottle after the deceased died. You have to expect the police to ask questions, Mrs. Prancer. It's our job. It's what the public pays us to do." Kyle looked into the garbage can at the cracked bottle of Crown Royal DeLuxe Whisky. He turned back toward her, frowning and asked. "Was his chest moving at all or did he make a noise when you first saw him or let me put it another way? It may seem like I'm asking the same question but tell me again. Why did you think he was sleeping it off?"

"I don't know. He looked unconscious when I walked by. I remember thinking he looked flushed all over, like his whole body was blushing. Maybe if he was alive, I could have saved him. I just ignored him and assumed he was drunk," said Bea, transfixed by the scene in the room.

"One more question and then I'll let you go. "Have you ever seen a corpse before?"

"Yes, I have," she said.

Nodding to himself, Kyle, with a light touch, grasped Bea's elbow and guided her out of the way so the scene-of-the-crime technicians could start measuring, fingerprinting, photocopying and gathering trace evidence.

“That's all for now. You can go back to your office. I’ll tell Detective Sanderson where you are. We will have many more questions for you later,” said Kyle, dismissing Bea with a firm but fatherly pat. It was really a push on the shoulder to move her out and away from the busy crime scene.

>>>>>

Evening, Tuesday

Thoughts can't kill people. Wishing doesn't make it happen. Maggie had never wished Fred dead so she knew she had not killed him but someone may have wished and made it come true.

She talked to the ceiling, “I hope it wasn't my mother.” Her Mom had always wished her ex-husbands off the face of the earth.

Totally gross! The police had made Maggie look at his body and the knife. She lay on her bed sighing wishing someone could hear her angst. Last week Fred had brought a carrot cake and Maggie had cut it, washed the knife and put it in the file cabinet drawer next to the coffee machine. Now the knife might have Fred's blood on it.

Heaving sobs rolled through her vibrating grief into the duvet and down into the metal coils of the mattress. Fred was the only person who had ever been nice to her when she was a kid. Maggie rolled onto her back and rubbed her stomach. Fred had treated her like a real daughter, not an inconvenience or unwanted expense.

About seven years after Fred divorced her mother, Maggie had moved to Toronto at age seventeen. She had been working at McDonald’s, living in a rooming house, trying hard to be an adult by not involving herself with the neighbourhood street kids when just before her eighteenth birthday, Maggie had seen Fred walking into the downtown Hudson Bay at Yonge and Bloor. He'd been a little chubbier and had walked with the rolling gait of one who has short legs and a substantial stomach. Pretending to be a secret agent she had followed him around the department store watching from behind racks of clothes as he tried on winter coats and looked at shirts. She had wondered, would he remember her or despise her? She had idolized him when she was six years old, hated him when she was nine and had forgotten about him during her teen years.

Fred had turned around a couple of time sensing an unknown presence. On the down escalator, he'd looked behind him and seen her at the top of the moving stairs. It had taken him a few seconds to age the child's face he remembered into the adolescent one staring down at him.

"Maggie Nichelton, my girl, is that you?" he had asked, smiling and squinting his eyes at her.

"Yes, it's me," she'd said, walking down the moving stairs. At the bottom of the stairs, he had enveloped her in a hug. His fox fur coat had made her feel like she was being hugged by a live teddy bear.

"I thought someone was watching me. What are you doing here? Shopping. Is your Mom in town too?" Maggie had grimaced and made a long face. Fred had laughed and asked. "What does that look mean? Mom hasn't changed but I love her all the same."

For lunch, they went to Hemingways on Cumberland Ave. The restaurant had been quiet but eclectic; the atmosphere relaxed and Maggie had looked around, with admiration, at the bookcases filled with used books. On the wall were pictures of the great writer and his Canadian friends, plus photos of Australian and New Zealand beaches and two large blackboards listing forty kinds of beers.

He had ordered them white wine, chicken wings, chips and salad. As they sat eating, she had poured her heart out to him. She didn't mean to; it just happened. Fred had said when he had an entry-level opening at his agency, she could come to work for him.

Two weeks after they met, Fred came to the hamburger joint with a written job offer. That was five years ago. Since that time she had gradually taken on more responsibility at the agency. Fred had deducted eighty dollars from her bi-weekly pay cheque which he invested. Last year, with him co-signing, she'd bought a one bedroom condominium near the Islington subway station.

And, now someone had killed him. She hated, despised, whoever did it. She wanted them to boil in blood. She wanted them to fall on a sword, be mauled by a cougar and be eaten by maggots. Who was going to look after her now? No one. She could look after herself.

The police had given her that look, the suspicious, contemptuous kind of look they reserved for hookers and druggies from the grungiest part of town. So! She liked to wear black grunge clothes. Her ebony hair was streaked with washable vivid colours, but she worked hard and she was never late. Only when the subway broke down in the winter. What did the police know?

"I hate everyone!" Maggie yelled at the ceiling. "Well, not everyone. I still like my friends and my Mom when she's not bitching about everything or feeling sorry for herself. And I like everyone at the agency, especially the new lady, Bea."

>>>>>

Bea was in rapid thinking mode and she talked back to her thoughts. "That policeman, Kyle Bottleman, talked to me like I was a dodo brain and so I was, but just for a few second."

Dead bodies, those she had seen before at funeral homes and in the hospital morgue. Too many corpses, her husband, John, her parents, and her father-in-law. Four years, one per year until this year.

She was sure, by the way the younger detective had looked at her, that he had recognized her. He was one of the uniformed policemen who had knocked on her door on August 24th, at 12:48 a.m. She had opened the door, looked into his eyes and known something terrible had happened. But like a well-trained seal, she had politely waved them into the living room and offered them coffee or tea.

'Are you Mrs. John Prancer?' he had asked too calmly, carefully enunciating each word. She had nodded.

'We have bad news. Your husband was in a car accident. Hum, I'm sorry to have to tell you this. He's in the morgue at Sunnybrook Hospital.'

'No!' She had said no, over and over again and told them to please check their facts. When her daughter, Samantha had come home, she had believed them right away. In retrospect, the police had only been in the house a few minutes before the sad truth had sunk in.

The police patiently asked her. 'Could she come and confirm the identity of her husband's body?'

'Yes,' Bea had replied. Silence, that's what she remembered the silence in the police car. Not a word had been spoken on the way to the hospital. She had wanted to take her car but there was no family car to take. It was totalled.

She had sat worrying about getting home because the bus service to Sunnybrook Hospital is and was terrible. In the police car, Bea had kept thinking over and over again. How was she going to get home? How was she going to get home? She would have to walk, in the dark, across the hospital's massive, dangerous parking lot to Bayview Ave. There she would have to stand, in the cold, waiting for hours for a bus.

At the morgue, a kind and knowledgable attendant had taken over. Bea had looked at her husband's still face and nodded her head. Next she had been guided to a side room where the attendant had asked her questions. Questions to help her make necessary decisions. Decisions based on lists of funeral homes close to her house or near the cemetery where her parents were buried.

Today she had explained to everyone what usually happens to the body after someone dies. Detective Sanderson had looked right into her eyes as if to say - better you then me this time, lady.

Once again Bea added up the people who had passed away, departed this earth, gone to a better place, gone to heaven which she believed existed or to hell which she didn't believe existed. Think positively. Who was alive? Her daughter, Samantha; her opinionated mother-in-law, Nora; her sister, Gail and her two sons. Samantha would one day have children and I, thought Bea, will make an excellent grandma. Probably, better than I was a mother.

Just before nodding off, Bea observed to herself. I found a dead body twelve hours ago and because I didn't know the man, it's not stressing me out. Maybe.

>>>>>

Niels Wolfe sat on the couch, tapping his foot, clicking from channel to channel and reading a magazine. He was a slim man of average height about five feet, nine inches tall and his appearance, like his personality, was contradictory. Blue-black hair, naturally glossy like the haunch of a brushed stallion, was drawn back into a braid that he kept hidden inside the collar of his Armani shirt. His face, inherited from his Dutch mother, was round like waxed cheese, with high cheekbones and almond-shaped eyes. From his father, a Blackfoot, Niels had inherited sensuous lips and a flat nose. When he smiled, it was with perfect strong white teeth that made his face instantly likable.

He didn't look at his fiancee, Debbie, when she brought him a glass of white wine. Each time she started to open her mouth, he said sh., sh., shush and pretended to listen intently to the idiot box. During the commercials, she would make a grab for the converter, mute the TV and try to continue their conversation.

"So, Fred was under the table in his birthday suit. The police came and then what happened? Niels, don't be so obtuse. Tell me what happened!"

He was ready to explode at her, scream profanities so he stood up, and said with restraint, "I'm going to the corner store, alone."

As he walked, he talked to himself in an angry whisper. The dark empty street listened to him like the forest listens to a tree falling. "The second those cops started to talk to me, their tone changed. They were so, so nice to Bea and Danni because they're nice middle-class, nice middle-income, nice pale middle-aged ladies in office clothes. The cops asked those two if they would like a cup of coffee and apologized when they explained that the police had to ask a few questions in private.

"When they called Maggie to be questioned, the empathy was turned way down but not completely off. They gave up questioning her pretty fast because she's such a cry baby. They probably never understood a weepy word she said. Bet that irritated the bastards.

"When it came time to question me; all I got was a - `Hey, you. You're next.' They just pointed to the only uncomfortable hard wooden chair in the interview room. I asked Bea afterward where she had sat and she said the couch. What about Danni? She got the couch. Now Maggie was assigned the hard wooden chair too. Well, I guess the cops just can't help it. They are conditioned, brainwashed to stereotype. What was I supposed to say in the middle of the interrogation? Me rich half Injun treat me like middle-class white man. What should Maggie have said? Me not trash, treat me like middle-class white woman.

"The questions were ridiculous. Where was I last night and early this morning? Where the hell do they think I was? In bed with Debbie. Could she confirm your presence? I better warn her that the cops will probably ask her what position we did it in. I'll tell her to say the missionary position with one foot out the window for ventilation.

"Was I here on an employment program? An employment program! Had I ever done time? So I answered. I didn't know what they meant. Did they ask anyone else those questions? No, I checked."

Niels mentally fumed around the block three time. He saw a police car and had to will himself not to run. On the last walk around, he muttered about his mother. Shit, he better phone her just in case she sees something on the effing ten o'clock news. Mom would tell Aggie, the one sister who still lived at home, and she would tell the next sister and the next sister would tell the last sister and then all five sisters would be on the phone pestering him. He was the last surviving male of the Wolfe family until his sisters' had kids.

He walked into the door and looked at Debbie's expectant face just waiting to hear the dirt. Death and scandal are a fascination for many especially his family. His mother even bought the *National Enquirer*, every Wednesday, when she went grocery shopping. Debbie helped him off with his coat and he started talking the moment their eyes met.

"The cops questioned all of us. Starting with Bea because she found the body. Well, she found the body about an hour before she told anyone but she thought Fred was drunk and sleeping it off under the table."

"Who's Bea? Is she a temp?" asked Debbie.

"No. She's the new employment representative. Fred hired her when she came in looking for a temporary job. He was such a soft touch but she's pretty good at dealing with the clients and temps. She knows her Employment Acts like the back of your hand because she worked for a provincial human resources branch. And she's a widow." With a touch of sarcasm he emphasized the word `widow'.

"Niels, what does that mean? Was Fred attracted to her?"

"Maybe, but he was attracted to anything in skirts over the age of thirty. Fred once told me he only dated women over thirty-five because they could think for themselves and he didn't have to drive them home after nookie. Nookie that is what he called it. Just like a twelve-year old. He loved his nookie. He would say; I love my nookie because it is better than a cookie. I'm going to miss him."

Niels emitted a sigh when Debbie started to massage his upper back. Her fingers moved up and down over his neck and shoulders muscles. Next she pressed the palm of her hand in small circles moving up the side of his head to the temples. She stroked his pale brown forehead and asked. "Then what happened, honey?"

"The cops questioned poor Maggie. You know what a flaky chick she is. They asked her about his next-of-kin. The only thing she knew was that Fred's parents are dead. He might have ten brothers and six sisters but no one knows. Maggie is the closest thing to family he had. She cried and cried and looked scared and guilty. The cops asked everyone where they were last night and this morning. I hope Maggie remembers whose bed she was in last night.

"Niels, come on. Didn't you sow a few wild oats before you settled down with me? You're not usually this miserable. Maggie's always nice to me when I phone."

"Yea, you're right, honey, Maggie's okay. God, only knows what she's going to say to the pigs. I better go into the office early. Set the alarm clock for five a.m. Someone has to look after the agency's and our investments."

>>>>>

First I would make him rub tree sap or honey all over his disgusting torso. Next I would force him to roll around in fresh faeces-filled kitty litter. Then I would stick his head in a bottle of bleach and shove his stinking body through a glass window. He would fall twenty-nine stories tumbling down onto Highway 401 to be run over by a shiny red Mack truck. His body parts smashed, smeared and scattered across eight lanes of traffic.

Danni Thompson always had half-awake daydreams whenever she was stressed. She let the revenge fantasy play out before she rolled out of bed and ritualistically said, “I'm getting pretty good at keeping the day dreams succinct because hatred does not pay the mortgage.”

What a mess at work today. She had to protect herself from it. The drive home had disappeared from her memory, she only remembered arriving and looking at her car keys lying on the coffee table.

Her co-workers didn't help, especially Maggie who never shut up and who knows what she said to the police. After explaining how the interview process would work, the detective had sent all the staff back to their respective offices to await his beck and call. Questions, questions, questions. The police were fools and their questions had been nonsensical.

“What is your name?” The older detective with the expressive blue eyes and the Scottish accent had asked.

“Daniella Thompson.”

“Do you have a middle name?”

“Linda.”

“Where were you born?”

“Montreal.”

“How long have you been with the Common Sense Employment Agency?”

“Just over six years.”

"When was the last time you saw, the deceased, Frederick Waddle?"

"This morning. I looked at him, in his office, with the rest of the staff. He was laying under the table. You already know that."

"Alive, Ms Thompson, when did you last see him alive?"

"I don't know, yesterday evening."

"What time?"

"6:30ish.

And on and on and on it went. Intrusive questions.

In retrospect, she had been an excellent witness, back straight, ankles crossed, calm, honest demeanour. She answered each question formally and, as her mother had always said, actions speak louder than words. She had conducted herself like a lady. When they asked about relationships between Fred and his staff, she had replied that she did not gossip.

>>>>>

Detective Alex Sanderson plopped his feet on the coffee table and took a satisfying slurp of rum and coke. She was gorgeous. Four years ago, she had been sad and gorgeous. Now Beatrix Prancer was his witness and still gorgeous.

By far the worst task that a policeman has to do is to tell a parent that their child has died. The second worst task is to tell someone that their spouse has died. He hadn't told her the whole truth and nothing but the truth, so help me God. What would it have accomplished? He had told Bea that her husband had died in a single vehicle accident. The car had smashed into a square cement post in the highway meridian. He still remembered wanting to put his arms around her, kiss her and make it all go away.

What he didn't tell her was that when the ambulance approached to take John Prancer's body away, the female passenger had walked up to him and asked. "Who will tell his wife?"

"Are you a friend of hers?" Alex had asked with a touch of relief in his voice. "Would you prefer to tell her? It's always easier if a friend or relative is there."

The woman, who had walked away uninjured from the accident, shook her head back and forth. "No, no, that's not what I meant," she replied, in a quavering voice. "Please don't tell her. Please don't tell his wife that I was in the car. It was an accident, it would have happened whether I was here or not. John took a drink after taking his blood pressure medication." She had stopped talking when a car pulled up beside them.

A young man, in his late teens, had opened the window and called out to her, "Hi, Mom, are you okay?"

Sloppy police work. Alex had never gone back to interview the woman. He had quickly typed up the report and left it on his desk. The next week he had been promoted to Detective so he had decided not to pass the file onto his replacement because John Prancer's blood alcohol level count had been just a smidgen above the legal limit of .08 milligrams of alcohol to blood and he had a bad heart.

Alex spread out with a drink in one hand, one leg on the couch and the other on the coffee table. Outloud, he said, "Bea, Beatrix, what an old-fashioned name, a memorial divine name. A name belonging to Tuscany and a fine red wine matching the colour of her hair. Dante's pure princess."

Bullshit, talk about a classic case of denial. Strange that she waited for over an hour before figuring out that Fred Waddle was dead. A cadaver was a cadaver. It smelled, it didn't move, its cavities overflowed. He must have been alive at 8:15 a.m. when she quietly shut the door, hoping that the problem would go away.

Ignore and everything will be fine. Beautiful Bea is probably just a classical ostrich with her head stuck in the sand.

Chapter 2

Wednesday, October 8th

The next morning, at the agency, the staff exchanged dejected good mornings; their routine forever altered. Maggie didn't bounce in talking a mile-a-minute and Danni and Niels didn't bet a cappuccino on who would fill the first job order because Fred wasn't there with the donuts.

"All I know is that each of us better be able to prove where we were early yesterday morning and the night before," said Niels, squinting his eyes, nodding his head and waving his index finger up and down in the air like the caricature of a lecturing professor.

"We're not suspects, you idiot," said Danni frostily, "because we don't even know how he died. He may not have been murdered. He could have had a heart attack while eating a donut, then the knife fell out of his hand, then some nutcase snuck into the office and stole his clothes after he died. Fred always left the front door unlocked after he came in the morning. Any Tom, Dick or Harry could have marched in here. Strangers are always wandering around the agency. That's what I told the police."

"Listen to what it says in *The Toronto Star*. The article quotes Detective-Sergeant Bottleman, as saying; *We are treating the case as a suspicious death. Until the results of the post-mortem are known, we have no comments*." Niels continued talking like a tabloid newscaster. "How could a perfect stranger know that the file cabinet, next to the mini-fridge, in the third drawer, contained the office's party supplies including the handy-dandy utility knife. This knife was found next to the body of the late and dearly loved Frederick Waddle. Don't say I didn't warn you: TO BE PREPARED. The police will be back this morning. What are you going to say when the police ask you about his personal life?" Sucking his breath in, he continued in an exaggerated domineering voice. “And tell me, MIZZ Thompson? Tell me. Tell me now! What was your relationship with your beloved boss? Was it really platonic?”

“Shut up, Niels. Just shut up. You're such a jerk, grow up. Don't you ever get sick of being sarcastic. This is serious and everyone is upset. Just shut up,” retorted Danni, slamming her fist onto the table and spilling her coffee over the newspaper. Streaky black water, stained with ink, rolled off the paper onto the table top and dribbled down the side onto the carpeted floor.

“That's enough,” said Bea, in mother mode, as she wiped the table with paper napkins. “Why don't we discuss work? We haven't cancelled any interviews so maybe we should try to have as normal a day as possible. Temps will be coming in, clients will be phoning and interviews and testing are scheduled.”

Maggie looked at Niels, her eyes narrowed and she said, “You, bastard, you should apologize to us, especially to Danni. And, like, I think, a maniac must have sneaked down the hallway and killed Fred. There are real psychos out there and maybe the agency hired one of them. The police have a list of everyone who came to the agency yesterday. I gave it to them. Maybe he died of a heart attack and maybe he took his own clothes off to help him breathe.”

“So where did his clothes go? Anyway, I'm sorry, Danni. I didn't mean to bug you. I'm just stressed. I hate the cops. We should check out our offices because the police were here all night and who knows what they did. There was fingerprint powder around my office door. Is there still a pucky yellow ribbon across Fred's office door?” asked Niels, talking fast in an apologetic tone.

“Invasion of privacy, that's what it is. A drawer in my desk was ajar so they must have searched them last night too,” said Danni.

“Yea, for sure,” said Maggie. “I gave them duplicate keys for the whole place and all the computer passwords. I knew everyone's password, except Bea's, because you all gave them to me when you went on vacation."

Danni and Niels looked at each other and took off.

>>>>>

Bea was at the front desk reviewing the day's typing test schedule, with Maggie, when the two detectives returned. A beam of sunlight moved across the floor and quickly faded as the door closed behind the two men. "Good morning ladies. Maggie, could we talk to you for a few minutes?" asked Detective-Sergeant Kyle Bottleman.

"Sorry, can't leave the phone," said Maggie.

"I'm sure Mrs. Prancer will be happy to answer the phones for you," said Kyle. Bea nodded her assent.

Maggie followed them to Fred's office where they removed the yellow plastic ribbon from across the doorway. She stood reluctantly just outside the doorway, and asked. "Can we please talk out here? I don't want to go into Uncle Fred's office yet."

"We would appreciate it if you would help us go through his papers," said Kyle.

She looked suspiciously at him. "Yesterday, you talked to me like I was a criminal. I didn't kill him. I loved him. Now, you, like, want my help."

"It's our job to ask questions so we can find out the truth. Now we need your help going through your stepdad's things," replied Kyle.

Maggie puffed up her cheeks with air, exhaled and bravely walked into the room. She started to gag when she looked around at the desk, bookcase and table so she ran and tried to open a window but it was sealed tight as a plumber's weld. The only way to open the thermopane window was to take it out of the frame. She turned to the two detectives and stated, “I hate this building, none of the windows open, it's sick, it makes me sick and I'm going to be sick.” With that statement she sat down and burst into tears.

The two detectives simultaneously rolled their eyes upward and Alex said, “Why don't I find someone to stay in the room with you? I'll get that guy, Nellie.”

“His name is **not** Nellie, it's Niels Wolfe. You should at least pretend, like, you're not prejudiced against him,” sniffled Maggie.

Alex walked down the hallway. He glanced sideways at the painting, stopping briefly to admire the James-Jacque-Joseph Tissot prints of serene Victorian women painted in rich yellows, blacks and greens. He wondered who had chosen them. Alex's favourite Tissot painting was the one of the slender lady, dressed in a layered flowing black coat trimmed with black feathers, set against a background of blowing yellow and gold leaves floating and falling around her. Tucked under her arm was a tattered pale-blue cloth-covered book. The original painting was in the Musée des beaux-arts de Montréal where Alex had bought the print. Once home it stayed rolled up in the hall closet waiting to be framed.

He stood outside Niels Wolfe's partially closed door and listened to him interviewing a woman for a secretarial position. It sounded like the interview had just started because Niels could be heard asking how long had she been at her last position.

As Alex sauntered down the hallway he pondered what Maggie had said. The girl was right. These sealed buildings, where no windows could open, were sick, full of reconditioned air, recirculating bacteria like the phlegm, from the cough, of a man with full-blown tuberculosis sitting on the subway. He looked into the next office to see if Daniella was free. She was talking on the phone so he motioned to her that he needed to talk. She nodded her head and turned her back to him.

After standing outside her door for a minute, Alex shrugged his shoulders and gravitated towards Bea's voice in the reception area. He stood examining her until she had hung up the phone and looked up to see him standing next to the desk, then he asked. "Mrs. Prancer, Maggie is upset, do you think you can help us in Mr. Waddle's office? Is there an answering machine or something?"

"Sure, first let me see if Danni is free. Yesterday was pay day and today is invoice day so we receive tons of phone calls. Clients want to discuss bills, continue or cancel contracts and temps want to discuss their pay or confirm the hours on their timesheet," said Bea.

As she followed behind the detective; his neck blushed soft red. She wondered if he was embarrassed about something or if he was nervous when someone followed close behind him. Perhaps he thought she would jump onto his back and stab him or worse yet tackle his legs and throw him on the ground to kiss him just like in kindergarten. Now, maybe, the poor girl or boy child would be charged with assault, be forced to attend anger management classes and have imbedded in a shaded area of his file, probably in capital letters the words - *possible anti-social sexual tendencies*.

Like a woman on a mission, Maggie rushed past them as they entered the office where twenty-four hours ago Fred had been found under the table. Kyle Bottleman was sitting at the desk wiping the fingerprint dust off the files he was lifting out of the desk drawer. "So, lassie, do you think you can help us. Miss Nichelton rushed away to find someone who knows the deceased's lawyer. Alex , here, needs assistance with the files."

>>>>>

Alex and Bea were alone in the office reading through file after file. No mention had been made of the fact that a body had lain where their feet rested. He had explained to her that every item, in the office, had to be documented by content and location. She could not do the documentation but he would appreciate her explaining what and how information was used. She wasn't to worry about touching anything because every scrap of paper had been photocopied the previous night.

He admired Bea's dark auburn hair when she was reading and her head was tilted forward. There were strands of silvery grey wandering amongst the thick locks. While he showed her papers, made lists and asked questions; she explained how a private employment agency worked. When his head was down writing, Bea also contemplated his strands of mousy hair tapered to a square on a strong neck.

Two hours later they looked up to see Maggie standing in the doorway with her arm around the shoulders of a solid woman dressed in a black sweater, black skirt, black hose and sturdy black walking shoes.

"Look who I brought over," said Maggie, "Josie!" The two people looked at her in bewilderment.

"Josie, what can we do for you?" inquired Alex.

"Do for you!" Maggie put in, answering the question in Josie's stead. "She's the cleaning lady extraordinaire. She's the best and the nicest. Today is her cleaning day at Fred's house so I went to get her and to look for Tony's last name and phone number. Remember you asked me for the name of Uncle Fred's lawyer. It's Anthony Eco."

"It wasn't me who asked you to find out the name of Fred's ..."

Maggie interrupted Alex. "Oh, yea. It wasn't you, it was the other older policeman with the cool Sean Connery accent. I knew that Josie cleaned for Tony too and that she would be at Fred's today if she didn't know that he had gone, passed away." Maggie started to sniffle so Josie patted her back and put her arms around the girl's shoulders.

"This lady was at Fred's house cleaning? You're not joking, are you? You mean she was cleaning his house this morning," said Alex. He shook his head in disbelief.

"Maggie knows. I clean Fred's house every Wednesday morning and other office afternoon. Then Maggie tell me to come clean office today. So sad he pass over. When you finish meeting I come back. You finish. I clean offices. Come, Maggie, we go for coffee," said Josie, grasping Maggie's hand in hers.

"Hold it right there. Just a minute! Didn't you see the notice the police tacked on the front and back doors of Mr. Waddle's house stating that no one is to enter the house without contacting the police first?" Alex asked out of principle, knowing the answer in advance.

"Josie can't read English. Were the instructions on yellow paper? She left them with Fred's mail on the kitchen table. I saw them there," answered Maggie for Josie. "Can Josie clean while you talk to us? This room smells."

"No, Josie cannot clean here or at Fred's place until we say so. Is that clear? She can stay with you if that makes you feel better but that is the only thing she can do. So you found the name and number for your stepfather's lawyer."

"Yea, I already told you. His first name is Tony and his last name is Eco. Somebody has to talk to him about the temps' payroll. They'll need their cheques next week. Like, who's going to tell the bank that he died? And, who's going to pay us? Can Fred's lawyer pay us?"

"Can I please have Mr Eco's number? I'll give him a call right now. You can talk to him the minute I'm finished," said Alex, ushering the three women out of the office and closing the door behind him with a bit of a bang.

"Jerkface," she said to the closed door, then turned to Josie and Bea. "Come on, let's go have coffee. I'll make it while we're waiting for the dumb detective to get off the phone so I can talk to Tony. I don't know what I'm going to say to him."

"Maggie, I suggest you ask Mr. Eco about Fred's will and ask who the executor is. That person usually knows what the deceased wanted in the way of funeral arrangements," said Bea.

"Oh, gross. A funeral. Do I have to? I hate this stuff. He wasn't supposed to die. Tombstones and graveyards, yuk. But, he should have a nice one with lots of flowers." Maggie's eyes glistened and started to overflow.

Bea put her arm around Maggie's shoulder and suggested, "Let's let the detective call the lawyer and then we'll talk to him together. Maybe you can help with the funeral. Think of it as something you can do for him. It's the final and only something a person can do for another person. While we wait, I'll help you make a list of questions for the lawyer."

>>>>>

Tony Eco came to the office in the afternoon to speak to the staff. He was a wavy silver-haired fiftyish man, who walked and spoke confidently giving off vibes that said. Don't worry, I'm here. I am confident, moral and reasonable. The stress level decreased and the atmosphere lightened. Someone was going to tell them what to do.

Maggie looked at Tony, in disbelief. She said, "I'm his main beneficiary, no way man."

"Yes, dear, he left his business assets and his house to you. I'm not sure what that includes but probably his house on Walmer Park Avenue, the agency and this building. His remaining personal estate is to be divided amongst his stepchildren. His wishes are, I mean, were quite clear. As far as I know, he did not have any living relatives so I would, as his executor, appreciate your kind assistance,

Maggie, in planning the funeral. Ten thousand dollars have been left, on deposit, with me for that purpose."

"Everyone wants my *kind assistance today.* Why, so much money? No way, I mean, yes. I'll help with the funeral. It's the least I can do."

"Thank you. You'll find that funeral arrangement can be quite expensive," said Tony Eco opening his arms and elegant hands like a minister inviting the congregation to stand for a hymn.

She looked at him in admiration, and asked, "Who should we invite? The other stepchildren. How many are there?"

"Four or five. Well, Fred may have had a wife or two that I didn't divorce him from, but that is unlikely because I've been his lawyer for over thirty years."

Chapter 3

Afternoon, Thursday, October 9th

Bea didn't quite know how she had been volunteered to help Maggie make the funeral arrangements but somehow the staff had voted her into the position that morning. Thinking back she realized that Niels and Danni may not act like the best of friends but they had worked together long enough, to communicate well enough, to finesse her into offering to help arrange a funeral for a man she had only known for three weeks. Yup, her co-workers had conned her, big time.

First, Maggie had come back from the lawyer's with a list of names and phone numbers of the ex-wives and the confirmation that the estate would pay travel expenses. Then she had laid her head on the table, emitted a despondent moan, and had said, `I don't know what to do. I told Tony I would arrange the funeral and he even suggested that I could have a party in Fred's memory. He said to call Jerrett Funeral Chapel. That's where his body is right now. It's totally gross. Can you please help me?'

Niels had patted her on her head with one hand and whipped out an electronic device with the other hand. He pressed a few buttons and the device beeped. Looking at it, he had shaken his head in dismay. "Look at this, I'm booked solid today."

Then he had passed the gadget to Daniella who had glanced at it, and said, "Wow, are you ever busy. How boring, you have interviews all day. Here let me check my calendar." She had bounced up and came back, a minute later, with her desk calender. "I have someone every twenty minutes and lunch with a client at noon. How's your time, Bea?"

"I'll have to look," she had replied.

As she had started to stand up, Niels said, “Yesterday, you were telling us that your husband had passed away a few years ago. I'm sorry. Did you have to arrange the funeral?”

“Yes. I did. It was almost five years ago. It's a lot of work.”

“Maggie, I have a brilliant idea. Why don't Danni and I take Bea's interviews and job orders for today and she can help you arrange the funeral?” asked Niels.

“I don't mind,” said Danni. “We can split the commission or Maggie, you're the boss. You could double the commission so we both get paid.”

“Sure, you could pay Bea's commission out of the fund Fred left for the funeral. Just call it consulting fees. I'll prepare an invoice for you to submit to the estate,” Niels had said, with a satisfied smile.

Later Bea remembered seeing a detailed handwritten calendar on his desk. The electronic gadget he'd whipped out had probably been a video game.

>>>>>

Bea and Maggie started to make the arrangements for the funeral. They had planned to hold it on Friday but changed the date to Saturday, when they realized that only six or seven people would attend on a work day. Discussing the menu, type of coffin, denomination of the minister, whether to have the service at a church or funeral home or at the cemetery chapel evoked memories of other funerals Bea had organized and attended.

At the funeral home after they had finished choosing a display coffin and urn, Bea sat in an alcove room waiting for Maggie to pay the bill. The room was small and warm so Bea found herself nodding off. To wake up she pulled out her note pad. Her pencil doodled a baby duck, a dead chicken, a car, a lion and a giraffe. After a few minute, she scribbled over the stick figures and started a picture list.

She wrote, in order of appearance, the names of the people that she had met at the agency. Beside each name she drew a picture.

Mrs. Fundy was a donut with a rag pulled through the hole because Bea remembered seeing her, sitting on a subway bench, eating a donut while, at the same time, wiping the arms of the bench with a folded dish cloth.

Maggie was drawn, as a hippie in daisy print bell bottoms and a striped shirt, laying under a tree. Danni was a simple stick person with a triangular skirt and no breasts. Fred, of course, was the dead chicken. Niels, he was hard to draw. No image of him came to Bea's mind. So she moved onto Josie, the cleaning lady, and depicted her as a Greek pillar of stone.

The two detectives were each a shoe, one a right shoe and the other a left shoe. The right shoe was scruffy and plaid, while the left shoe was ordinary and shaded grey.

Bea stared at the list. It was bothering her that she couldn't think of a picture for Niels. What was he? Finally, she drew a cyclops, with a happy face.

A few minutes later Maggie came back. The moment the door shut behind her and her foot touched the sidewalk, she burst out, “That guy was so cute, Bea, I think he was hitting on me but yuk, he touches corpses every day and maybe he’s that nice to everyone or else he's used to dealing with old people most of the time and was so happy to talk to me because I'm, like, under thirty and not wrinkled. It was so *weird* but look at the list; almost everything is done. The cremation, the urn, the cemetery plot and the announcement will be in two newspapers tomorrow morning. So far it's cost $6,362.45. We're going to order the flowers next, right? Then food for the party? I'm going to spend the whole ten thousand dollars. Wow!”

>>>>

At the police station the two detectives were reviewing the information they had compiled. When another report was thrown into Kyle's in-tray, Alex picked it up.

"It's icing sugar. That's what the white powder is that they found on the knife and on the bookcase. He must have eaten some kind of pastry just before his demise," he said, reading another scene-of-the-crime report that had just been delivered warm from the printer.

"Donuts. That's right. Hand me the sheets from Tuesday's interviews. Look. Each and every person mentioned it. Fred Waddle usually brought in boxes of donuts, muffins or cakes on Tuesday morning, payday, and he usually left them in the coffee room also known as the file room," said Kyle.

"He wasn't a miser from everything we've heard. So, where did the bags or boxes of Tuesday morning goodies go?"

"Good question. Let's find out his favourite donut shop or bakery. How long did the coroner's office say they were going to be?"

"A week, maybe two weeks," said Alex.

"Bloody hell, they're slow. No way, let me get on the phone and tell those scientific buggers to hurry up. For all we know he keeled over of a heart attack from eating too much cake and cookies. Maybe his trousers cannae do up and his shirt buttons popped off so he stripped them off," said Kyle, expanding his round stomach till one of the shirt buttons almost popped open. His face became serious. "No joking aside, we will continue to treat the case as a suspicious death."

Chapter 4

Morning, Saturday, October 11th

October was temperamental, it couldn't decide whether to be sunny and breezy, grey and gloomy, or tepid and foggy. By early afternoon, the weather became comfortable, just right for standing outdoors at a funeral, because the sun lazily moved between clouds in unison with the wind which disappeared, on a moment's notice, just to swing upwards to hurry a slow cloud.

Although she hadn't attended the church service, Bea wanted to go to the internment at Prospect Cemetery. Her late husband, John, was buried in section nine of the same cemetery so she made a quick detour to visit his marker.

"Hi, dear," she said, brushing the leaves off his grey-green granite marker. The grave was under a fern leaf beech tree. In spring the leaves were jade green and in autumn became yellow, then jaundiced and brown. She thought of the tree as John's tree and section nine as her section. It was about a block and a half north of the St. Clair gates just past the war memorial. She didn't think of it as John's section because he had never been there and the saying was true, cemeteries are for the living. Visitors walk on the grass, the trees provide shade for walkers contemplating life, living grief, taking a short cut or playing hiding-go-seek.

Four times, the tulips have gone to sleep and woken; four times, the grass had turned from green to brown; four times, the trees have moulted and three times, those ugly purple and pale green ornamental cabbages had been planted besides the stone steps leading up to the Veterans' Section. A cannon memorialized the graves of those who had fought in both great wars and greeted people who came to visit the over 5,000 veterans' graves. In front of the gun was a boulder inlaid with a bronze plaque that read: 17 POUNDER ANTI-TANK GUN USED BY THE CANADIAN ARMY DURING WW II.

She would have to have a quick chat or else she would miss the internment. Bea spoke, her voice barely audible. "John, I'm not here to visit you today but a Fred Waddle. You didn't know him; he died on Tuesday at my new job. It was terrible. The police haven't determined the cause of death but everyone thinks it's murder. You can tell me to mind my own business but it seems like the police aren't doing much except focusing on one guy. He works at the agency. His name is Niels. He's a smart guy in his early thirties. When he came to work yesterday, he said that the police showed up at his house at six-thirty in the morning, banged on the door and yelled, **'Police'.** Then they just asked his girlfriend one or two questions about his whereabouts Monday night. It sounds like they purposely humiliated him because he has a juvenile record and maybe he was a little stink when he was a teenager but now he talks like every investment company's dream client, portfolio this, rollover that, stock option that, watched *Venture* on CBC last night. He doesn't fit the stereotype of a Metis. I think that's what he is."

Bea sat down on her haunches, pulled out the grass from around the granite marker and continued to whisper. "Last week he was giving his opinion on welfare reform and how Workfare should be mandatory. I asked him if he thought maybe we should recruit temps from the Ontario Works office. He said, 'the agency already has enough charity cases that Fred brings in from the front stoop.' Took him a minute but he twinged onto his own hypocrisy. I like him but he's a dichotomy maybe because his mother is Dutch and his father was aboriginal. Appearances can be deceptive but he seems a hard-working man. Have to go or else I'll be late for the service at the mausoleum."

At first glance the mausoleum seems huge and hard with its slabs upon slabs of red granite plates. Visitors have few secluded corners in which to hide, no grass to sit on, no tree to lean against or bushes to shade them when emotions overwhelm. However, softening the harshness of stone are tranquil stained glass windows of the Stations of the Cross depicted in opalescent and iridescent shades of blue, green, creme and pink coloured glass. In the afternoon, the sun filters through the windows creating rainbows on the glossy panels of red stone.

As she walked over to the immense edifice, she thought, opportunity, that was the question. Who had the opportunity to kill Fred? How did he die? She didn't remember seeing any blood. Did he die in the office or somewhere else? Maybe he wasn't murdered, maybe it only looked like that. Last night on the news Bea had watched Detective-Sergeant Kyle Bottleman read a statement that sounded like an approved sentence from an approved police manual. *We are treating the death, of Frederick Waddle, as a suspicious death until the results of the post mortem are known. Until the report is received, I cannot make further comments.*

Bea followed the sound of voices until she saw about thirty people standing, in a semi-circle, inside an alcove of stone walls. From the back she recognized four of them. Maggie Nichelton, in an ebony pant suit, stood beside the Anglican minister. Every few minutes her shoulders would dramatically move up and fall down as grief bubbled up and fell down like water in a boiling pot.

Niels Wolfe stood, directly in front of Bea, dressed in a wool black blazer with grey dress trousers. One foot in front and back leg bent, he seemed ready to sprint, at the crack of a starter gun, except his shoulders were rigid and his head was drawn uncomfortably forward. Then he shrugged his shoulder and shook his hands to release tension.

Danni Thompson stood on the outskirts of the crowd dressed in her office uniform consisting of a straight navy-blue skirt, matching jacket and white blouse with a red and navy scarf neatly tied under her stiff collar. Suddenly, she crossed herself and bowed her head.

Watching from the edge of the right side of the crowd, stood Detective Alex Sanderson looking Columboish in a rumpled beige trench coat. When Bea glanced towards him, she found him staring at her. He raised his eyebrows, smiled and winked. She blushed. Then she turned her head to listen to the minister's final prayers and watch the bronze urn being placed into its final resting place.

Mary Nichelton was the only ex-wife who attended the funeral. However, four ex-stepchildren, including Maggie appeared. The three women and one young man had also been invited to hear the reading of the will on Monday morning.

Red roses identified the stepchildren. Maggie's idea. Around her head was a black head band covered with delicate fuchsia rosebuds onto which was sewn a black mesh veil that floated up when she spoke. Bea watched Maggie talk to the rose-adorned young adults who came in various shapes, sizes and shades of Caucasian though they were all bright and healthy-looking.

The youngest, Pierre Tremblay, looked to be about seventeen or eighteen. He was gangly, uncomfortable and restless, shuffling and occasionally scratching his head or straightening the belt on his trousers. Maggie smiled at him but regretted it because his face immediately matched the rosebuds on her headband.

After the urn was interred, she walked up to him and said, “Hi, Pierre. It's over. Is this your first funeral?”

“Hi, yea. Sorry, I forgot your name. Now what?”

“Maggie Nichelton. Are you coming to Fred's house? The police gave us permission.”

“I don't know. The police gave you permission for what?”

"To use Fred's house for the wake. Come on. I found a bunch of photo albums full of pictures. Maybe there is one of you and your Mom," said Maggie.

"So. How did you know my Mom was married to Fred?" Pierre asked. "And now I might get some money. My Mom made me come because she thinks Fred owes her something."

"Don't talk to me about the inheritance. That's Tony Eco's job. He's Fred's lawyer. They have court on Saturday now, so he isn't here. Anyway, I don't think it's appropriate to talk about money at funerals," said Maggie, lifting her veil with authority.

"Sorry, I don't know what's appropriate to talk about at funerals," said Pierre looking straight over her shoulder as if he was talking to a tree half a mile away.

"Come on, don't be a cold blizzard. I don't know any of these people either. Come to Fred's party, please. Please, look how old everyone is except you and me. There's Bea. She helped me organize everything for the funeral because her husband, mother and father, grandfather and grandmother died. She said that a wake or a party gives people a chance to remember a deceased person. I want everyone to remember good stuff about Fred."

"Yea, right so I can remember him visiting. Just because he's dead doesn't mean I have to think he walked on water or something," said Pierre, still avoiding her eyes.

"Are you always this miserable? Fred walked out on your Mom, not you, shithead. That's what he told me years after he and my Mom broke up. There's going to be lots of food and even liquor. Come on," said Maggie pulling on his arm.

"Yea, you're so *special*," said Pierre, with an inflection on the word special. "He must have liked girls better than boys because he only visited us on Sunday."

"Don't you like girls better than boys? I'm just teasing you. Fred left my Mom alone too but it had nothing to do with me. She drank. You'll understand when you are older."

"Yea and how old are you?" sniped Pierre.

"Almost 23. Oh, come on, stop being such a jerkface. I'm like almost your stepsister so I can hit you." Maggie reached over and gave his arm a playful swat.

>>>>>

Like Bea, Alex watched the people in the gathering. Everyone looked reserved and respectable. No arrow fell from heaven or up from hell pointing an accusation at that exact person standing right there. The killer, if there was a killer, was probably in the crowd of mourners, pleased with his or, maybe, her work, absorbing others' grief, as if it were his. Usually it was a 'he', but this time Alex wondered. Most masculine crimes were violent, sudden and harsh. This one was tidy, not a drop of blood on the carpet. Not a raging bull, with elevated testosterone, in sight.

If only Fred could send a message from above. What would he say?

Look there, Alex, can't you see I'm pointing at the smug bastard who did me in. Look, you dumb detective. Look! There she is, the self-righteous bitch. It's written all over her face. Over there. You, asshole, you're looking at the wrong guy.

He had only once interrogated a serial killer. The psychopath had looked Alex straight in the eye and lied and lied and lied but the killer couldn't sit still. Though barely noticeable, he moved from buttock to buttock, constantly shifting from side to side, rolling from right cheek to left cheek.

As Alex scanned the small crowd, his eyes stopped on Bea Prancer. Kind of a strange last name but better than her maiden name, Draft. She looked up and he, for some inexplicable reason, winked and waved. How unprofessional. Oh no, she was walking towards him.

"Detective Sanderson, hello."

"Hello, Mrs. Prancer. Please call me, Alex."

"Thank you. You can call me, Bea. Do you always wink at suspects or am I no longer a suspect?" She let her eyelids flutter closed, then flip open revealing twinkling grey-blue eyes. The laugh lines, around her eyes, were like half spider webs reaching outward to catch the humour as it spun from her eyes.

His face tensed but relaxed when he realized that she was teasing him and no one was watching them. "Well, no, you're not a suspect. We've confirmed your alibi. You were at your next-door neighbours, the McElcherans, making salsa. Is it difficult to make?" asked Alex.

"No, it is really simple. Just a bit of chopping. Would you like the recipe?"

"No, thanks. I don't cook much because I live alone."

"Really," said Bea, feeling disconcerted but compelled so she asked. "How's the investigation going? Have you determined how he died yet?"

"No, I'm not at liberty to discuss the case," said Alex.

"Okay, I was thinking about how complicated it must be getting. Did Maggie tell you we contacted three of the ex-wives and their stepchildren? Would you like a list of their names and addresses?"

"Sure, I could come by tomorrow and pick it up."

"Tomorrow is Sunday. I won't be at work but I have a copy at home." Bea said, unconsciously pushing her hair off her forehead and moving her weight to one hip.

"Fine. What ..."

Maggie came rushing up to them with three or four mourners in tow and interrupted, "Bea, This is Yolande and Peggy, they are like my stepsisters but older. Can they follow your car to Fred's house because I have to stop at the liquor store on the way? I promised Pierre some rum and there was none in Fred's liquor cabinet."

"Who's Pierre? Isn't he the youngest one? What does he need rum for?" asked Bea.

"I promised him and now he's like a brother too, sort of. His Mom drinks too."

Bea looked pointedly at Alex, and asked. "Aren't you going to say something to her?"

"What do you suggest? A lecture on underage drinking at funeral parties. I wouldn't know, I investigate homicides; not adolescent drinking infractions."

Maggie and Bea started to laugh, then looked guilty as heads turned towards them in curiosity, then condemnation. "Okay, Maggie, you take the kid and whoever can follow me. My car is the green Ford Taurus with vanity plates that read - Bea Me," said Bea, in a loud voice, to the people standing behind Maggie.

Alex watched them walk away. Cemeteries are a great place for surveillance, all the suspects together. His eyes followed Bea, her confident walk, her jacket cut to accentuate her figure with its ample bosom and tapered waist. He felt like a teenage boy staring at a Marilyn Monroe pin-up calendar.

Watching the cars as they drove, single file, out of the olive-green wrought iron gates, onto St. Clair Avenue West, Alex again thought, Of those at the funeral, how many were really mourning? Did one of them hate Fred enough to kill him?"

>>>>>

The detective was not the only one watching the crowd of mourners leave the mausoleum. Fuming, Niels walked behind the procession; his eyes bored into Danni's back. That witch, he would get her. She had been sitting, in her office typing away, when he had left the agency on Monday night. How could she say he was there when she left? He wanted so much to confront her, call her a two-faced liar in front of all these people. But he had promised his bloody mother, he wouldn't. She, like any good but irritating mother, and he, like an obedient son, had agreed that he would go to the police after the funeral.

'First pay your respects,' Mom had said.

'Fred's dead,' he had said to her.

'That doesn't matter, dear, just pay your respects and then go and sort this little misunderstanding out.'

Who would they believe him or Daniella? Her. The police had gone to his mother's house yesterday afternoon and she had immediately called him. Upset, that was an understatement, she was more than upset, she was fearful. Tammy, his oldest sister would verify that he was at her house just after seven o'clock. He had called her on his cell phone to say he was stuck in traffic at 6:37 p.m. Do the cops ever believe the family?

Niels jogged up beside Danni just as she approached her car door. He grabbed the door handle, and said, "Here let me open that for you." He yanked the door open forcing the metal hinges to expand and vibrate when they reached their maximum flexibility.

Danni smiled at Niels pretending to be oblivious to his angry gesture and just said, "Thank heavens, the worst part is over."

"Well, this part is over."

"What's eating you, Niels? Fred died, not you. Are you going to the little party Maggie planned?"

"No," he said. "I've got work to do. I have to call Bell Mobility to find out how to get a record of the phone call I made Monday night at precisely 6:37 p.m. I'm sure, Danni, you remember I left the agency before six o'clock or does your selective memory move time."

She looked at him, incomprehension written on her face, and asked. "What are you talking about? I don't remember when anyone left the office last Monday night. That's what I told the police. If they told you any different, it wasn't from me."

"Swear on a stack of Bibles that's what you told the police," said Niels.

"I swear I told them that when I left the agency Monday night the only person I saw was Fred. I also told them I didn't know when anyone else left because I was working, not gossiping, until just after 6:30," said Danni.

"Really." He looked at his co-worker, nodded his head, then kicked a stone across the roadway. Close to the ground, the stone flew until it hit a gravestone. When the stone hit the grey granite, Niels swore, "Damn, look what they made me do. Thanks. I believe you. It's those effing pigs. I hate them."

"Don't worry. It'll be okay. The police ask questions of everyone regardless if they are innocent or guilty. They make everyone feel guilty, even children. Go home and have a drink," said Danni, from the driver's seat.

"Okay, bye." He stomped back to his car muttering, "I hate them. I hate them. I've hated them ever since I was ten years old."

>>>>>

Attending the funeral was not on Detective-Sergeant Kyle Bottleman's agenda. Seniority has its privileges. He stayed home to have breakfast with his wife and putter around the garden. While digging and preparing the vegetable garden for winter, he mulled over the suspects in the Fred Waddle case.

The potent smell of deteriorating tomato plants reminded him of chemicals. Suddenly, his stomach lurched into his throat forcing him to slide down the handle of the shovel onto his knees. After a few seconds rest, he stood up and walked into the kitchen. His wife looked at him with concern. "What's the matter, honey?" she asked.

"Flashback, I just 'ad a nauseating flashback about the '65 laboratory deaths. I cannae forget it. I've got to phone Marcus."

Back in Scotland when he was a young constable, Kyle had seen a dreadful case of hydrogen cyanide gas poisoning. Two young men had broken into a laboratory during an animal rights protest. They had released a few rats and dumped all the chemicals, in the laboratory, onto the floor. Within two minutes, the boys were in convulsions, three minutes later they were unconscious, two minutes later they were gone. It was Kyle's first death scene and he had never forgotten the rosy hue of the poor boys' skin.

After calling Marcus, the pathologist, Kyle went down to the police station. He was a methodical man who kept detailed notes, made charts and created time-lines. Already the victim and each of the main suspects had two full pages in his new three hundred page ringed scribbler. The first page described the person and the second page set that person into two periods of time - Monday night and Tuesday morning.

Every time a question came to mind, he wrote it down. When the question was answered. He moved the question and answer to any other suspect's page who could be affected even by coincident.

Until an estimated time of death was confirmed, Kyle had cast Maggie as the primary suspect. She would probably lose the staring role because her alibi, for Monday night and Tuesday morning, was almost verified. Dancing she was at an after-hours club, on Queen Street West, until the wee hours of the morning. And with a young gentleman the rest of the night. That young man had a roommate who also saw Maggie arrive and leave the apartment.

Niels Wolfe was suspect number two. He claimed he had phoned his sister, Monday night, from a car phone while he was driving on Highway #401 to her house. Kyle had spoken to Niels' mother and heard all about his five sisters and how he was the only son. He could do no wrong. He had seen it before where entire families were willing to tell lies for one bad sheep, apple, seed, maybe murderer.

Kyle sat there wondering, would he tell a lie for his son to save him from prosecution. No bloody way, even if he did have a living son. What about his daughters? Maybe.

Once to protect his sister, he had lied when her first husband had accused her of theft after she had left him. Kyle could still remember the bruises on her back and arms and her adamantly refusing to lay a complaint so he told a uniformed policeman that his sister had just flown to Scotland. Some lies are just common sense but murder; can it ever make sense, be moral?

The third suspect was Danni Thompson. She reminded him of his sister; trying to be conscientious, working so hard that sometimes it appeared she was doing something because she felt guilty. Danni had said that she went home around 6:30ish Monday night and that Fred Waddle was still in his office. During the interview, she had sat rigid and kept looking at her hands.

Late Afternoon, Saturday

Was it the colour of diluted blood? Danni looked at the wine. Their affair had started in April and now it was October. She really didn't want to go to the wake. That kid, that rotten kid, why did Fred leave Maggie the agency?

She craved alcohol. It was supposed to be an analgesic. It was supposed to be a form of self-medication, she had read that somewhere, a legal mental pain-killer, not as addictive as morphine or Valium. Excellent substitute. She poured another glass. After two more, her vision wavered; she saw double. Who was that in front of her? Her father, her mother, dead from her realm, dead from Montreal, Quebec, Canada, North America, the world. A person could be dead and still be here. Fred, she had just attended his funeral. What a waste of money. How much had that nitwit spent? Thousands? She hated him dead, dead as a door nail. What did that mean? Dead as an exterminated rat. Dead as a fallen tree.

Danni stumbled up the stairs, spilled her drink and said, "I should wipe that up. Wipe them out of my life. Was that a song; a melody of melancholy? Where was her mind? I better go to bed. No, I am supposed to go to the wake. It's not even Fred's house any more. It's Maggie magpie's house."

At the top of the stairs, Danni lay down to watch the wavering shadows in her mind's eyes. Fred's nose and eyes appeared looking down on her, his foot appeared, his private parts turned from brown to blood red then disintegrated, shrivelling like hair in a fire. Why did he have to die?

She moved her legs, in slow motion, toward her bed. The alcohol had slowly impregnated her brain so her thought processes were slowing down and as she shut her eyes they stopped for a sleep.

>>>>>

Maggie stood, beside the food-laden table, looking at the guests. They were eating the lasagna, salad, cheese, devilled eggs, shrimp, sandwiches and desserts that were laid out on the dining room table. On a narrow rectangular table, at the side, of the living room, was the contents of the liquor cabinet, twenty-five bottles plus a 26-ounce bottle of Woods Old Navy rum she had bought at the liquor store. Everyone was eating and drinking like starving POW soldiers. She heard someone grunt, then burp his appreciation of the feast.

Playing on the stereo was Fred's favourite music, the Platters. Mary, with two of the stepchildren in tow, walked up to Maggie, and said, “Pierre, Yolande, this is my daughter, Maggie. She organized the wake. Isn't it lovely? Believe it or not she was the teenager from hell, so much trouble. But all my hard work before she was fifteen years old paid off. Now, she's great,” said Mary, giving her daughter's arm a proud squeeze.

“Thanks Mom. I met these guys at the cemetery. How are you doing? Like, how's the food?”

>>>>>

Following orders from the two women, Pierre moved tables and carried dishes into the kitchen; at the same time, he followed Maggie with sorrowful and admiring eyes. They were loading the dishwasher for the second time when he stated, “I think I missed the last bus to Hamilton.

“When was the last bus?” asked Bea. “Your mother will be worried, you'd better give her a call.”

“I'll be eighteen soon. Maybe I could stay here in Toronto tonight. Someone told my Mom that the estate would cover expenses for the weekend. It's kinda late to go home,” said Pierre.

Maggie gave him a hard stare. “What if I said NO, you better, like, go home. I think the buses run between Toronto and Hamilton all night. Or you could sleep at the bus depot but I heard that the rent-a-cops there are sadistic and love to beat up on young good-looking guys. And so what if you are almost 18. Until Fred gave me the job at the agency I was almost starving, almost sleeping on the street, barely surviving. Is that what you want? You can't run away on the night of Fred's funeral. I won't let you. And your Mom will blame it on me.” She started to cry and looked at Pierre with steaming eyes. “You can stay here, you jerk.”

"Don't cry. I didn't say I was going to run away. You're really emotional, aren't you," said Pierre, standing in the middle of the room holding two dirty coffee cups.

"Look at my Mom over there sleeping it off on the couch. Looks like she's going to spend the night too. Tony said that the house is registered as part of the business so I guess I might own this house so everyone can stay."

Pierre's eyes lit up as he realized that he had won his wish. His hang-dog expression changed to delight.

Bea looked at the two of them and restated her advice, "He should call his mother."

"It's okay, I already called my mother, from the cemetery, and told her I might go to my grandpa's. He lives in Richmond Hill. She's only interested in the money not in anything else. Anyway it's good she didn't come. She would hate this house."

Maggie laughed and said, "You sneak. Okay, let's go upstairs. I've only used the bathroom and looked in the spare room. There's fingerprint dust in Fred's bedroom. I dare you. I double dare you to sleep in his bed."

"No problemo. I'll race you up the stairs. On your mark. Get set. Go!" yelled Pierre.

As the two galloped up the stairs, Bea called after them. "Good night." On the way out she covered up Mary with a throw and looked at her watch. It was almost ten o'clock. Long day.

Chapter 5

Sunday, October 12th

Bea was in the early stages of waking up when the doorbell rang. She rolled out of bed, stumbled down the stairs towards the ringing and pushed the lace curtains across the front door window. There standing on the front porch was Alex Sanderson looking fresh out of the shower, his thinning hair still damp. He had traded his rumpled coat for a Norwegian-braided sweater coat and faded jeans.

Her heartbeat accelerated as she opened the door, looked down at herself and realized that she was in her nightie. What did he want? "Hello, come in," Bea said. Then she turned and ran up the stairs, halfway up she turned and pointed at the living room. "Have a seat, I'll be right back."

"You said you were an early riser. Sorry," said Alex.

What was the matter with her? She scurried around the bedroom, yanked on a pair of pink stretch pants and a hand-knit sweater. No! They made her look like a 1960s housewife, all she needed was pink curlers and a cigarette dangling out of the side of her mouth. She looked in the closet for a dress. Who wears a dress before they have morning coffee? Finally, she pulled on a pair of jeans and left the long sweater on.

"Sorry, I was at Fred's wake last night. Would you like some coffee?" said Bea when she came into the living room.

Alex jumped up. "Yes, please. I came to pick up the list of his ex-wives and stepkids," he said, following her into the kitchen. Lounging in the doorway, he watched her prepare coffee and open cupboards to find mugs and the sugar bowl.

"Would you like some cinnamon toast?" Bea asked.

"Thank you, yes," replied Alex.

She glanced at the digital clock on the microwave; the numbers glowed 8:22 a.m. "What time do you start work?"

"I'm off today but I forgot when we spoke at the cemetery. Yesterday, you said you were going to Fred's wake. Was he Irish? Waddle sounds like an English name."

"It wasn't really a wake, just a subdued get together, because most of the guests didn't know each other. It was tiring especially making small talk with strangers or people I hardly know."

"I'm glad it was you and not me. I hate going to things like that alone." Alex almost knocked his cup over but he continued talking to cover up his nervousness. "The one thing that I noticed yesterday was that the women weren't crying even when the minister placed the urn in the wall. Other than, what's her name, the girl from the agency, none of them appeared too distraught. They were all looking around. Craning their necks this way and that way. They looked more curious than sad."

"Curious George. They acted like Curious George. That was one of my favourite books as a child. The mourners were keeling over with curiosity. They were, excuse the pun, dying of curiosity just like in a bad soap opera. The stepchildren appear unknown to each other at their stepfather's funeral wondering how much did he leave me. I was surprised that the two other ex-wives didn't show up just to see what Fred's other families looked like. Most people must wonder what happened. What kind of lives do their old lovers live? What kind of homes have they made? What kind of wealth have they acquired? I always thought ex-spouses would enjoy the assessment so they could say to themselves either, it was a mistake to dump old Fred or boy, was I ever smart to dump that jerk. What about you, would you do that?" asked Bea.

"I never think about my ex-wife. It's a waste of energy and time." Alex stated with no intonation in his voice.

"Sorry, I didn't realize that you had an ex-wife. Maybe we should talk about something else. Have you found out how Fred died? Your partner said on the news that you were waiting for a post-mortem report."

"The autopsy report should be issued tomorrow. Before I discuss this with you, I need your assurance that what we discuss is confidential. That it won't be broadcast across the internet or appear in the newspaper tomorrow morning," said Alex seriously.

"I know how to keep secrets. I've done it all my life. I've kept secrets from my parents and from my husband. When my daughter had her first boyfriend, she didn't want her Dad to know, I didn't tell. I'm not a blabber mouth though my husband used to say I was a bit of a nosy parker. On that subject, I have an inside track at the agency. I could help you investigate," said Bea. Her eyes lit-up with questioning eagerness.

"Well, maybe we can discuss the investigation. You do have access to some of the people Fred was close too. One thing I was curious about is and who knew that Maggie was the main beneficiary of Waddle's wacky will?" asked Alex chuckling. "Waddle's wacky will was warped."

She started to laugh and said, "Waddle's wicked will will work wonders. I was there when the lawyer told Maggie about the will. She was shocked. Maybe her Mom knew about the contents. I could find out. Mary seems nice but they aren't very close. I gather she drinks a tad too much. Are you going to interview them, the ex-wives?"

"Yea, we'll be interviewing them. But we are curious about Maggie. She's the main beneficiary and she seemed pretty pleased with herself yesterday."

"Take my word for it, she really didn't know about the will. She was pleased with herself at the funeral because she had arranged the service, the cremation, the internment and the party. She should be proud of herself. It's hard work and she didn't fall apart. I think she did Very Well. I don't know why everyone is so hard on that girl. At the agency too, she keeps the payroll, maintains the files and schedules tests. It's that old story of judging a book by its cover!" exclaimed Bea, her motherly instincts raising their lioness ire.

"Hold off, I didn't accuse Maggie of anything. She has a pretty good alibi. It's her mother that I might have questions for," said Alex looking at Bea's protective eyes.

"Her mother, I don't think that Maggie has had much to do with her over the last four or five years."

"That may be. Mamma Mary has a record as a minor fraud artist, two charges, one conviction for using someone else's credit card. She claimed, she had their permission," said Alex raising his eyebrows in disbelief.

"Maggie pulls a face every time anyone mentions parents. I don't know if she knows her Dad. What difference can that make?" asked Bea, pouring them another cup of coffee.

"No one likes to admit it because we hate to label people but specific crimes have personality profiles. If it's murder, we check out the family first. We look for the known symptoms of a violent criminal. Previous convictions or charges of assaults or rape, unstable work history, history of family violence and so on."

>>>>>

After he left Bea hugged herself and hummed, "She loves me, yea, yea, yea. He loves me. Yea, yea, yea," as she cleaned up the kitchen.

Four years ago he had been one of the policemen who had come to the house to give her the news that John was dead. She had liked Alex's eyes then and she liked his eyes now. They were compassionate but reserved.

He hadn't reminded her that he had been the one who had driven to the morgue the night her husband had died. Maybe he had forgotten. That terrible night he hadn't said a word to her on the way to the hospital. She had wanted to ask questions but had been too stunned to form a coherent sentence.

A few weeks later, she had considered phoning to find out more but it seemed morbid. Now four years later she was still ambivalent about wanting to know the answer to questions about the accident. *How fast was her husband driving? How could someone die in a single car collision? Who called the police? What were the results of the autopsy?*

And then, there were the questions that were unanswerable. *Where had he been going that night? Driving in the opposite direction of their home. Why did he have five hundred dollars in his pocket? Was he planning a major purchase without discussing it with her? Was it a gift for her, Samantha or himself?*

While she tidied up, Bea thought to herself, Damn, just what she needed to start herself thinking again was a funeral. That first year after John died, she had worn herself out thinking about death and what it means, why it happens, how it happens and who it affects.

Grieving and thinking about death expended an immense amount of mental and physical energy so after about a year she vowed to only grieve once a week, on Sunday, when she went to the cemetery. But thoughts of life and death, rather like the sun on a partially cloudy day, wandered in and wandered out so she let them.

They weren't always depressing thoughts. Last week when she was reading an article about silicone breast implants, she wondered. *Does the mortician take the silicone implants out and are they recycled? What if the body is buried with them, do they ever decay? If they are filled with gel, do they freeze or burst erupting against decaying skin leaking into the lining of the coffin?* Another good argument for cremation.

A few years ago, Bea had attended a bereavement group for widows and it had helped but she wished she had someone to discuss these things with when the mood hit her. Samantha would listen but was unsuccessful at hiding her discomfort. She preferred her mother happy and enjoyed her company best when all was well.

Tomorrow was Monday. Work. No one at the agency seemed to know who was going to run the place because it had been a one man operation. Maggie would eventually take over the agency.

Young women were interesting, Bea thought. Her own daughter also permanently resided in her mind, coming forth several times a day. She and Sam had become closer after her daughter had moved to Newfoundland. She talked to her Mom every Sunday and came to visit once or twice a year. A typical Canadian baby-boomer family. Parents and children in different cities, different provinces, different but connecting worlds. What would Sam think if her mother started to date?

>>>>>

Alex's apartment seemed dank and depressing. The clothes on the floor and the dishes in the sink were pressuring him to clean up. He kicked a pile of laundry into a plastic basket and filled the sink with soapy water before he opened his balcony door. On the balcony were two cheap white plastic chairs and three black pots containing brown plants. Alex threw himself into one of the chairs and looked, over the railing, down to the ravine. Couples and families were enjoying themselves, walking dogs, riding bikes and skateboarding taking advantage of the Indian summer day.

Damn, he could have asked her to go for a walk but, no, what did he do? Talked about his stinking marriage. They had talked about other things and she did laugh at his joke about the wacky will and the story about the cop who found the skeleton of a monkey and thought it was a child. Every cop uses that story as an ice-breaker.

Alex went back into his demanding apartment, picked up the dirty clothes and walked out the front door. The laundromat in the basement was full of running kids and tired parents so he threw his laundry into the trunk of the car and drove to the police station.

Wives, wives and more wives that had been Fred Waddle's problem. One wife had been enough for Alex. She had gone to the Calgary Stampede, with her sister, four years ago and before he could say abracadabra she'd a new job and a house in Red Deer, Alberta - the land of the marriage-free and the fiscally conservative. He had wondered if it was another man but more likely she had become bored with him, his hours and his obsessions with police work.

After a year he had given up doing the *what if* scenarios. *What if I wasn't a cop, would she still have left? What if I had been better in bed, better endowed? Would she have stayed? What if we hadn't decided to wait to have children? What if we had lived in a house instead of an apartment? What if I was black, French and played a mournful sax?*

At police headquarters Sunday afternoon was quiet time so his favourite machine was free in the central computer room. He input the approval passwords needed to access personal information on Canadians citizens, landed immigrants and refugees. Under provincial legislation revised in 1997, a police officer's misconduct would first be investigated by the chief of police so officers felt free to access personal information databases knowing no senior officer would ever discipline them for it. Though he had initially been uncomfortable with bending the law, he enjoyed the intellectual exercise of searching for classified information. Technically, without a duly authorized search warrant, personal and third party information collected for other purposes by government should only be assessed with that person's knowledge, not necessarily their consent but their knowledge so they could correct or advise of wrong information.

The amount of data that is available on individuals at the push of a button was astronomical, amazing and scary. A person only had to know where to look and the police were excellent at hacking into the most confidential databases in Canada.

Alex typed in Beatrix Prancer, nee Draft, her date of birth and Social Insurance Number. Within an hour he had information about her: credit rating, marital status, bank balance, investment portfolio, market value assessment of her house, property tax, charitable donations, citizenship, place of birth, insurance coverage, motor vehicle licence abstract, charges and criminal convictions, small claims court settlements, prescription history, name of family doctor, chiropractor, and so on and so on. The printout was four pages long.

Initial searches had already been done on Maggie and Fred. Next Alex typed in Daniella Thompson's demographics. While the computer was searching he sat back to read up on the financial health of the beautiful Bea Prancer.

Her house was mortgage free and he rented an apartment. She had an investment portfolio of diversified mutual funds worth over a hundred grand and her Registered Retirement Savings Plan,(RRSP), was maxed up each year. He had a small RRSP and a few Canada Savings Bonds which he really shouldn't cash in for seven more years. No fingerprints so she had not been arrested.

Maggie had less than half a page of financial history, no credit cards but a mortgage co-signed by Fred two years ago. Danni had a mortgage-free townhouse but few savings.

While the computer was searching and processing data on Niels Wolfe, Alex stretched his legs. He went to the vending machine down the hallway and bought a healthy lunch consisting of canned orange juice, a bag of chips and two chocolate bars. When he sat back down, his eyes almost popped out of his head. Niels, now there was a search worth its weight in bonds, had accounts with two major mutual fund houses. His net worth was estimated, not including his home, to be over a million dollars. "Working as a employment counsellor must be pretty lucrative," muttered Alex to the computer screen. "He's going to hav'ta prove he won it, inherited or earned."

When Fred's financial information came up, Alex quit slouching, sat up straight and picked up the phone. It rang at the other end; voice mail picked up. *You have reached the Metro Toronto Forensic Accounting Department. Our office hours are 9:00 am to 5:00 p.m., Monday to Friday. Please leave a message after the tone. If this is an emergency, call 911.*

Chapter 6

Monday, October 13th

In the morning, Niels, Maggie, Danni and Bea sat, around the table in one of the interview rooms, munching on homemade butter scones, freshly-beaten whipping cream and peach jam. Niels had brought in goodies to apologize for being stand-offish at the funeral and as a tribute to Fred's love for pastry.

“Oh, I accept your apology, Niels. The police upset me too,” said Danni. “They bombard people with questions and accusations. Paparazzi style but it's worse because you can't run away even if you are innocent.”

“I wonder why the police haven't told us what Fred died of. He wasn't stabbed or shot or beaten up so he most likely died of natural causes. A heart attack or maybe alcohol poisoning,” said Niels.

“Like, then, who left the knife next to his body. I bet it was a temp. who despises the agency. Maybe we sent someone to a horrid job where he was abused and treated like a bag of maggot-infested garbage. A terrible negative reference was sent in by the abusive employer but we ignored his complaint and never found him another job. Homeless and starving he comes to the agency because he knows there are free donuts every Tuesday morning. Finding no pastry the famished man yanks open the filing cabinet, pulls out the knife and rushes into Fred's office. In a moment of raging hunger, he knocks a jelly donut out of Fred's hand, grabs the box of donuts and throws the knife on the floor. Two minutes later, Fred drops dead of a heart attack.” Maggie stopped her story because jam and whipping cream slid out of her scone onto the table. She swiped up the goo with her finger, licked it off and resumed talking. “He had to steal Fred's clothes too.”

"So he stripped him of his clothes and stole his donuts too. Come on, Maggie. I bet it was one of Fred's girlfriends. He had lots of them," said Niels.

"Who told you he had a lot of girlfriends?" asked Danni. Her eyes narrowed with irritation at his suggestion.

"Oh please, Fred loved women and they loved him back. Look he had more wives than your average Joe Blow. Maybe one of the ex-wives did him in," said Niels.

"My mother is one of the ex-wives so I don't think that is a very nice thing to say," said Maggie.

"If Fred was murdered which we don't know yet; it was probably a man because most murderers are men. What motive would one of those women have? Not money because they don't directly inherit," said Bea, answering her own question.

"Motive, why does she need a motive? She might just be crazy, like she ..." said Maggie.

Niels interrupted, "Control and jealousy those are the motives that drive women to kill. Men kill for greed and power. No, I revise my statement. Power, jealousy and greed that is what drives men to kill, extreme lack of or want of any of the three can turn into rage or war."

"That's so male. And it's a delusion. Most men kill their wives because they are control freaks. Revenge, greed, jealousy is just another name for wanting control, wanting everything your own way," said Danni. Her face was intent and angry.

"I think Danni's right. Wanting control of something, that's it, even in mystery novels. The detective looks for the motive, the reason why the murder was committed and the most common is the villain wanted control or wanted revenge for losing control of a given situation. Maybe we should be asking different questions. Did Fred make anyone feel powerless? Did anyone owe him money?" asked Bea.

"Yea, right! That's all anyone talks about. It's like now Fred is gone, no one cares about him; just his money. I still think it was a stranger, a maniac, who sneaked into the front door," said Maggie, clicking her spoon on the table as if demanding silence. "I hate talking about this."

"Well, I've had enough of this deep discussion. I'm going to work." Danni gave Maggie an exasperated look of mild contempt. "I assume as long as I'm working, I'll get paid. And you're going to discuss that with Tony today after he reads the will, aren't you?"

"Oh, sorry, yea, he already talked to me about that. I forgot to tell you. Everyone is gonna get paid just like before except that Tony and me will sign the cheques," said Maggie.

"It's Tony and I will sign the cheques. Fine, let us know how it goes today," said Danni. She walked out shaking her head.

>>>>>

Karen, the new receptionist, watched from behind the front desk as Detective-Sergeant Kyle Bottleman strode into the agency. Following him was Detective Alex Sanderson and a man in a dark-blue double-breasted blazer with gold buttons. He carried a laptop computer case and a square black box. Just as she stood up to greet them, the phone rang. She picked up the receiver and said over it, "There's no one in."

They nodded and continued to march past. Over his shoulder Kyle said with a grin, "It's okay, lassie, we are the police."

The three men went directly to Fred's office. They stood in the doorway staring at a sturdy woman standing on a chair spraying blue cleaner fluid into the upper edges of the window. Just as she reached up to wipe downward, Kyle bellowed, "Why are you cleaning in here?"

The woman wobbled in the chair, put down her bottle of window cleaner and squeegee, and turned around. She looked at the three men looking at her and said, "Maggie ask me to come clean the poor man's office. It upset her, all the mess. Paper on the floor. If you not finished here, you tell Miss Maggie. I work for her now. Fred, he was good man. Why you always yell when I want clean? That is my job. You can't arrest me for cleaning. I don't even know you policeman. You should wear uniform," said Josie, the cleaning lady extraordinaire.

"We're not going to arrest you for cleaning but stop it. It wasn't me who yelled at you last time. That was my partner," said Kyle pointing at Alex. "We must all look alike, except I have less hair."

"I only wipe the window, the desk and the table. The floor, I vacuum but not scrub. Maybe need new carpet. Maybe not. You talk to Maggie. I go home. You tell her. She say that the police took the yellow ribbon away so all finished," said Josie, gathering up her cleaning supplies and pursing her lips. The man in the blue blazer moved forward to help her. She shot him an appraising look, nodded indicating the vacuum cleaner and signalled him to follow her.

"Just a minute," Kyle said. "Where did Maggie and the rest of the staff go?"

"Maggie go to nice lawyer, Mr. Tony. I clean his house too. He have seven children, three grandchildren. Very nice wife. She work too hard so many children."

"Okay, do you know where Bea Prancer, Danni Thompson or Niels Wolfe are?" asked Bottleman in exasperation.

Josie looked at her watch, tapped the crystal and said, "Lunch, the two girls tell me they go lunch, ten minutes ago. I go home now. You tell Maggie. She phone me. You can't arrest me for cleaning, my grandson say so and he goes to university for study psychology."

She handed her cleaning supplies to her well-dressed helper who followed her, out of the agency, to her car. Kyle wished he had a camera to take a picture of the forensic accountant crossing the street with a vacuum cleaner hose hanging over his back and a bottle of commercial strength cleaner in his hand.

"Look, she reminded me of my sister's mother-in-law," said the helpful man when he walked back through the door which Kyle held open for him.

"I didn't say anything. We, the police, are here to serve and protect. Don't ever apologize for doing the serve part of our commitment. While you set-up your paraphernalia, we'll look around, then we have to go see this bloody lawyer, Tony Eco. He talks like he has an unbroken egg in his oh-so proper mouth."

Since the agency was devoid of staff, Kyle decided to do a walk-about. He glanced at Niels' desk calendar in admiration. Small meticulous notes outlined what he had been doing day by day and hour by hour. Niels had noted who he interviewed, how much he paid for lunch and who to phone the next day. Last Monday, Niels had highlighted in yellow - Go to sister #3 - birthday party.

Kyle leaned over the desk and said, "Looks like Niels did go to his sister's Monday night. He's written for Friday, October 10th, call Bell Mobility - confirmation of Monday phone call; confirm bank transfer. Good lad, checking his own alibi. Ah, today - October 13th - The Cyber Café; 11:30 to 1:00 - lunch."

The two detective walked back to the office where the man in the blue blazer sat typing on his laptop which was hooked up to Fred's computer. He looked up and said, "Nothing untoward so far but I'll be here for awhile. I don't think this guy used his computer much even though the agency has a sophisticated database and upgraded software."

"He probably didn't use his computer. I suspect the computer expert in this office is Niels Wolfe. He has a shelf of computer manuals and what looks like an expensive computer in his office. He also has a strange note in his calendar about checking an Internet bill," said Kyle.

The man in the blue blazer hit himself in the forehead, and sarcastically said, "That is so suspicious, he has a note in his calendar about an Internet service fee. That's irrefutable evidence. Throw the guy in the slammer, throw away the key, hang him by his fingernails. Don't even think about taking into account the fact that millions of Canadians and Americans are paying the same monthly fee.

Kyle's dislike of computers was well-known. He didn't hate them but he did find that they were given time and a reverence far above their station in life. He agreed they had advanced police investigations one hundred fold but when did a computer have a revelation, an instinct or see, or hear or give birth to an idea.

>>>>>

While the two detectives were arguing with Josie about where and when she should clean, Maggie was humming as she walked to the lawyer's office. The sun was shining and the air was cool, crisp and invigorating.

She swung her arms up into the air and skipped along.

The offices of Davis, Eco and Pearson were located in an historical home on Huron Street just north of Bloor Street. The street was a mix of large brick homes which were either renovated or decrepit. Tenants in both types of housing were charged exorbitant rents except that the down-and-outs only received a tiny cockroach-infested room for their five hundred bucks.

When Maggie arrived she stood outside the law office and took a deep breath. The bevelled stained glass windows framing the carved oak door distracted her for a moment. She pulled open the door to see a crowded waiting room. All the seats on the two harvest green leather couches were filled. She recognized everyone from the funeral. A couple of people half-heartedly raised their hand to welcome her but no one spoke so she stood looking at her shoes. Behind her the door slammed and Pierre rushed in. He looked around, walked over to Maggie and whispered, "Hi, I skipped school. The lawyer told my Mom she couldn't come for me because I was over sixteen. She's so pissed off."

From a door behind the reception desk a slim woman, dressed in a tailored raw-silk burgundy suit, appeared. She announced, "Ladies and gentlemen, good morning, I assume you are all here for the reading of Mr Frederick Waddle's last will and testament. The reading will take place in the library where Mr. Eco is waiting for you. Please follow me."

The crowd followed the sophisticated woman up three flights of stairs to the law library which encapsulated the entire third floor. Other than the entrance doors the walls were floor to ceiling books. In the centre of the room was a grand circular conference table where Mr. Eco sat with reading glasses perched on his Roman nose.

He looked up from the thin file and said, "Come in, have a seat. I will try to be brief. We seem to have more people than we have beneficiaries. If Fred Waddle was never your stepfather, could you please wait downstairs? Coffee is available from the receptionist."

One man looked at his wife and shrugged his shoulders. After the minor exodus there were four people sitting around table. They smiled nervously at each other. Tony Eco looked around, nodded his large grey head and picked up the file in front of him.

"Frederick Waddle's will was fairly simple. He left his personal estate to stepchildren whom were born before he married their mother. I believe we have contacted such children except one, the daughter of Sophia Augusta Hemming who Fred married in 1960 and divorced in 1963. A few years later Sophia passed away in Montreal. We have initiated a search for her daughter. Unluckily, when we drafted the will, Fred could only remember his first stepdaughter's nickname, Lallie. He instructed that his personal assets were to be divided equally between the surviving stepchildren and his business assets and his home will go to Miss Marigold Maria Nichelton."

Pierre whispered, "Marigold Maria." The lawyer stopped talking to gaze, without blinking, over his reading glasses at the teenage boy.

"Ah, Mr. Pierre Merlin Tremblay, you also are mentioned here specifically as the youngest and only stepson. When Fred revised his will last year, we discussed how he wanted your share of the estate administrated. He, like myself, felt that age twenty-one or even twenty-five should be re-declared as the age of majority. So until you reach the age of twenty-one, I will, with the kind assistance of Nova Scotia Trust, manage your investments."

"Oh shit," said Pierre. "My Mom's not going to like that. Can we change it?"

"No," said the lawyer, matter-of-factly. "Now does anyone have any other questions?"

One of the stepdaughters waved her hand in the air and said, "How long will it take to probate the will? Is it complicated? It took my grandmother almost a year to sort out grandpa's stuff but she didn't hire a lawyer. I guess the estate is paying you if you are the executioner."

"Executor. To your first question. It will probably take many months, hopefully no more than a year or so. One thing I should make you aware of is that the police informed me yesterday that they will be conducting a forensic audit on both Fred's business and his personal estate. As his executor, I will, of course, co-operate to the best of my ability with the police. Should anything come up that would affect probating the will. I will inform you. To your second question, yes, the estate is paying me. My fees are outlined in the last section of the will.

"How much is the estate worth?" asked the same woman.

"I'm sorry, I don't know. We have applied for access to his bank accounts and safety deposit box. Taxes and debts must be paid first. The will was simple but the estate is quite complicated for a number of reasons including the fact that he had overseas investments. I will be providing you with updates."

Maggie put up her hand, and asked, "What's the difference between a personal asset and a business asset?"

"Good question. Let me give you an example. The Common Sense Employment Agency, which your stepfather owned, has a number of bank accounts open under its incorporated name. These accounts are business assets. Fred had a number of bank accounts under his own name, the money in those accounts are personal assets. Any other questions."

The four people shook their heads so the lawyer closed the file, placed his glasses on the white folder and stood up. He walked to the door and said as the people filed out. "If you think of anything else you would like to ask me, let me know. The receptionist will give you one of my cards. Good bye. Oh, Maggie, could you please stay behind for just a minute? I need to talk to you."

Chapter 7

Morning, Wednesday, October 15th

A steady wind from the northwest signalled that winter was coming. Each morning the temperature was half to one degree closer to zero Celsius, the wind was colder and the sun rose later in the eastern horizon. In fifteen days daylight savings time would end, the clocks would be set forward and dawn, unlike death, would begin one hour later.

Alex looked at his watch for the tenth time, flipped through a report and lackadaisically wrote notes. He sat waiting for his partner who was the senior detective assigned the responsibility for supervising the testing of the new area code software. This meant that Kyle would be grouchy when he came back from his meeting. Placing him in charge of testing a computer application was similar to asking a bulldozer to build a mountain. Installation was already a few days behind schedule because a qualified systems officer had still to be found to replace the one that didn't show up the day Fred died.

Kyle walked into the homicide office shaking his head. “Laddie, I don’t understand the problems, bugs, they call them. These people just cannae speak the Queen's English. They cannae speak any pidgin English, either. I just don ...”

Alex interrupted his partner. “Dr. Christie's secretary called; the autopsy report will be ready at 11:30 this morning. She said that he wants us to come over. The witch wouldn't tell me boo, not even the cause of death, just that the doctor has some concerns that he would like to discuss with Detective-Sergeant Bottleman and if Detective-Sergeant Bottleman has time, Dr. Christie is free for lunch.”

"Okay, let's go," said Kyle. "Marcus just has a real secretary. He says she's worth her weight in gold, diamonds and emeralds. You've met her, she's missing an arm. Next time you talk to her try to be charming, like me. Have a conversation with her. She's the administrative power at the morgue."

The Coroner's Court building was two blocks away on Grenville St. The detectives walked down a back alley that Kyle claimed was once called Morgue Alley. It had been named that, in the late 1800s, when the alleyway was the only throughway to the morgue door in the original hospital built on that site. Over time the hospital had closed but the morgue remained, in the basement of the old building, until it was demolished in 1948. Now the home of the coroner's office was an ugly cement government building. The morgue still resided in the basement and on the second floor was the Office of the Chief Pathologist, Marcus Christie.

Dr. Christie had a comfortable grey beard, an intelligent doctor's beard; shaped like the soft toe of a worn leather shoe. It hung straight from his invisible chin, down over his Adams' apple to his collar. It was grey masculinity hiding possibly sensuous lips. His balding head was bent over a picturesque reference book and he murmured as he read the text in front of him.

Colourful primitive pictures from South America and peaceful scenes of the Quebec Laurentians decorated his office. He was so absorbed that he did not see the two large detectives standing in his doorway as he swivelled his chair around to the computer on the table behind him and said out loud, "I know it's here, where the hell did I read that?"

"Where the hell did you read what, Marcus? Maybe you should keep a reference list on the computer, isn't that what you told me last week when the wife couldn't find a recipe. As a matter of fact, I remember your words exactly, you said, 'I never lose anything because I keep track of all my information electronically and any idiot can search for it if they know how to spell," Kyle gloated. "So what did you lose, my dear friend?"

"Stick it in an outhouse, Kyle. Well, tell your partner to come in, don't just stand there at the door. I was working on *Your* case." Dr. Christie emphasized as he winked at Alex who was holding up the door frame with his shoulder. "I have been researching *Your* case and the draft post-mortem report is typed. One week and one day since we received the body. Good turnaround time, eh? I heard from my wife who heard from your lovely wife that you might be irritable this morning, Kyle. Seems someone finds it difficult to accept the advantages of new technology. Some people realize that advances are being made to help mankind, save time and ensure innocent people, usually men, are not thrown in the clink. Of course, some people enjoy learning new things that tax their mind," he said in lecture mode as he turned once again to search the bookcase behind him.

Alex looked at Kyle who he could see was preparing to enter full debate mode especially when the pathologist turned his back on his audience. Alex intercepted before his senior officer could start his usual counter attack which he so enjoyed.

"Your secretary mentioned on the phone that we would find the autopsy report interesting and that you wanted to discuss it with us. That is why we walked over here," said Alex.

"Really," replied the doctor, "I thought I had asked your partner out for lunch so I could bug him. More importantly, we may wish to discuss Kyle's fascinating colour-enhanced flashbacks and our wives' non-poisonous cooking."

"So I was right, you bastard, it was cyanide poisoning. I knew it. The minute I smelt those tomatoes and remembered those poor pink boys," said Kyle. He leaned over the desk and tried to read the autopsy report upside down. Marcus straightened him with a push on the shoulder and shoved a document in his hand.

"Here I printed a copy for you. It wasn't pure cyanide, Kyle, but a poison that produces toxic cyanide-like symptoms. Hydragin killed our fat friend. The poison probably came from the *hydrangea macrophylla* plant. I've only seen one other similar case. Some dippy broad got hibiscus leaves mixed up with hydrangea leaves and brewed herself a poisonous pot of tea. The public health department must be notified. But considering the time of year it's strange, not indicative of accidental poisoning. Here in Canada the flower blossoms outside from early June to mid August. Then it goes to seed or is cut back in the fall and by now is almost finished moulting. Your suspicions were right."

"Whoa, what is hydra what macrophylla, anyway? I've never heard of it but I bloody well knew it was poisoning," said a pleased Kyle.

"Symptoms are similar to cyanide poisoning but there is no residual almond smell. The stomach lining was bright red but toxicology couldn't determine the cause. What we did find was a seed and a fragment of a leaf lodged between Fred's two back molars. This plant material was sent to the botany department at the University of Toronto and they identified the seed as coming from an hydrangea pod. Amazing. Did anyone see him die? More importantly, where did he have his last meal?"

"Don't know. No one has come forward. He was found in his office. A woman saw him prior to his death but she though he was sleeping off a drunk."

"He was in a coma, comes after the convulsions."

"Dr. Christie, can tell us more about this poison?" asked Alex.

"As I said, there is evidence that the poison came from the seeds or leaves of the hydrangea plant. Originally from Japan and China, the plant is now popular in North America. It says here there are over eighty species. The most common is *Hydrangea Macrophylla*. You've seen them, they have wide ball-like flowers, usually white or pink. They will turn blue if a few grams of sulphite of ammonia per quart of water are added to the soil when the plant is blooming. Very interesting," said the pathologist, reading alternately from a thick gardening book and a medical abstract on his computer screen. "The glycosides must decompose by reacting with water in the gastrointestinal tract before releasing the poison. When I opened him up, there was the stomach; inflamed. And the colour of the blood, definitely poisoning. The test results came last night and confirmed my hypothesis, well really Kyle's hypothesis."

"Hydrangea, we have some in the garden. So do you, Marcus. The wife gave you a plant when you removed the hedge in the front yard and replaced it with flowers. Those flowers were white. How would you extract the poison?"

"Easy, piece of cake. Harvest the seeds or buds, chop up the leaves, squeeze them in a garlic press or chop `em in a grinder and mix them in with a good strong cup of coffee better yet a cappuccino with cinnamon and sweetened whipping cream. A caustic cocktail, excellent way to hide the taste; if there is one. Toxicology found coffee in the stomach contents. I'll have to find out the flavour of your average deadly *hydrangea macrophylla*. This book says that the most toxic part of the plant is the flower bud."

"Thanks, Marcus, reminds me of lunch, where do you want to go? How about healthy vegetarian?" asked Kyle, with a wicked grin.

"Fat chance. That's a prescription for malnutrition," said the solidly built doctor making a face and putting on his coat.

"Marcus, tell Alex about the restaurant we went to in Stratford last summer where the wives ordered soup with purple and yellow pansy leaves floating in it."

"It was crap. All I remember is the cost. Pansy soup for rich pansies, seven bucks a bowl. I had watery chicken soup with two carrots and one slice of unpeeled zucchini."

"Oh, sweetheart, I said to the wife as the spoon entered her delicate but open mouth; there's an ant on your pansy," chuckled Kyle.

The two laughing men walked out but Alex stopped and stood in front of the secretary's desk. "By the way, thanks for calling about the report," he said, smiling a forced smile. "I suppose you've heard all his tall stories before. Do you think any of them are true?"

"Of course, Dr. Marcus never lies or exaggerates. Your Scottish partner is another story," said the secretary. After a few seconds of silence, she asked, "Can I help you with anything else?"

Alex shook his head and ran to catch up to the two old friends who were standing at the elevator still deciding whether to eat Chinese or Greek food.

Afternoon, Wednesday

While the two detectives and the pathologist were eating lunch, Maggie was walking east on Bloor Street discussing semantics with Tony Eco. "Stepchildren, we're not babies. Can't you find another word for us."

"It's just a term. How about step-adults or step-siblings or simply beneficiaries. What do you prefer?" asked the lawyer.

"I like the word beneficiaries the best. Oh, Tony, I'm having a really hard time. Everyone at the agency is, like, doing their job as usual but some of the phone calls don't make any sense. Some guy phoned to tell me not to bother sending him an invoice and then I couldn't find him on the computer anyway. Another one called for Fred but when I told him he was dead, the guy slammed the phone in my ear. Niels is helping me but he said I need to talk to you about running the business efficiently so as to continue making a profit and something about due diligence. Whatever that is. Can you give him signing authority for cheques and stuff at the agency?"

"He's right, Maggie, you need to manage the business efficiently and I am sure you can do that with professional assistance and training. Thank Mr. Wolfe for his kind offer and advise him that you and I will retain signing authority. Fred must have believed you would make a fine businesswoman or he wouldn't have left you the agency," said the lawyer crooking his arm so she could put hers through his; which she did with a slight curtsey.

"Fred didn't expect to die. He probably figured he had twenty more years to teach me whatever I needed to know. I guess this means I shouldn't spray a purple streak in my hair this weekend."

"Whether you paint a purple or blue streak in your hair, you will remain the sole proprietor of the Common Sense Employment Agency. To change the topic. I would like to send someone down to the agency to start auditing the accounts, both receivables and payables. At the restaurant we can have a serious talk about managing the business."

"Okay," said Maggie. She pulled her arm out and skipped a few steps ahead, then turned and waited for him to catch up. His tailored wool coat and even pace made her want to pull him along like a toddler on the way to her favourite park. They walked down St. George Street and strolled through the walkways through the university to McCaul Street. A few blocks south was Baldwin Street where delegates from the United Nations would have been comfortable with the ethnicity and price ranges of the restaurants available.

She picked Japanese where Tony insisted that they not eat in the communal area but in a private room where there were chairs and tables laid out with knifes and forks.

"Maggie, you know how much I enjoyed being Fred's lawyer. I was looking at his file again this morning. The first time he came to see me was in 1966. While I'm settling the estate, I'd like you to retain separate counsel," said Tony quietly with equanimity.

She looked flustered and said, “Like, why would I need a second lawyer? I like you. You were Fred's lawyer. You don't treat me like I'm an idiot face. And anyway it will cost more money soooo, no, I won't retain separate counsel.”

“Fred didn't ask for my advice about his business dealings or about how he ran the agency. How do I put this tactfully? He may have been involved in a number of dicey business practices that the police are investigating,” Tony said leaning back in his chair and shutting his eyes. A moment later, he opened his eyes to see her shocked face.

“That's bullshit, Tony. Why don't you say what you really mean instead of talking crapola. Are you saying Fred was a criminal or maybe a con artist. I do need another lawyer. How could you, after being his friend for over thirty years. You know he helped me get a job and buy the condo at almost half the regular price. I hate you.” Maggie jumped up and ran to the rice paper doorway. She turned and yelled, “Screw off. You're fired. I'll look after Fred's stuff, all by myself.”

“Shut up. The entire restaurant is listening. Come and eat. I'm the executor so you have to deal with me. Look, it doesn't mean Fred didn't care about you. Regardless of the circumstances, you should retain separate counsel for your own protection.”

“No, I want you to do it,” said Maggie. She stood for a minute looking at Tony like he was the Grinch that stole Christmas.

“Come on,” he said dishing food onto her plate. “I'll recommend someone that you'll like. What do you prefer? A man or a woman? I've also retained an accountant to look over the books at the agency and Fred's personal assets. Why don't you come tomorrow to meet him?”

“Maybe, I'll see. I suppose he's going to want to snoop around Fred's office too, just like the police. They're so bossy but I think Bea likes one of them. What are you going to tell the police?”

"Nothing at the moment. We'll see. Eat up," said Tony.

"I'm not hungry." She looked at his plate and said, "You only ate half a piece of sushi. You should have told me you didn't like Japanese food. Next time you pick the restaurant."

After the disastrous lunch, Maggie walked like a speed walker, anxiety rang through her footsteps each time her foot hit the sidewalk. She stopped for a hamburger, fries, onion rings and two small pops before she could think straight enough to go back to the office. On the way back she said to herself, "I'm the boss. I'm the boss. I'm an adult."

Tony Eco made a quick detour home to have a hot sausage, fried onion and mushroom sandwich with tomato sauce made by his wife who never served raw fish.

>>>>>

Bea sat at her desk looking at her two weeks at-a-glance calendar - the weeks of October 6 to 12 and October 13 to 17 were laying in front of her. She had ten minutes before her next interview so she wrote:

Tuesday, October 7th, *Fred dies- how and exact time - unknown*

8:15 *I walked in the door and sat at my desk.*

8:20 *I saw Fred unconscious on the office floor so I shut the door*

8:25 *Maggie came to work, walked down the hallway to coffee/file room*

Fred's office door not visible from my cubicle

8:30 Temporary workers started to come in to pick up pay cheques from Maggie.

8:55 Mrs. Fundy appeared at my desk, Maggie forgot to phone to advise that Mrs. Fundy is there - maybe Maggie was not at the reception desk.

9:00 Danni and Niels arrived, walked down the hallway and also commented on Fred's door being closed.

9:00 to 9:20 Listened to muffled conversation of temps and staff walking up and down the hallway discussing new assignments and pay cheque discrepancies.

9:20 Detective-Sergeant Kyle Bottleman called, Maggie at the front desk. Niels and Danni both say they were in their offices.

9:25 Found Fred's body - not breathing

Suddenly Bea heard an angst-ridden sigh. She looked up to see Maggie standing at the entrance of the cubicle.

"Maggie, are you okay?" she asked with concern.

"I'm fine. I just talked to the new receptionist, Karen. She's doing my job. She seems to be okay." Maggie lifted her shoulder and let them drop down as if the burden of feeding the world's homeless rested alone on her slender shoulders.

"It can't be that bad. The day is more than half over. Why don't you come over for dinner tonight? I'm making chicken and pasta salad," said Bea.

"Okay, I'll come. First I have to start reading all the stuff Tony gave me to study and then I have to see my Mom. She's in town this afternoon. I don't know why."

>>>>>

Later in the afternoon, when Bea was walking down the hallway, she heard raised voices. “Mom, you were still seeing Fred. Where? Here or in St. Kitts or maybe Africa? I don't believe you. He was seeing another woman, someone younger, I know more than you know,” stated Maggie in a know-it-all voice.

Mary's voice radiated, around the corner, through the partially opened door into Bea's ear. “You ungrateful little bugger. I fed and clothed you, and did you ever say thank you? No. You know what a hard time I had bringing up a child on my own. Who do you think bought groceries, paid the rent and put a roof over your head? Me! Your mother, no one else.”

“Mom, okay, okay, I'm sorry. I know it was hard on you. How much you suffered. That's why I left, you just saw me as a financial burden. Fred dies and all of a sudden, I'm a useful daughter and you want me to ask Tony for money for you. What you really want is, like, you want me to lie for you. I'm not going to pretend Fred invested your money for you. Forget it.”

“Fine. I'll talk to the lawyer myself. You don't understand this. I gave that man over eight years of my life.”

“Get real, Mom, he left us after two years, two years and I'm almost 23. So two years out of 22 years of my life he lived with you. And you drove him away because you nagged at him every day.”

“There's no talking to you, as usual,” said Mary. “I give up.”

Bea heard Mary leave and followed her into the washroom just in time to see her fling her purse onto the counter and rush into a stall. When she came out she stood in front of the mirror trying to repair the streaky damage the tears had caused. The smudged black eyeliner mixed with pancake make-up made her look like a depressed racoon.

“Hi, are you okay?” Bea asked.

"I'm fine but my own daughter doesn't trust me or believe me," said Mary to the mirror. The reflection showed a fiftyish woman wearing a grey Persian-wool coat with black embroidered buttons. Underneath the coat was a tight red sweater over an equally tight black skirt which accentuated the extra roll around her waist.

Bea came up beside her and said, "My daughter, Sam, short for Samantha, is a year older than Maggie. She lives in Newfoundland. Sometimes, Maggie reminds me of her. They both have strong healthy personalities. What do you think, maybe they inherited their brains from their intelligent, independent mothers?" She winked at Mary and they both started to laugh. On an impulse Bea asked. "Do you want to have a quick coffee?"

Mary smiled wryly and said, "Okay, where?"

"Starbucks. It's two doors away."

They sat in art deco chairs near the window drinking coffee and nibbling on over-sized, over-priced cookies. Physically Mary looked like her daughter with the same oval face, round eyes, aristocratic nose and smooth skin. Her gestures were also similar because after a moment silence, she had a ready smile and ran her hands through her hair as she prepared to start talking.

"I loved Fred and I saw him almost every Saturday. He phoned me when he hired Maggie to tell me not to worry about her. A week later we resumed our relationship. He kept me updated on how my daughter was doing. Sure I drink a bit and smoke up a bit. And I spend way too much money on bingo. All these years, I knew Fred was looking after Maggie. If he was alive and standing here, he would tell you. He loved me but we couldn't have stayed married. I don't do day to day aggravations very well. Oh, once in awhile I saw other men but Fred was the one. I even gave him my savings to invest but my daughter doesn't believe me."

>>>>>

Later that evening at Bea's house, Maggie stood at the kitchen counter shaking the chicken parts in a clear bag and said, “My Mom always had more than one kind of Shake and Bake in the cupboard too. I like the original flavour best but I never buy it because it's like an old lady food. Shoot, that came out wrong. I didn't really mean you were an old lady.”

“Would you like a glass of wine from a lady who will one day be old?” asked Bea, with a stern frown.

“Okay, I had a bad day. Wait till I tell you what Tony said and what my Mom said. She just drives me insane, up the wall, crazy. I wish my Mom was more like you.”

“Don't say that, I drive my daughter, Sam, up the wall too. I talked to your Mom today. I like her. She was really upset about the fight you had with her.”

“Yea, right.”

Bea and Maggie ate dinner in the living room while watching the news. There were no announcements about the investigation so they continued their discussion about mothers.

“Pierre's mother was really pissed off at him when I drove him home on Monday afternoon. He'd skipped school to come hear Tony read Fred's will and he didn't tell his Mom he was coming. When we arrived at their house in Hamilton, she ran out the house like the steel ball in a pinball machine, walked up to Pierre and softly slapped him across the face. She glared at him and said half in French and half in English, `Tell that putain to get Fred's car out of my driveway.' So I turned around, walked to the car and never said good bye to Pierre. Maybe I should phone him but I don't want to get him into more trouble with his Mom. But maybe I misunderstood because I almost failed French in high school. What do you think I should do?”

"Sure, give him a call. At the funeral he looked like he enjoyed being friends with you. But remember you haven't heard his mother's side of the story," said Bea, enjoying her role of surrogate mother.

Chapter 8

Evening, Thursday, October 16th

The sun disappeared from Alex's rearview mirror and the car interior darkened. He looked at Kyle, with unconcealed irritation, because in the increasing darkness he could sense that his partner was continuing to be energized by the day's activities.

"It's not that funny, the man was a philanderer, he took advantage of those women," said Alex.

"Yup, no woman can have free choice or sexual desire. He was an on-the-road kind of guy, king-of-the-hill, many hills it seems," said a chortling Kyle.

"He was an old manipulative two-timing, three-timing Don Juan."

"Old, hardly, fifty-six that's not old. I'm going to be fifty-four next year. What do you think, a man or woman hits fifty-five and they should become celibate? From what I hear you're regaining your virginity and you're only forty-four years old. Maybe that's what you need. An ex-wife or two or three to borrow and boff in the buff. Damn good show, Fred saw two or three of them most weekends. I think they loved him. And not one of them mentioned sex. Why didn't we ask them about their sex lives, Alex? We'll have to bring a female officer with us next time to ask whether he got it up every weekend."

"It's none of our business. We're not talk show hosts. We are, as you've stated hundreds of times, homicide investigators," Alex said. He pressed hard on the gas. The car leaped forward and swerved into the outside lane speeding up to pass a transport truck lumbering along at 110 kilometres per hour. As the car accelerated, he thought, The whole stinking damned police force knows I'm not seeing anyone and the next thing you know they'll be saying, I'm a faggot. If he wasn't my superior officer I'd stop the effing car and throw him out the door. Tell him to get out and walk home."

"Whoa, Alex slow down, the highway is almost empty. Just think what a twist. Wait till I tell Marcus. He'll love it. This is going to make the news, for sure, when the trial starts. Murdered man poisoned by exotic Japanese flower, sleeps with younger woman and three ex-wives, all in different towns, almost every week-end."

Kyle pulled a road map of Ontario out of the glove compartment. While opening and folding the map he accidentally hit his partner on the head but continued talking. "Okay, where's the scale? What kind of scale is this 1 cm = 100.5 km or 1 inch = 160.8 miles. What happened to one inch = 100 miles. Okay here goes, I am marking a big O, for you know what, on the map for each ex-wife, O-one, Hamilton; O-two, St. Catharines and O-three, Stoney Creek."

"I don't know why you are enjoying this so much. What if your wife lied about going to a women's therapy group at a hotel Friday nights? She even gave her husband the room number so he could call her if there was an emergency. So that made it acceptable. I would kill her if she ever pulled a stunt like that."

"I think Fred was addicted to these woman. He told each one that he couldn't live with them or without them. Tomorrow we will to do some in-depth checking on the wives. Could it be the Case of the Wives' Revenge?" asked Kyle.

"I already did a computer scan on the stupid wives. Only Mary Nichelton has a record for minor fraud. Used her ex-boyfriend's credit cards without his permission. None of these women's elevators made it up to the top floor," said Alex.

"What the hell does that mean?" asked Kyle.

"The elevators are their brains."

"Aren't we a cheery little misogynist tonight."

"Screw off. Twenty minutes max and we're home."

The sky was black and cloudy when they approached the city limits. The lights from office towers, streets and houses glowed upward acting as a beacon for incoming drivers.

>>>>>

In a well-practised motion Alex flopped on the couch, kicked off his shoes and hit the play button on the answering machine. When Bea's voice came on; he sat up.

"Detective Sanderson, Alex, this is Bea Prancer. You asked me to call you if I heard anything. I didn't realize this was your home number. I'm sorry, maybe I should have called the typed number, not the hand-written number, on the card you gave me. Anyway, could you please give me a call? Thank you."

Alex poured himself a drink and zapped frozen lasagna in the microwave. While eating his dinner he replayed the recording three times and he stymied an urge to clean up.

Bea wasn't a suspect so there was absolutely nothing wrong with calling her tonight. There were strict regulations on seducing and socializing with the suspects and witnesses of a criminal investigation. But Bea was not a suspect and not really even a witness. She hadn't seen the murder; she had only found the body. And she could become a valuable informant. And he wasn't planning on sleeping with her until after the investigation was over. Satisfied with his rationalization, Alex picked up the phone and dialed her number.

"Hello," answered a sleepy voice. "Who is this?"

"Mrs. Prancer. Bea, It's Alex Sanderson. I'm returning your call."

"Oh, thank you, it wasn't an emergency. What time is it?"

Alex looked, in dismay, at his watch. It was a few minutes after midnight. “Sorry, I just got home. It's too late for me to talk to you now. Right?”

“It's okay, I'm awake now. I was wondering how the investigation is going. I spoke to Maggie's mother today and found out some things about Fred that might be important. There was much more to this man than meets the eye.”

“Yea, that's an understatement. There was definitely more to him than meets many eyes,” laughed Alex for the first time that evening.

He stifled a yawn and Bea said, “Come for breakfast. Then I can tell you a little more about Maggie's mother.”

Chapter 9

Noon, Friday, October 17th

At the police station, Kyle spent his morning catching up on paperwork. He transcribed his notes from the previous day's trip, prepared a travel claim and was talking on the phone to a botanist about hydrangea plants and shrubs when Alex sauntered in. He whistled as he walked to his desk, twirled his chair around and started his computer with one elbow and his monitor with the other elbow. Then he turned and with perfect aim threw his parka, across the room, onto the coat rack hook.

Kyle looked up at him and said, "Nice shot, but get your coat. I was just going to leave without you. I got your message about interviewing Bea Prancer again. It took you three and a half hours. Were you planning to stay for lunch? Tony Eco called to say he was doing his duty as an officer of the court. Yea, right. There seems to be some discrepancies that he felt we might like to look into. We're meeting him and his accountant at the agency in fifteen minutes."

"I knew Fred was running a scam," said Alex. "The Suits couldn't find anything because there was nothing either on his computer or in the agency's files. The evidence must have been kept somewhere else." Like a certain Toronto tabloid, Alex used the nickname, the Suits, to mean accountants and anyone who worked in the tax or financial services sector.

"Eco was ambiguous. The accountant hired by the estate has noticed discrepancies in the invoices when compared to the payroll. We are taking along our own accountant, what's his name? The fraud guy who always wears the double-breasted suits with the shiny navy button."

"I wonder if Anthony Eco is related to Umberto Eco?"

"Who's Umberto Eco?" asked Kyle.

"Some Italian who wrote a book called the *Name of the Rose* and funny short stories about salmon and smoking in the States," said Alex.

"Now what the hell are you talking about? You hate smoking," said Kyle, looking at his partner as if he was a man from Mars. "You're very talkative today."

His partner continued, "I should start reading fiction again. Women like novels especially mysteries, don't they?"

"I gather your interview with Bea Prancer went well."

"We had breakfast."

"So you discussed books while you were on duty? I'm having lunch with Marcus today. He reads or I can ask the wife tonight what books, she thinks you should read to attract the opposite sex. Is it vitally important for you to become fictionally literate today?" asked Kyle.

"No," said Alex, ignoring his partner's teasing tone of voice. "Look, here comes what's his name. The blazer guy."

>>>>>

Bea and Maggie were on their way out for lunch when they acknowledged the three men coming in the front doors. Watching the police stroll into the office had become an ordinary sight for staff at the agency so they merely acknowledged each other with a nod.

"Tony and a special accountant are coming to meet them," said Maggie. "I might be inheriting tainted money. Did you know Fred had a Swiss bank account? After the party I cleaned up the living room and found a bank book taped to the bottom of a tarnished silver teapot. Do you want to see it? Maybe it's not really a Swiss bank book. See it says - Bank Suisse Internationale. What if the money he bequeathed me was made from awful war crimes?"

"Maggie, war crimes, what war? Your stepfather was born in 1941, the Second World War ended in 1945. And he was too young for the Korean War too. Did he ever leave Ontario?" asked Bea, trying to stop herself from going into mother mode.

"No, he didn't go anywhere. But, he was an excellent businessman, wasn't he?"

"Excellent, he was so excellent that two policemen, a lawyer and two forensic accountants are all meeting to examine his books," said Bea.

Afternoon, Friday

Her head appeared at the top of the circular snakeskin's strangulating hold. As she crawled out of the narrowing straightjacket, her real skin, herself emerged in creamy mucus. The bodiless pile of scales shrieked and moulted rage.

Danni moaned, exhausted from the image of the primeval urge to flay herself. Her daydreams had not obeyed the rule of coming only once a day either early in the morning or just before going to sleep. She concentrated on closing the images by reciting the last two lines of Dicken's *Tale of Two Cities*.

It is a far better thing I do, than I have ever done.

It is a far, far greater place I go, than I have ever gone.

She wanted someone to confirm that she had new skin, that the degraded covering had flaked away into the air, blown through windows over the years into the soil joining billions of minute epidermis particles pulled down by gravity, disintegrating into the earth. If there are thirty-two million people in Canada and each of them regenerated a new layer of skin every ten to twelve years, how many microscopic freckles there must be floating around?

Not one cell remained. Not one wrinkle had the same cells. They had reproduced and regenerated. Fred had not touched the same skin as that murderer. She wished she had told him before he died. Just as she lay her head on her desk, someone knocked on the door.

"Danni, your one o'clock is here," Bea called through the closed office door. "Are you on the phone?"

Danni rose from her desk, opened the door with a jerk and said, "I don't have a one o'clock appointment."

"Well, he's one of Fred's temps and I think Maggie told him that you would see him when he called yesterday. It's on the e-mail calendar."

"Okay, I'll be right out. Sorry. I forgot to check my e-mail this morning."

"Are you okay? Do you want me to see him? I don't have an appointment until 1:30," said Bea.

"Excuse me," said Danni. "There is something wrong with an office that depends on a computer to communicate." She brushed past Bea as if oblivious to her offer of assistance.

In the waiting room the receptionist jumped up and in a perky but pesky voice said, "Hi, Daniella. I tried to call you but your line was busy and I think the voice mail isn't working. Who should I tell?"

"Tell Maggie, she's the boss." She turned toward the man who was waiting for her. "Mr. Clarke, please come in. Have we met before? You look familiar." He appeared to be in his late thirties and was wearing an expensive tartan shirt and faded blue jeans.

"I believe, I saw you when I was here a couple of weeks ago," said the man as he followed Danni to her office.

"Let me bring up your file," she said, keying in his last name and first initial.

"I really came to find out what happened to the contract position at the police station. I spoke to Fred last Tuesday morning and told him that I would be back in the country the following Thursday. That was yesterday. I'm sorry he's not here."

"Fred. Oh, you don't know," Danni stammered, stared at the computer screen, then abruptly stood up. "Wait here a minute. There's someone you have to see. Let me go get them." She backed out of the office.

>>>>>

"You, sir, were to report to me last Tuesday at nine a.m. sharp. If you had been under my watch your behaviour would be considered insubordination and abandonment of your post. Do you know the trouble and money you have caused me?" Detective-Sergeant Kyle Bottleman asked as he stood, military style, in the doorway of Danni's office.

Mr. Clarke looked up, with amazement, at the man accusing him of not reporting to work at the police station. "No! You're wrong. I didn't not show up! I told Fred that I had to go to my grandmother's funeral in England. I even gave him the number of a guy who could do the work instead of me. Where is Fred? I told him," he said, looking at the man who had suddenly started examining him as if he was an interesting diagnosis, not a live person.

"I'm sorry, Mr. Clarke. Let's start at the beginning. When did you last talk to Mr. Waddle?" asked Kyle.

"Tuesday morning. I called him from the airport. My grandmother died on Monday afternoon and I decided, at the last minute, to go to the funeral because my grandfather is also ill," said the befuddled systems officer.

"What time did you call?"

"It was really early. I expected to talk to an answering machine but Fred answered the phone. My flight left at 8:10 a.m. so it was just before 7:00 a.m. when I talked to him. I had already gone through customs because I used the phone in the departure gate waiting area."

"Ah ha. What's your first and middle name, Mr. Clarke?"

"Tom, hum, Thomas Harry, sir."

"Not your fault, Thomas. Fred Waddle passed away last Tuesday morning. My partner here, Detective Sanderson will take a statement. We'll need a few more details."

Night, Friday

It was a five minute walk from the Islington subway station to her apartment building. Fred had said that property near the subway would always appreciate in value and it was safer for a woman without a car to live within walking distance from the subway because she would be home lickety split.

As usual Maggie went to the side entrance door of her condominium because it was closest to the mail room. Shrugging off her knapsack she reached into the back pocket for her keys, opened the door and walked down the silent hallway. Just as she inserted the tiny key into the rectangular metal mail box door, she heard a noise.

Turning her head, the word, hello was just coming out of her mouth when - Whack! She fell forward, arms out, the weight of her torso and the force of what felt like a two by four smashing against her made her collapse onto her stomach and chest. Instinctively, she tucked and covered her head with her arms, then she rolled into a fetal position so as to protect her face from the unrelenting force striking her body. When she tried to get up, a foot kicked her back down. "Help," she squeaked as something hard and spiky hit her again and again.

Maggie tried again to stand up to defend herself, she kept her shoulders hunched over and went onto one knee. Her arm reached out to grab the assailant's leg when suddenly a deep male voice yelled. “Hey! Whatsa going on in here?” She turned her face with relief toward the Hungarian accent and saw black shoes with tassels run out the door past the building superintendent.

“My God, child, can you move? Your back, stay here. I'll call an ambulance,” said the superintendent as he took off his coat, folded it and placed it under her head. Splinters of wood, the tips oozing blood could be seen lodged in her skin.

He hesitated for a second uncomfortable at leaving her alone. “I'll be back soon. Don't worry. My wife will come. She'll bring you a pillow.”

The urge to escape overcame Maggie so she crawled into the corner hugging the superintendent's jacket like a baby blanket. Once in the corner, she started to cry but stopped when her body realized that sobs made the pain worse. Where was he? She remembered that he had taken weeks to fix the leaky pipe to her washing machine.

As the ambulance attendants carried her out they argued about where to take her deciding finally to drive to the emergency ward at the Toronto General Hospital. In the emergency ward, while waiting to be examined, a nursing assistant, assuming Maggie's boyfriend had assaulted her, started a standard lecture in a voice dripping with disdain on how no woman has to take abuse. Maggie shut her eyes and croaked, “It wasn't my effing boyfriend. If you really want to help me, you'll call this number and ask Bea to come.”

“Is she a real friend?” asked the stupid woman.

“No, she is my worst enemy,” said Maggie, “and she runs a safe house for torture victims of biker gangs. Call her please.”

Chapter 10

Saturday, October 18th

Maggie lay on her stomach with her head turned sideways when Bea pushed the thin curtain aside and asked, "Hi, how are you doing?"

"Bea, like, am I glad to see you. They can't find my clothes. The nurse put my clothes somewhere, then she went off shift. I heard the police say they only needed my jacket and shirt. Now the hospital is saying that maybe the police did take my clothes. But whatever they can't find them."

"It's okay, honey," said Bea. She sat on the edge of the bed stroking Maggie's hair. "It's okay. I phoned your Mom. She guessed you would need a change of clothes so she's making a pit stop at your apartment."

"Good. Do you think my Mom will bring me some food? I'm starving. They gave me a dirty look when I asked if they serve lunch. Getting beat up makes you hungry. I think I must have pissed the people here at the emergency ward but I don't know how. They're probably rude to everyone with blue streaked hair."

"I'll go to the nursing station and see if you're allowed to eat. If you can, I'll go get you something good after your Mom comes. So, what happened?" asked Bea.

"I went to the mail room and suddenly someone is hitting me. There were splinters in my back. It's so gross and it hurts, hurts, hurts. I only saw the back of his legs and shoes. He had small feet in black loafers with sissy-boy tassels and black dress pants with a sharp crease. The chicken-shit hid his face with a brown wool hat with holes for his eyes and mouth. The policeman said, it's called a balaclava. Whatever he hit me with felt like a machine gun shooting me in the back."

Alex came into the room while Maggie was speaking. He placed his hand on Bea's shoulder to say hello and interrupted, "It was a piece of broken fence with nails in it. You're lucky, young lady. You can say thank you to your leather jacket; it saved your life. What were you doing in the mail room so late at night? It was after midnight."

"Da, it's the mail room. I always pick up my mail on my way upstairs. But I'm never going in that room again by myself. I wasn't doing anything wrong."

"Maggie, you didn't do anything wrong. Whoever hit you is vicious and dangerous," said Bea, turning around to give Alex an accusing look. "Someone tried to kill her. What are you going to do about that?"

"Well, she'll be fine here in the hospital. We're working on it," he replied just as a nurse and doctor came into the room. The nurse flipped her head and pointed her finger at the door and said, "Out."

"Ah, would you like us to *please* leave the room. Okay. I have to get back to work," said Alex. He rolled his eyes at the nurse's curt manner.

"Bea, don't leave too. Can she stay? Please, please," pleaded Maggie. The nurse looked at the doctor who nodded in the affirmative.

While the doctor was shining his light into Maggie's eyes. Bea asked. "How long will she be here?"

"She can go home this morning. Someone should stay with her for the next day or two. I'll arrange for a home visit to check the wounds and bandages. She should see her family doctor on Monday," said the doctor.

"She's still bleeding," said Bea watching the doctor and nurse remove long strips of bloody gauze bandages, examine the wounds and reapply clean bandages. "Shouldn't she stay in the hospital till the bleeding stops?"

"I know it looks bad but the nails didn't puncture any vital organs such as her lung or heart. She should be okay at home. The bandages need to be changed every four hours so I'll show you how to do it," said the nurse with a that's-life-folks shrug.

During the bandage changing demonstration, even the exhausted nurse cracked a smile when Mary Nichelton arrived. Pulling the curtain aside, the mother of Maggie burst in. The first thing she saw was her daughter's bruised and bleeding back. She dropped her bags on the floor and rushed over to her daughter and exclaimed, "My baby, the devil must have attacked you. Tell me who did it and I'll shoot them through the heart with a bullet with your name on it."

Maggie looked at her, and said, "Hi, Mom, It hurts but they gave me mega-drugs. I'm really starving."

>>>>>

It was late in the morning before Mary and Bea brought their patient home. Bea made up the spare bed for her unexpected guest. Maggie was happy when the two women served her pain killers, cookies and tea in bed. They were all upstairs watching a movie video when they heard a loud noise downstairs.

Bea stood at the top of the stairs and listened. Mary stood behind her. The two women tiptoed downstairs and when they were half-way down a menacing male voice called out, "Hello, ladies. Are you alone?" Mary stopped abruptly on the spot causing Bea to almost fall over her.

There reclining in the easy chair, in the living room, reading the *Saturday Globe and Mail*, was her now favourite detective. Alex looked up at them and said, "The door was wide open indicating an invitation to enter and a complete lack of security and common sense at the Prancer residence."

"We didn't hear you come in," said Bea.

"I know. I knocked on the open door three time. No one answered so I called up the stairs to announce my presence but all I heard was laughing and talking. Every time I heard laughter, I heard Maggie scream, `Don't make me laugh, it hurts.' You, ladies, wouldn't have heard a herd of elephants come in the front door or a mugger or..."

"We were watching a kids' video, *Matilda.* It's hilarious, a comedy about a little girl with terrible parents. I better get up to my daughter or she will say I'm a negligent mother," said Mary. She looked seriously at Alex. "Maggie thinks a crack addict attacked her and it had nothing to do with her personally. You're a policeman, what do you think?"

"I don't know, Mrs. Nichelton, but I think that Maggie will be safe as long as you all take some precautions, like locking the front door." Mary nodded her head and went back upstairs.

"You look hungry. Would you like breakfast?" asked Bea.

"Sure," said Alex. "Breakfasting with you could become a bad habit, if I'm not careful."

"So are you complaining or just changing feet?"

"No, but I better change the subject. Is Maggie settled in? Tough girl and she's not as dumb as she looks."

"Is that your esteemed policeman judgement of Maggie's character? Who do you really think is doing this? It might be involved with Fred dying. Do you know what the cause of death was yet?"

"Three questions in one breath. The answer to question one is - Sorry, I shouldn't have been flippant. The answer to question two is; we don't know who attacked Maggie or if it had anything to do with Fred's death. And the answer to number three is; yea, we do know the cause of death but it's still confidential."

“Why is it confidential?” asked Bea, lowering her voice. “Was it natural causes? Please tell me. Everyone thinks it was a stranger that came into the office, robbed Fred of his donuts and clothes; then scared him to death.”

“Scared him to death. Never, in my twenty years as a cop, have I ever seen a victim who was scared to death. Murder by a stranger is a pretty rare event. Last year in the whole of Canada there were 555 homicides and only in few cases, the victim didn't know the assailant. We don't live in the United States, you know.”

“Alex, are you deflecting the question about how Fred died?”

“I can't say anything except, there will be an announcement soon about the cause of Fred's demise and he didn't die from natural causes.”

“Really,” said Bea. Her eyes lit up with curiosity.

“Yes, really. Can we change the subject again? What do you know about Maggie's family? When I asked her about her father she said, as far as she was concerned her Dad was vapour and if she met him, she would walk right through him,” whispered Alex afraid that the mother and daughter upstairs would hear them talking.

“Let's go out. Maggie will be fine with her Mom,” said Bea. She yelled up the stairs. “Alex and I are going out for brunch. Do you need anything at the store?”

“No, thanks,” yelled Maggie back to her as they walked out the front door. They heard Mary say, ‘Maggie, don't yell, this isn't your house.’

>>>>>

They drove to the Village Restaurant, on Spadina Avenue, for the best breakfast in the city or so Alex claimed. The special for $7.25 included three buttermilk pancakes, three eggs, four slices of bacon, an order of toast, fried potatoes, sliced tomatoes and coffee.

When their coffee had arrived, Alex started to describe the interviews with the ex-wives. "Three of them, he went to visit them almost every week-end. One of the ex-wives, Martha, has remarried and tells her present husband that she attends a women's therapy group every other Friday night. She gives her present hubby the phone number and hotel room number just in case he needs to talk to her. Saturday mornings Fred would continue on to St. Catharines where he visited Mary, mother of the battered heiress sleeping upstairs in your house. He usually spent the night but rose at the peak of dawn Sunday morning to drive to Hamilton."

"That's what I was going to tell you. Mary told me she was still seeing Fred on the week-ends. Maggie didn't know that her mother was dating Fred. So who did he see on Sunday? Let me guess. Pierre's mother."

"Correct. The lovely Martine Tremblay. She was Fred's Sunday favourite," said Alex. He looked with satisfaction as the waitress brought his breakfast on three plates.

"I thought Tony Eco said there were four wives," said Bea.

"Yea, one died years ago in Montreal. Can't remember her name," said Alex.

"What is the fourth wife, Martine Tremblay, like?"

"Oh, sophisticated, slight almost skinny but with large breasts. She's an attractive French-Canadian with a delicate facial structure surrounded by short wispy black hair and heavy black eyelashes framing haunted violet eyes."

"Really," said Bea in amazement. "She sounds like a Vogue model that floated into your eyes and out of your mouth as prose. Did you get a sense of her personality, by any chance?" Alex chose to ignore Bea's sardonic question and continue with his narrative.

"She was polite but extremely nervous. During the interview she kept hopping up to do things, she made coffee, opened the back door to air the house, moved a pot of flowers and filled the sugar and cream containers. Kyle finally asked her to sit down. Numerous times she mentioned that Fred's will was unfair to her. Resentful, that would be the one word describing her attitude."

"So did you like her?" asked Bea.

"Don't know. Can you do something for me? Find out who would inherit if Maggie died. I assume it's her mother, Mary," said Alex.

After the late breakfast he dropped Bea off at home. Maggie and Mary were sleeping so Bea also went for an afternoon nap but first she locked the front door.

Chapter 11

Morning, Monday, October 20th

Niels popped his head into Danni's office door and asked, "So has the princess boss arrived for work yet?" When Danni shook her head no, he came in, slumped down in a chair and pulled out a file cabinet drawer to prop his feet on.

"Look, it's nine-thirty and the little twerp still isn't here. Neither is Bea. The whole place is falling apart; maybe we should start looking around for another job," said Danni pointedly looking at her watch and raising her eyebrow in disdain.

"Twenty year olds like to party."

The sound of heavy footsteps came down the hallway. Niels turned around and was startled to see Kyle and Alex standing in the doorway. "Good morning," said the older policeman, "don't get up for us. We stopped by to tell you ..."

"You don't have to tell us why you are here. Ms. Nichelton is now the owner but she isn't in yet. My co-worker tried to call her but she doesn't answer the phone," said Niels to the detectives.

"Yes, we know she's not here. That's what we came to tell you. Maggie was assaulted Friday night at her apartment building. She has been released from hospital and Bea is looking after her," said Alex.

Niels leaped off his chair again and stated, "I was at home Friday night working on my investment portfolio. I phoned and e-mailed a change order to my broker. You can check the times with him. We ordered Chinese food around eight o'clock. What time did it happen?"

"Mr. Wolfe, how tall are you?" asked Kyle scrutinizing him from head to toe.

“Just under six feet,” said Niels, sitting up straight in his chair, then slumping down.

“And, what size are your shoes?”

“Size 12. Why?”

“Maggie's assailant evidently had small feet so relax you won't qualify as the resident mugger,” said Kyle. “Now I would like to speak to each of you privately.”

“Sorry, I'm just ... I don't know. How is Maggie? I should have asked that first,” said Niels.

“She'll be fine. She's in a lot of pain, excruciating pain,” said Alex over his shoulder as he walked out of the room.

“Ms. Thompson, I'd like to speak to you first,” said Kyle.

“I have an interview in half and hour and numerous job orders to fill. Maybe you should talk to Niels first,” said Danni.

“No, I'm sorry. I'll start with you. We should be finished in half an hour.” Kyle turned to Niels and said, “Mr. Wolfe, would you be kind enough to cover for Ms. Thompson, should I go over my allotted half an hour?”

Niels nodded his head in assent and said as he scurried out of the room. “No problemo. Don't rush for me.”

Kyle closed the door, pulled out his notebook and sat down beside Danni. With unconcealed irritation, Danni looked at the note book in his hand. “Aren't you going to ask me what shoe size I wear? Size eight. The most common size of women's shoes in North America.”

“No, I wasn't planning to ask you that. I would probably just look at your feet. I did want to talk to you about something else. You know in this electronic world, information is available from genealogical databanks across Canada. Even adoptions and divorces, rightly or wrongly, are now linked up to other personal information. As part of the investigation we have been looking into the background of the people Fred knew. I should start by reassuring you that unless the information we gather is used as evidence that information will remain confidential. We did find out that you were born Daniella Linda Hemming in 1959. In 1965 you were adopted by Günther Doses and became Daniella Linda Doses. In 1978, you legally changed your surname to Thompson," said Kyle reading from his notebook.

Danni did not respond but sat staring into her coffee cup. She picked up the spoon, started to wave it in the detective's face and said in a furious whisper, "My personal history has nothing to do with you or your investigation. Nothing. I am sure you are aware we have a Freedom of Information and Privacy Act. My emphasis is on the privacy."

"I'm well aware of F.O.I. but this is a murder investigation."

"Not F.O.I. but F.O.I. and Privacy, you keep forgetting the privacy part."

"Birth, death, and divorce records are public records as are records of criminal cases unless a minor was involved. You were just a young girl when ..."

"It was years ago, you have no right to bring that up, no right what so ever! You can't force me to talk to you about that murder. My mother's death has nothing, absolutely nothing to do with Fred's," said Danni, putting her head on the table and her hands around the empty coffee cup. "Just leave me alone."

Kyle sat studying the distraught woman beside him. He reached instinctively over to stroke her hair but instead placed his hand over hers and said, "Lassie, I wasn't planning to talk to you about your mother's murder but about the fact that your mother was married to Fred in 1961. Do you remember? You were only four years old when they divorced."

"You're lying! You're lying. My mom was never married to Fred. Married to Fred! Was she really? No. I don't believe you.

Maybe that's why I loved him, he loved my mother," said Danni. Her voice almost inaudible.

"Didn't Fred ever mention your Mom to you?"

"No. He told me a few times that I reminded him of someone but he couldn't remember who. I told him once that Hemming was my birth name. He never said anything to me. What if he knew and he didn't tell me?" Her face was the colour of pie dough and her eyes roamed around the room as if searching the walls and ceiling for reassurance.

"Are you okay? We assumed that you knew about Fred and your mother. I'm sorry about what happened. Life's not fair," said Kyle. "I didn't know about your Mom. Did it happen in Montreal?"

Her usual controlled demeanour dissolved into a wasteland of realizations and painful memories as she sobbed, "Oh Good! Your searching into my past didn't reveal the juiciest scandal. Too bad, you can find out yourself. There's more you don't know. I was dating Fred. Maybe he didn't really go to look after his favourite aunt in Niagara Fall on the weekends. So did he? She was supposed to be suffering from Alzheimer's. I hate stepfathers, I hate stepfathers."

"I'm sorry this has turned out to be so hard but it's necessary. We have to continue our discussion. I have a few more questions but they can wait. Maybe the office isn't the best place for this. I'll call you tomorrow to set up a time to continue the interview either at your home or at the police station. Do you want me to tell Mr. Wolfe that you're going home?"

"No, I would rather work. Please don't tell him anything. I don't want to think about it."

>>>>>

Kyle looked, out the car window, at the cotton ball clouds blowing across the sky as if rushing away from winter winds. He turned to his partner and said, "I didn't re-interview Niels Wolfe.

He's a write-off anyway because his alibi checks out. But that Daniella Thompson. I've been a cop too long to be surprised at much but this afternoon, she threw me a humdinger I wasn't prepared for. We have to find out what happened to her mother twenty-five years ago. She was murdered."

"Murdered! Her mother was murdered!" exclaimed Alex, sitting up in the driver seat so as to listen more carefully to his partner.

"No wonder she acts a bit strange and detached. Unless she's a great actress, she really didn't know that Fred was once her stepfather. And to make matters worse, she was having an affair with him," said Kyle.

"Yea, that confirms the office gossip. Did you ask her if she slept with him Monday night and poisoned him at breakfast the next morning?" asked Alex.

"No. I never got to that point. She's emotionally fragile. She'll seize up if we come down too hard on her. First, I'm going to find out who killed Danni's Mom and then I'll question her again. She hasn't got an alibi for the Tuesday morning Fred kicked the bucket or the Friday night when Maggie was beaten up," said Kyle. "So, Alex, what happened at your meeting with the Suits? They find anything?"

"Lots of suspicion and conjecture. I wouldn't write-off Niels Wolfe too quickly. He may not be a murderer but he's involved. I suspect Niels. Why would a 32 year old millionaire spend his work day interviewing temps for clerical jobs?" asked Alex taking a deep breath and continuing. "He said he made his money on the stock market in derivatives and farm animals. Whatever that means. Where did he get the start-up capital? He didn't inherit it or win the lottery. I checked. I want to apply for a search warrant for Niels' house and computer. They found five invoices where the company didn't match the actual work location of the worker. And more importantly, the short-term contract was always for a provincial ministry or municipal agency like the police. The temporary worker worked at a government office, got paid but the invoice was made out to private company. Typos, that's what the lawyer suggested. Yea right."

"Enough, Alex, donnae forget we are with the homicide department, not the fraud squad," said Kyle.

"Niels is guilty as sin, maybe not murder but something nefarious. And what about the computer guy, Tom Clarke, what about him? He was on the agency computer but your specific job order couldn't be found, anywhere. I think our dead friend, Fred, kept two sets of books, and someone got a kickback," said Alex in a stubborn tone.

"Are you saying Fred could have involved the police in whatever scam he was pulling? Come on. Alex. Human Resources Branch arranged to hire this systems guy to install the area code software. The job is being done as we speak and the guy will get a pay cheque from the Common Sense Employment Agency. They'll bill the police. I've signed the guy's timesheet in triplicate, sent copies to Human Resources who will approve the payment and send it to the Finance Branch. They'll match it with the appropriate invoice; then they'll pay the agency. Where would the "conspiracy to defraud" take place? At the Finance Branch or at the Human Resources Branch or with me, I'm the one who signs the guy's timesheet."

"The fraud took place at the agency. We don't know how but we know that Fred was raking in money from jobs that were not recorded on the regular job order and invoice system," said Alex.

"The Suits can talk to Revenue Canada. You know how happy a complicated tax scam makes them. That's their job. Our job is to find a poisoner before he or she poisons again. We shouldn't bother ourselves with some cheap tax scam. So someone works for Company A but Company B gets the tax credit for that work. For sure, it is against some tax regulation, somewhere in some unreadable act. Don't get fixated on that part of the investigation. It could be important but I doubt it," said Kyle. His tone of voice was that of a patriarch upbraiding his son for disagreeing with the family's religious beliefs.

"I'm not fixated. It's past lunch time," said Alex looking at his watch. It read 1:00 p.m. "Maybe I'll go see how Maggie Nichelton is doing instead of having lunch with you and Dr. Christie. You can take the car if you drop me off at Bea Prancer's house."

"Bea, Bea, you would rather see Bea than have lunch with Marcus and me," sang Kyle. "Okay. But seriously, don't get involved until the case is over."

"She's barely a witness," said Alex.

"I just said be careful and make sure that girl, Maggie, stays with someone and doesn't go home alone until we find out what's going on."

Afternoon, Monday

Kyle met Marcus at their favourite Greek restaurant, Knossos, which is located on Yonge Street four doors south of College Street. They serve generous portions of chicken and pork shishkabob or slices of moist lamb with boiled parsley potatoes, rice and warm heavy bread.

Though he no longer smoked at home or at work Kyle kept a red pack of du Mauriers in his briefcase. He only pulled them out when a suspect needed a smoke or when he had lunch with the pathologist because cigarettes were the catalyst of their debates about how to protect the public, especially the poor, in a capitalist society or medical rehabilitation versus correctional rehabilitation of drug addicts.

After they had ordered a beer and settled into their favourite seats beside the window, Kyle updated Marcus on the Fred Waddle case and his interview with Danni.

"It sounds like a movie of the week. Was the prim and proper Daniella suffering from post-traumatic stress syndrome? Could she have metamorphosed into a cold blooded killer or was she framed and re-victimized by the deadly murderer of her saintly mother?" asked Marcus, eating his tender lamb and rice with enjoyment. "You're right, it would make excellent material for my book."

"Post-traumatic stress syndrome, yea, I've read about that. Danni is our primary suspect and after this morning's session she might just be it. I hope not, life just isn't fair. I don't think she'll take-off so I didn't take her down to the station. She was so focussed on the past; she didn't even realize that she might be a suspect in the present," said Kyle.

"Does she have a garden?" asked Marcus.

"She lives in a townhouse, probably has a postcard yard. I'm going to question her at home tomorrow. Did you bring the flower book?"

"Yea, it's right here," said the pathologist pulling out a slender soft-cover book. On the cover was a picture of a beautiful, sky-blue hydrangea. Inside the book, pictures of the large round pink, blue and white flower heads filled every other page. "It's an interesting plant, really a blooming shrub. By the way, I reported the poisoning to the city's Public Health Department but advised them that it was probably not an accidental poisoning. I noticed that you still haven't released the cause of death. Soon, Kyle, you have to do it soon."

"Marcus, I know the protocol," he replied. "What else did you find out?"

"The seeds, bud and leaves are all poisonous but I still don't know if they have a strong taste. Should try it myself but my stomach has been a bit queasy of late. Your gut is like a steel trap.

Come to my laboratory to nibble the deadly dried hydrangea leaf," said Marcus. With an evil gleam, he beckoned with his head at the same time moving his eyebrows up and down.

"How generous. Maybe. How desperate are we to know this victual fact?" asked Kyle totally ignoring his friend's antics.

"Not important. There's no way he died in that office. Hydragin poisoning has similar symptoms to cyanide, but takes longer to react. Usually there is vomiting, convulsions and coma, finally death. Phewff, the way the body was laid out and the office was not in turmoil indicates that the first stages of dying took place somewhere else. Also I'll send you the chemical analysis of the skin residue. It indicates Fred was cleaned up with a blue liquid cleaner, probably window cleaner. Looks like someone gave him a good wash after he died."

"I don't have any info on where he was poisoned or where his clothes went or who tidied him up. It's driving us crazy. Availability, that's also on my list. Not that that would prove anything except availability. You and I both have the bloody plant in our yard and we don't run around poisoning people. I wouldn't have even known, how to do it, would you?"

"No, but it wouldn't be hard to figure out. Look even this book has a warning that the plant is lethal. You would be better finding out who had the access, knowledge and hatred. How intelligent is this Daniella woman?" asked Marcus.

"She's smart and proud of her independence. I don't know all her history but I can already guess it's gruesome. This afternoon I'll find out who killed the poor girl's mother."

"Poor girl's mother. Are you developing a soft spot for your suspect, Kyle? I'm disappointed in you. I have heard you tell your junior partner that feelings have no place in police work. And intuition is only useful if it is supported by evidence."

“Bullshit,” retorted Kyle pulling out a cigarette. When he lit it, he leaned back in his chair, raised his chin and blew an almost perfect ring of blue-grey smoke. The smoke like the spoken word floated up and disappeared never to be seen or heard again.

“Your smoking is like our present government who is lacking in common sense. They, like smokers, believe their own lies about the lack of negative consequences of their actions. The solution is simple. I'm going to tell your wife who, like the voting public, should choose to vote you out of the bedroom,” said Marcus obviously pleased with his analogy.

“Clever, fine, I'm going to tell your wife that you ate potatoes, rice, a double order of lamb, half a loaf of bread and walnut baklava. Pretty fattening.”

“No wonder Alex doesn't want to have lunch with you. You're obtuse.”

“Bullshit. The kid isn't lunching with us because he's in love with one of the witnesses and I had to warn him. Bea Prancer is the woman who found the body of ...”

>>>>>

Alex walked up to Bea's house and frowned when he saw the front door propped open with a winter boot. He knocked and looked in to see Maggie lying sideways on the easy chair talking on the phone.

“Pierre, gotta go, that policeman, the one who l-o-v-e-s Bea, just walked in. Ha, ha, he just gave me a dirty look. Don't worry about your Mom, she'll find another job. I'll ask someone to look her up in the computer. Bye, you can call me at home tomorrow. Call collect. I don't want you getting into trouble.” Maggie hung up the phone and gave Alex a radiant smile.

She tried to push down the foot rest on the chair but squealed in pain as her back turned. Alex put his hand on the foot rest and started to push down but stopped when the chair was halfway up. “Why was the front door open, young lady?” he asked.

“Because I was hot.”

“If I help you out of this chair, you have to promise me that you won't leave the doors open and that you'll have someone with you at all times for the next few days.”

“Da, who are you? My father.”

“I'm serious, Maggie, we'll ask Bea if you can stay here for a few more days. Whoever beat you up meant serious business.”

“Who would want to poison me? Also I can't figure out who hated Fred enough to poison him,” said Maggie. When she answered him back, there was a touch of contempt infused with bravado in her voice.

“How did you know he was poisoned?” asked Alex. He pushed the foot rest upward throwing Maggie backwards.

She squealed in agony as her back hit the chair and screamed, “Ow! You bastard!”

He stepped back to avoid her kicking legs. “Sorry, I didn't mean to hurt you,” said Alex. He grabbed Maggie's hands and pulled her into a standing position.

She punched him in the arm and said, “I trusted you, you jerk.”

“Sorry, It was a reflex motion. Let me ask again. How did you know that Fred was poisoned?”

“What are you so pissed off about? It was on the news at noon. What kind of plant poisoned him?”

Ignoring her questions, Alex picked up the convertor and flicked the TV to the all-news channel. The Toronto Public Health Department had issued a news release about the cause of Fred's death. The news release warned the public, especially gardeners, that they should not eat any leaves, seed or buds of the hydrangea plant family as they are extremely toxic and could be fatal.

"What the hell are they doing issuing a press release?" Alex asked the TV.

"What the hell did they issue a press release on, Alex? Good to see you," said Bea as she walked in the door her arms laden with grocery bags.

He jumped up, retrieved the bags and said, "The Public Health Department announced that Fred died from hydrangea poisoning."

"Really! Never heard of it," said Bea.

"I have," said Maggie, jumping into the conversation. "Fred has two plants beside the stairs leading up to the deck. He loved them cause they have big pink round flowers."

"Fred grew hydrangea?" Alex asked her.

"Yea, when they were blooming he made me admire them every time I was at his house. Maybe he ate the plant and didn't know it could kill him. Fred ate anything that was green. He loved salads. He was like a rabbit nibbling lettuce and carrots even between meals. The only reason he was over-weight was because he liked hamburgers, sour cream, desserts and cookies too."

Bea looked at Alex and asked. "Why did the Health Department and not the police announce the cause of death?"

"We were waiting for more test results but Public Health must have an upcoming budget submission at municipal council and figured poisoning was sexier than TB or AIDS prevention."

"Sort of like the police releasing crime statistics the week before their budget submission," said Bea. She winked and walked out of the room.

"Touche," said Alex. "Talking about budgets. Maggie, who did the agency's bookkeeping?"

"I only kept the payroll. Fred did his own bookkeeping and paid the bills for the agency and the office building. Niels helped him with his investments. I talked to Tony and he's hired a management consultant to help me learn the business," said Maggie. "Starting next Monday, I'll be an apprentice just like a plumber." She started to giggle but it hurt so she went back to the couch and lay down on her stomach.

"Sorry, I forgot to ask. How are you feeling? I looked at the incident and medical reports. You were whacked eight times across the back and neck with a fence post. In the post were two nails that punctured your skin in seven places," he said all the while looking into the kitchen where Bea was putting away her groceries.

"I know how many times I was whacked but I have great drugs. I only hurt all over when they wear off. We're making homemade pizza. Will you stay and have some?"

>>>>>

After lunch Bea and Maggie laid down for an afternoon nap and didn't wake up until the doorbell rang. Remembering the stern lecture from Alex about leaving the door unlocked, Bea cautiously moved the lace curtain aside to see who was ringing the bell. There on the front porch stood Danni.

"Come on in. Are you okay?" asked Bea as she guided the pale-faced woman into the living room.

"I'm fine. Where's Maggie?" asked Danni.

"She's still sleeping. The pain medication zonks her out every four hours."

"How is she?"

"She'll be okay but it will take time for the bruises and wounds to heal."

"Does she think it's her fault? I wanted to tell her that it wasn't her fault that she was beaten up. People think that sometime after being assaulted."

"No, Maggie believes some psychotic crack addict did it. She'll be awake soon. Let's have a cup of tea or would you prefer a drink, wine, rum."

"I'd love a glass of wine. Your house is cosy." Danni followed Bea through the dining room and stopped to look at the pictures on the wall. "Bea, are these your parents?"

"Yes, that's my Mom and Dad and those are my in-laws. Only my mother-in-law, Nora, is still alive. This is my daughter's grade ten school picture."

"Do you have any sisters?" asked Danni.

"Yes, one, the pictures of her and her family are upstairs."

"Do you talk to them very often?"

"Most Sundays, we chat on the phone. I haven't seen her for over three months. She lives in Oakville, only an hour's drive away. Her kids are teenagers. She and I are as different as cats and dogs, different personalities, we even look different. She has naturally blonde hair and look at me, dark brown. She's petite and I'm not. She loves to participate in sports and I like to read and take walks. Like all kids when I was mad at my parents, I would wonder if I was adopted. Did you do that?" asked Bea with a giggle.

Danni laughed throwing her head back with an exaggerated fling. "I never wished I was adopted because I was adopted. Maybe I should tell you. I think I know who killed Fred and it was probably my fault. Well not really my fault, someone I know probably did it."

"Who! Why!"

"I never realized it. I really didn't until that Scottish detective started to question me. Nothing is ever secret, well it was never a secret. It was all over the newspapers in 1968. My mother was murdered because of me."

"Who murdered your mother, Danni?" asked Bea carefully. She looked up to see Maggie, eyes wide open, sitting on the stairs and shushed her with a look.

Danni continued her story while staring at the family pictures in the dining room. "It happened in Montreal. Maybe Fred knew about it but I don't think so. That's what confused me. The bad stepfather killed my mother because he wouldn't stop tickling me even after I peed my pants. He was mad because I screamed and struggled to get away from him. He wouldn't let me go so my Mom threatened to hit him on the head with a cast iron frying pan. He still wouldn't stop so she swung the frying pan, he grabbed her arm and the frying pan flew out of her hand and smacked him in the temple. She shouldn't have done that, that made him furious. He chased her into the kitchen, grabbed a butcher knife and chased her around the house. When he caught her, he stabbed her, ten times. She bled to death while I hid behind the couch."

Bea put her arm around Danni's rigid shoulder as she continued tell her story. "Today, the Scottish policeman shocked me when he said that Fred had been married to my mother over thirty years ago. I came to see Maggie because she had a list of Fred's ex-wives."

"I have a copy of the list as well because we used it to contact people for the funeral. It's right here. What was your mother's name?" asked Bea as she walked over to the hutch.

"Sophia Augusta Hemming."

"Sophia Augusta, yes, she's on the list as Sophia A. Doses."

"I always called him the bad stepfather. I can't remember his name but he must be out of prison by now and he probably killed Fred if he knew I was dating him."

"Danni, did you tell the police?"

"No. Don't worry. They'll come question me again and again and again. I've been through this before. Unless you leave town they won't leave you alone for years and years, reporters, social workers, lawyers, foster parents. Don't wake up, Maggie. I found out what I came for. I can see her another time."

"Don't go. I'm already awake," said Maggie from her seat on the stairs. "Maybe we are, like, stepsisters. That would be awesome. I would have, like, an older sister. Cool." She looked at Bea and said, "I came downstairs because my bandages are loose. Could you please change them? It really hurts." Maggie slipped the nightgown off her shoulders and Danni sucked in her breath with shock at the red welts and contusions.

"Danni, do you mind helping me?" asked Bea.

As they further removed the blood-stained gauze bandages; Maggie's black and blue back was revealed. The puncture marks were circles of crimson red and the bruises criss-crossed over them.

"That bastard, I remember his name. It was Günther. I'm going to find out if he did this," said Danni yanking her coat on. She grabbed Maggie's arm and said, "Don't say anything to the police. I'm leaving. I may be wrong but I have to find out."

"Danni, where are you going?" asked Maggie. "Don't forget you're like my sister now so you have to tell me where you're going."

She looked at the girl with dismay and exasperation. "I can't believe this, okay, okay. I'm reporting to a bloody kid. I'm going to Kingston Penitentiary, then to Montreal and if you don't hear from me by the day after tomorrow then call the cops and tell them to arrest Günther Doses."

Chapter 12

Morning, Tuesday, October 21st

It was two weeks to the day and the hour that the world had changed at the Common Sense Employment Agency. Bea and Maggie were the first ones to arrive at the agency and for once there was no evidence of police activity. Maggie inspected the offices acting as if she had been gone for eons and eons, not four days.

She went into Fred's office and sniffed the musty locked room odour. "I hate this room. Yuk. If I'm really rich. I'm going to redecorate and get rid of this ugly furniture." Maggie hit the bookcase, then in a reflexive motion she tugged the bookcase toward her and jumped back when it glided toward her like a smooth train on well-greased tracks.

"Holy cow! Look. Pull the bookcase over another foot toward you," said Bea pointing at the wall. An antique red oak door appeared as the bookcase slid along the wall.

"Awesome, this is so cool. A secret door." Maggie pulled the flat handle up and gave it a pull but it was locked. She kicked the red door causing pain to sear through her body. Next she collapsed onto the floor, rolled onto her stomach, punched the floor, and yelled, "Shit, shit, it hurts."

Bea rushed over to her. "Maggie, are you okay? You have lots of time. We can go up to the second floor to look for another entrance," she said helping the shaking girl stand up.

Determined to find out what was behind the door, Maggie knocked to see if it was hollow while resting her body against the wall. "No echo, it must be solid wood. Let's go upstairs now."

The two women walked out of agency and into the foyer of the low-rise office building. Beside the elevator was a name board which listed Victorian Investments and Victorian Payroll Services as the residents of the second floor. Maggie looked at the tenants' names. "Those names sound familiar. I should go and introduce myself to the second floor tenants, don't you think?"

"Sure, you're their landlord or you can call the property managers. Do you know who they are?" asked Bea.

"No, I don't think we have a full-time property manager. There's a part-time janitor but Fred called the plumber and stuff if things broke down," said Maggie as they walked into the elevator and pressed the second floor button. The elevator ascended but didn't open on the second floor, it descended directly back to the lobby. A second time she pressed the second floor button. The number two button lit up but the stainless steel doors did not open so she pressed the third floor button and the elevator moved upward. On the third floor, the elevator doors opened.

The two women exited, walked to the exit sign and down the stairwell to the second floor. The door to the second floor was locked.

"This is too weird, it is so, like, weird, really weird, isn't it that the elevator doesn't open on the second floor and the door is locked," said Maggie.

"Yes, especially since it's a fire exit."

"Let's try the elevator again."

"Yea, it's strange alright," said Bea. "Are you sure the building doesn't have an emergency superintendent?"

"Fred looked after everything. I'll have to ask Niels. He knows all about Victorian Investments." On the way down, they tried again to stop at the second floor but just like before the elevator didn't stop, it descended directly to the main floor.

When they walked back into the front door of the agency, Alex and Kyle were both standing, with hands on hips, looking around the waiting room. "We didn't see *Anyone* around and the door was

Open," said Alex looking at Maggie with accusing eyes as if she was a bad influence on Bea. "I told you *Both* yesterday morning, NOT TO LEAVE DOORS OPEN."

"Yes, Papa. I'm sorry, please forgive me." Maggie grabbed Kyle's coat sleeve and pulled him toward the back offices, "Come on," she said, "We found a secret door behind Fred's bookcase. It's locked and we couldn't find the key. And we couldn't lock the agency door because the new receptionist doesn't have her own key yet."

"Okay, let's go see this secret door," said Kyle with a chuckle. Maggie scooted ahead and Bea and Alex followed behind them. As they walked down the hallway, Kyle abruptly stopped in front of Danni's closed door and asked. "Didn't she come in this morning?"

"No," said Bea. "I almost called Detective Sandman about Danni last night."

"Detective Sanderson," whispered Alex in her ear. He, accidentally - on purpose, collided into her and placed his hand on the curve of her waist for a minutia longer than an accidental brush.

Up ahead the young excited woman stopped in her tracks, twirled around and glared at Bea. "How could you? Danni asked us not to tell the cops for two days."

"She asked you not to tell the police. She didn't ask me. You told her that you wouldn't tell and you don't have to break your promise," said Bea.

Maggie stared at her, and said, "How could you? You're only telling because you have the hots for Alex."

"Okay, I see you two have been busy. Let's see this door first and then we'll talk about what Danni did or didn't say last night," said Kyle.

"There, look. It's so cool but we don't have a key," said Maggie pointing at the antique door in the centre of the wall.

Everyone was staring at the door when Niels came up behind them and said, "About time you found Fred's hide-a-way."

Maggie swung around to face Niels. "You, like, knew about the door?"

"Sure, that's the door to the Victorian room where Fred conducted his other businesses. He kept it a semi-secret just for fun but lots of his clients knew it was there."

"Really," said Alex in amazement. "No one told us."

"I don't believe it. Are you telling me that the police had this room sealed off for almost two weeks and they didn't find the upstairs' office," said Niels, with a sarcastic laugh. "I wondered why four cop cars showed up at my house which, by the way, is why I'm so late. The police, with their usual consideration, banged on my door this morning and dragged us out of bed. So Maggie, my dear new boss, open the door, walk up the stairs and reveal to curious eyes the bounty of Fred's economic finesse which is what these dumb cop were so stupidly looking for at my house." Niels narrowed his eyes and spat out at the two detectives. "You could have just asked me about Victorian Investments instead of raiding my house, scaring my fiancee and confirming for the whole bloody neighbourhood, that yes, Indians are always getting in trouble with the law. Maybe you would prefer to line us up for target practise. Oh, but then who would you have to humiliate. Maybe the homeless. No, they're no fun, they're usually too weak to give you a good fight."

Alex opened his mouth to interrupt while Niels was taking a gulp of air but Bea shook her head as if to say, let him finish venting.

"In two whole weeks you haven't figured out what Fred was doing, have you? Don't the cops have anyone with half a brain working for them? Let me tell you the story, though I had nothing to do with it. Victorian Payroll Services was a service that allowed companies to claim payroll credits for non-existent workers. It was a tax scam. The temps worked for a government agency not the private business that claimed their salary against profits. Fred ran it all by his little own self but lots of the boys on Bay Street bought his services. I had nothing to do with it. And guess what Victorian Investments does? It provides advice and makes investments, nothing else."

Kyle interrupted, "I don't give a flying piss what you advised them. We are sorry, you're upset but I cannae do anything about it. So do you know where the key to this door is, Mr. Wolfe?"

"Sure, the key is in Fred's top right-hand drawer." Now that Niels had finished his tirade, he quietly said, "Sorry, guys. They had no reason to barge into my house this morning. Have fun in the room upstairs." That said, he walked out but muttered, "The cops can harass ten year old boys but they can't catch real criminals."

Maggie rushed to the desk and yanked open the drawer so hard that it crashed onto the floor. Contents flew out and as they landed she scooped up a key from the floor and shouted, "I found it."

The door didn't creak when it opened. A narrow staircase appeared lit with two sea-blue glass sconce. In each sconce was a single electric light that was shaped and flickered like the flame on a wax candlestick. Up the stairs, they trooped with Detective-Sergeant Kyle Bottleman in the lead. Behind him were Maggie, Bea and Detective Alex Sanderson.

The door, at the top, of the stairs, opened to reveal an elegant room transported as if from an English castle. An antique collector's dream of replicating the manor study with adjoining sitting room and library.

Feminine oohs and aahs filled the room and vibrated off the walls. Directly in front of the stairs was an enormous desk. To the left of the desk was an archway leading into a room with a settee and matching wing chair. Gold framed oil paintings and Chinese watercolours hung on the deep mustard painted walls. To the right, through the second archway, was a library. Mahogany bookcases filled with leather-bound books surrounded the room.

Maggie ran into the sitting room and said, “Awesome, why did Fred keep these rooms a secret? Look at the crystal booze bottles. There must be thirty bottles on this trolley. It's so shiny. Wow! I wonder who polished it up. I wonder if Josie knew about this.”

Sitting beside the huge desk was a wooden file cabinet. The detectives zeroed in on it while the two women ran their hands over the ornate hardwood furniture, felt the tightly knotted Persian carpets and admired the display of Murano glass figurines.

“Wow, it's so beautiful,” said Maggie waltzing through the centre room into the library. There she stopped beside the reading table and pulled out a chair to sit down. A second later she leaped up. “Ooh, stink, I stepped in something gucky. It's puke, yuk.” She looked under the table to see a large blob of dried vomit beside which lay an upside down plastic container. Under the container was decomposing salad greens, radishes and tomatoes.

The two detectives rushed over and said together just like a chorus. “Okay, ladies. Out we go.”

Alex herded Bea and Maggie down the stair. At the bottom, he said, “You two stay right here until I get back. I have to call the scene-of-the-crime technicians. While we're waiting for them you can tell me all about what Danni said you weren't supposed to tell the cops.”

“I'm not telling him because she asked me not to and I'm, like, almost her sister,” said Maggie standing Cossack style with her arms folded across her chest and her feet wide apart.

“I'm, like, a mother so I guess, I can tell,” said Bea, with an indulgent smile.

“Fine, but I'm not talking to either of you tonight.” Face like a chunk of cement, shoulders stiff, she sat pretending to read a magazine while Bea chatted with Alex. Every so often Maggie would look up, catch, then avoid Bea's eye.

"In a nutshell, last night Danni came over to my place and told us that her stepfather, Günther, murdered her mother. She saw the bruises on Maggie's back, over-reacted and said she was going to find out if Günther had killed Fred. Maybe she drove to Kingston last night to see if he is still in prison there. Or maybe she has gone to Montreal to talk to his family. That's where she grew up."

"Why?" asked Alex.

"Danni freaked when she saw my back and she thinks maybe her horrible stepfather killed Fred. Her Mom should have stayed married to Fred, he wouldn't hurt anyone. But then he wouldn't have become my stepdad. Maybe you should put a tail on her," said Maggie her eyes beaming with logic and concern. Her silence mode ended almost as soon as it had begun.

"Okay. Thanks. Could you two, please, each write out a statement? Here's a pen and pad of paper. No one downtown is going to believe this. We'll call the Montreal police and see if Günther Doses is known to them. And the minute you hear from her, let me or Kyle know," commanded Alex.

>>>>>

For some reason memories can't replace reality. Danni looked with disappointed amazement at her childhood home on Bartholomew Street. The front curtainless window was enormous and she could see a canary yellow, sienna and ruby red glazed sarcophagus leaning against a grand piano in the living room. The house had been renovated into a monster home that was squeezed between two narrow, normal sized houses. From her car she sat transfixed. Who owns this house? Did that bastard Günther sell it when he was released from jail?

Every ten minutes or so she turned on the car heater but still shivers of cold rippled through her body and a chill had set into her bones. She talked to herself, "Now that I'm in Montreal, what am I going to do? I have to do something."

A few minutes later, Danni drove to the local shopping centre and went to a sporting goods store where she bought a down-filled sleeping bag, a ski suit, arctic fleece gloves, scarf and headband, a pillow and a wool blanket. Finally, at Reitmans, she bought new jeans, underwear and a sweater. After shopping, her stomach started to make hungry noises so she drove downtown to Warshaw's Supermarket. There she wandered around the store, touching and looking at products. After recovering from the nostalgia attack, she paid for the Montreal smoked meat, caraway rye bread, brine dill pickles, coleslaw, olives, Neuhaus chocolate bars and a bottle of red wine.

With her favourite boulevard St-Laurent food beside her, she continued her vigil. All through the early evening hours, she sat, sighed and watched her childhood home. Upstairs and at the back of the house lights went on and off, but she never saw a person walk past the empty front window though shadows would appear at the far right end of the room. By ten o'clock, Danni stuffed with bread, wine and questions climbed over into the backseat and fell asleep, in the sleeping bag, with her head resting on a pillow supported by the armrest.

Chapter 13

Morning, Wednesday, October 22nd

As she stretched Danni smacked her head against the hard door knob and twisted her ankle against the even harder car door. Each knee, shoulder and hip muscle, attached to their respective joints, ached and resisted when she crawled from the back seat over to the front seat of the car. She slithered out of the car door and stood on rubbery legs just as the front door, of the house on Bartholomew Street, opened. A mink coat containing an anorexic-looking woman walked down the street towards the bus stop.

A few minutes later, a man, also gaunt and wrapped in fur, appeared rolling a garbage can down the driveway. Danni pretending to fix her windshield wiper eyed him with vague recognition. She combed her hair with her fingers, then walked over and stood on the sidewalk. "Hello," she called to the man fiddling with the garbage can lids. "As a child I lived in this house and was just stopping to look at it."

"Really. This was, my brother, Günther's house. He bought it in the fifties. Other than him, no one else has owned it. When did you live here?" The man asked but he immediately answered his own question. "Oh yea, I wondered if you'd ever show up. You must be Lallie."

"Daniella, people call me Danni," she said rubbing her eyes of sand and shock. In front of her stood an older version of the man she had despised for over a quarter of a century. His eyes, sunk deep into his head, were small, almond shaped and more intelligent than she remembered. The liver spots on his forehead and hands reminded her of mangled coins that had been placed under a train's wheels by pre-adolescent boys.

"Um, I'm Siegfried Doses. Wanna come in? My wife's gone to work. She never knew your mother. I forgot her name."

"Her name was Sophia. Why are you living here? Did you buy the house from Günther? Sorry, I didn't mean that. I didn't mean that. I don't care about the house." Danni stammered looking over his shoulder at the house.

"Why don't you come in?" asked the man sensing her curiosity. He extended his arm in a welcoming motion.

"Thank you. I came for a reason. I'd like to ask you some questions about Günther," said Danni. The brother put his hand on the small of her back so as to guide her into the front door but she stiffened and shrank away from his touch. She straightened and apologized, "Sorry, I'm quite stiff this morning."

She hadn't expected the inside of the house to be so different, so renovated or so gaudy. On the main floor the walls had been removed creating a long space leading to a stainless steel kitchen which extended into a sun room. Inserted into the half wall between the kitchen and the living/dining room was an enormous aquarium and a gas fireplace. Instead of making the rooms airy and comfortable, it made them pretentious and phony.

"We never use the living room and with that dead mummy in there, it reminds me of an Egyptian tomb. Over the last twenty years my wife has decorated that room, this way, that way. You know, I've never told her your mother died there. Let's go in the kitchen."

Danni glanced again into the room, took a panicked shallow breath and followed Siggy into the kitchen. Her mind and body reacted like a two pack a day, fifty year old smoker going into severe nicotine withdrawal. Three second bursts of anxiety, anger and proud resolution followed by steely will to hide these surges of emotion engulfed Danni as she sat watching the brother, of the man she despised, reheat coffee in the microwave. He looked so old and ordinary pushing button on the microwave.

He placed a mug in front of her and he said, “Call me Siggy. I always wanted to say how sorry I was that Günther lost control.”

“So, why didn't you?” asked Danni. She looked down into her coffee cup. “Nobody talked to me, they only asked thousands and thousands of questions. Where's your brother now?”

“Long gone. Günther never forgave himself. I warned him that he would cross the line one day and he did.”

“Well, he's doing it again.”

“Doing what, where, again? It's impossible.” said Siggy to the exhausted woman.

>>>>>

What a waste of time. Reality strikes as the saying goes, she thought. Günther had been released from prison over sixteen years ago. After his release he had drunk himself into a daily stupor which one day turned into a permanent frozen stupor. Three, 9-year old girls, in the Eastern Townships of Quebec, bumped into him while tobogganing down their favourite hill. How inconsiderate to die where a bunch of little kids would crash into your frozen carcass. In his pocket was a picture of Danni's mother, Sophia.

Danni left Montreal and drove fast, passing slower cars with a heavy foot on the gas pedal and her eyes locked on the horizon. Sign posts indicating turnoffs to Valleyfield, Cornwall, Brockville zoomed in and out of her peripheral vision. The children, in a yellow school bus, smiled and waved at her as she drove around them. She looked in her rearview mirror to see the mini-bus slam on its brakes because she had changed lanes too close. “Oh, I hate you. You bastard. I have to get off this highway,” Danni said to herself.

In a motel room she opened the mini-fridge to find that it was empty. No booze - so she ordered a pizza and lay on the bed watching a movie.

Questions, she needed protection from the questions. She had to go back to Toronto and face the questions. That older detective would be back and she had to be prepared to explain why she had left the province.

Questions marked her like a felt pen permanently marks thick black lines on a garbage can or flip chart paper. The questions would re-scar her new skin. After her mother had been buried in a pauper's grave, the question terrorists had asked and asked and asked, the social workers, the psychologist and the revolving door of hapless foster parents kept demanding she talk and talk and they forced her to speak by asking questions.

Questions, she had practice listening. It was answering that would kill her.

>>>>>

When someone is missing time passes as if in a kaleidoscope, swirling with the dominant colour of the lost presence. Daniella, Bea had decided, was red blood, old rage bleeding new pain. Maggie was greenish brown, new growth, fresh compost and poor grammar. Niels was sky blue with intermittent showers and the odd lightning bolt.

She tried to pick a colour for herself and for her, maybe, favourite detective, Alex. Yellow, sunshine and cleanliness, no, that wasn't either of them. Purple passion and black agony - definitely not. The black tulip was the deepest purple and unique. Tulip black, that could be their colour.

At the agency business was trying to continue. The police had finished examining the luxurious second floor office and Maggie was talking about redecorating Fred's office in between taking lessons on how to run a business. Niels and Bea were back to their regular timetable of interviews and job placements, plus they were covering for Danni. The new receptionist, Karen, was dealing with clients, handing out cheques and checking timesheet under Maggie's critical eye.

Bea noted, as she had numerous time, that when someone goes away there is an atmosphere of strangeness but the everyday things just move along at their usual pace. The buses keep running, workers keep working, food is cooked, people eat, people sleep and most of them bathe. The phone keeps ringing and the world keeps rotating on its solitary axis. Tick-tock, tick-tock goes humanity.

Late afternoon, Wednesday

"Hi, Bea. Can we please go soon? Remember Pierre is coming over after school and my Mom phoned to say she's coming to make sure I'm okay my first night at home. She's been treating me like a three year old ever since the attack so I better be home before it's dark or she'll go on and on about how worried she is," said Maggie.

"Sure we can leave anytime. I didn't realize that it was past four-thirty. Before I forget, you asked me to look up Pierre's Mom's file. Let's do it before we leave. What was her name again?"

"Martine Tremblay."

"There's a good chance that Fred was paying her through his other company, Victorian Payroll Services," said Bea looking at the message, on computer screen, that read, *Not Found*.

"I'm so tired, I could sleep on the floor. I still don't understand about Victorian Payroll Services. Do you?"

She didn't answer Maggie's question because it had become a rhetorical question having been asked over and over again. Those who might know replied in monotonic repetitive sound bites.

Niels would say, 'I manage Victorian Investments, not Victorian Payroll Services.' The accountant would say, 'I suggest you address your questions to Mr. Eco.' The management consultant would say,'That's not my area of expertise.'

Bea searched the archived database and Martine Tremblay's file popped up as ***Inactive***. This message meant that a pay cheque had not been issued for over two years. The electronic file only recorded tombstone data including name, address, Social Insurance Number, birthday and last day worked.

"Let's go," Bea said. "We can look for the paper files tomorrow."

"Okay, my Mom is picking up barbecued chicken with Portuguese hot sauce and those little round roasted potatoes for supper. It's the best."

As they climbed into the car, Bea sang to Maggie. "I've grown accustomed to your face. I'll miss the coffee brewing and the dirty dishes too."

"Yea, right. You won't miss me because, like, that hunky policeman is going to call you more now. I heard him say he would phone if he heard anything about Danni. You'll call me too. Right? I wonder where she is. I think the cops know something they aren't telling us. Maybe you should seduce Alex, ask him to tell you everything; then call me the minute he is asleep drugged by your passionate love."

Bea coughed an *I'm ignoring you cough*, and said, "I'll call you if I hear anything. Meanwhile, don't forget to rest once you get home."

"Do you want to come up to say hi to my Mom? She really likes you. I don't know if Pierre is there yet. He has such a problem with mothers, he hates his. He's coming for dinner but he has to catch an early bus home because he told his Mom he was going to a movie."

"Most teenage boys find their parents more than irritating."

"Yea, but Pierre says that his Mom sits at the kitchen table writing weird angry letters that she never mails and picking fights with him. She sounds strange. Maybe she won't be so bitchy to Pierre if we find her a job," said Maggie.

"That's not nice. She's probably depressed because she's unemployed and her ex-husband just died. And didn't you fight with your Mom when you were a teenager," said Bea. She turned an inquiring face toward the girl sitting next to her. "So you never thought your mother was strange?"

"Yea, I suppose. But my Mom only grew up after I left home."

"Don't be so hard on her. Maggie. She told me the other day that she knew Fred was looking after you all these years. He gave her regular reports. Alex told me that Fred maintained an intimate relationship with all his ex-wives including your Mom."

"Intimate relationship. You mean, like, she was still sleeping with him. Gross! I didn't believe her when she told me that. She isn't that bad, she just doesn't know how to manage her life. She said, Fred invested her savings for her."

"It's probably true. Check with Niels to see if Fred asked him to invest funds on your Mom's behalf. If he didn't, your Mom should contact Tony Eco to make a claim against the estate and she should retain a lawyer."

"Retain a lawyer, retain a lawyer, you sound just like Tony. He said that I should retain my own lawyer too. Maybe he can look after Mom's stuff too. Did you know Pierre calls his mother, Martine? Does your daughter call you, Bea? I don't call my Mom, Mary." Maggie sighed, closed her eyes and laid her head against the headrest.

By the time Bea drove up to the entrance of the condominium, the worn out girl was sleeping slouched forward with her chin almost resting on her upper chest. Bea telephoned upstairs to see who was home. Both Pierre and Mary had already arrived.

Mary looked into the car. "Maggie told me; she was feeling fine. Those were her exact words,`Mom, I feel fine.'" Mary opened the passenger car door and kissed her daughter's forehead to wake her up. When Maggie opened her eyes, Mary said, “Hi, honey, you’re home. Let's go upstairs. Why did you go to work today? You look terrible.”

They walked into the building bickering about what Maggie should and shouldn't do. She could be heard saying. “Mom, my legs are fine. I can walk. The asshole hit me across the back. He didn't break my legs.”

“Do the police know who did it yet?” Pierre asked Bea as he helped unload the luggage. “She told me it was a mugger, probably, high on crack. If I were a mugger I wouldn't attack her, she doesn't look rich enough. I would only mug women in expensive clothes as they came out of an Instabank in a really rich neighbourhood. I'd mug men too. I'm not sexist.”

“Lovely logic, makes sense to me,” said Bea. She smiled and handed him a box with plants and a plastic grocery bag filled with cards, stuffed animals and books.

>>>>>

After dropping Maggie off, Bea had an urge to speed home to call her own daughter. The moment she walked in the house, she picked up the phone and because she was calling on a Thursday instead of a Sunday, the first question out of Samantha's mouth was “Is something wrong, Mom?”

“No, I was just thinking of you and decided to phone.”

“I'm fine. How are you? It's getting cold here. Last night it went down to minus one,” said Samantha.

“It's not that cold here yet,” said Bea.

“It's always warmer in TO.”

After chatting with her daughter, Bea said goodbye but stayed on the phone and dialed Alex's number. “Hi, it's Bea. Have you heard from Danni? We're still worried about her.”

“No, we haven't heard anything. An officer is driving by her place as part of his rounds. He'll let us know if her house lights come on. “Is Maggie with you?” asked Alex.

“No, she's moved back to her condo. Her Mom and Pierre are there tonight. Why don't you come over here?” asked Bea.

Fifteen minutes later, she opened the front door. Ten minutes after that Alex followed her into the kitchen to watch her open a bottle of Valpolicella. Two drinks later, Bea helped him slip under the covers.

>>>>>

At the same time that Alex was pulling the two-inch duvet over Bea's warm sleeping form, Debbie was standing with exasperated hands on her exasperated hips glaring at her fiancee.

“What do you mean, Niels, we have to leave the country? What about your bossy family? Would you rather desert them or embarrass them? You're always doing something for your dippy sisters who adore you. Now you want to leave them and not tell them where you're going. Come on, Niels. Grow up. Nothing can be that bad. You always knew what Fred was doing, wasn't kosher. We can move to a smaller house if you end up owing Revenue Canada a bundle. I don't want to leave Toronto and I don't want you to leave either. Fred and his Bay Street buddies conspired to defraud the government, not you. They can't put you in jail for something someone else masterminded.”

“It was fraud, outright tax evasion. I invested the profits for Fred. They might throw me in jail for being an accessory or something. I knew what was going on. I knew the money coming from Victorian Payroll Services was dirty. Just wait, people will start avoiding you. Debbie. Don't think our friends won't ostracize us. I've already started to move our money out of the country. Whatever I do, I'm going to pay big time. My Mom is going to keel over and die."

"Your Mom is not going to die. She'll be disappointed that you didn't show better judgement and that you were a greedy boy. That's all. And don't move my money out of the country, I'm not going anywhere."

"Shut up, Deb. You're about as supportive as the water under a sinking ship. What are you? The cheerleader for the torpedo?"

"It's going to be rough but no one died," she said sticking her tongue out at him.

"What a dumb expression and in this case someone did die. You trivialize everything. It makes me want to puke," shouted Niels. Out of the room he stomped.

Debbie followed in close pursuit, "Stop it, just stop it. I'm sick of fighting about this. I don't even know what we are fighting about except that you're upset all the time and you take it out on me. Let's go to bed and vent laying down." She threw a pillow at him and gave him an affectionate push up the stairs.

"So, Deb, you wanna to sleep with a loser?"

"No, Niels, I don't want to sleep with a loser, or a whiner but I do want to sleep with you. Even though you're an effing pain. Come on, it's after midnight. We both have to get up for work."

>>>>>

The express bus to Hamilton motored down the highway at a cruise control speed of a hundred kilometres per hour. With his coat bunched up under his head, Pierre leaned up against the window and looked south. He watched the city turn into Lake Ontario and the Great Lake turn into dark suburbia then black countryside. Tiredness engulfed him so he shut his eyes and replayed in his mind the evening conversations between Maggie and her mother, Mary.

'Sounds like a woman to me, small feet and a small head. Picking up and hitting someone with a piece of fence is cowardly. Your father enjoyed bar fights when there were men's only bars. But he always said a real man uses his fists not a stick or iron knuckles,' Mary had said.

'Iron knuckles. Mom, what are iron knuckles?' Maggie had asked.

'They are stainless steel contraptions with finger holes that thugs slip over their knuckles to beat people up with. Your father was wrong. A real man or woman doesn't hit anyone. That's why I kicked Maggie's old man out. And me, I only smacked Maggie once. I lost it and whacked her across the face. Left a bright red hand print on her cheek as big as her face. It took a week for the bruise to disappear. Maggie was four and she threw a piece of cat poop at me. It scared me so much. I couldn't sleep for days but I learnt my lesson. I was enormously strong compared to my baby. Whoever beat up Maggie is a sick yellow-belly sap-sucker with no self-control, no consideration for others and no guts to talk things through instead of beating people up. No anger control but that is no excuse.'

'Mom, I don't remember you ever hitting me. Compared to the guy who beat me up; your smack must have been like a butterfly wing brushing my cheek. I think it was a she too. You know what, Ma, I remember you coming after me with a fly swatter because I had eaten all the dessert that you had just baked for some new man you met at bingo.'

'You're going to give this boy the wrong idea about our family,' Mary had replied laughing and winking at Pierre. 'I just yell. And don't forget to tell him how often you ignore me or argue back.'

He had sat on the couch and listened while Mary changed the gauze dressings on Maggie's back. They even joked about the wounds, the scabs and the massive yellow and purple bruising. He had laughed when Mary called him over to confirm that, yes, the bruises were the same colour and matched the purple streaks in Maggie's hair. 'Bruises talk to you,' Mary had said, 'each colour is a message from your body telling you about the stage in the healing process.'

The regular dull roar and vibration of the bus started to lull Pierre to sleep. Suddenly, he sat up as if to shake away an impending nightmare. After a minute he lay back down, his hands ran down his side and outer thighs. Then tears ran down his cheek into the pocket of his coat folded under his cheek.

Chapter 14

Morning, Thursday, October 23rd

"Jingle bells. Jingle bells. Jingle all the way," hummed Alex. He saluted the people in the homicide squad room. In response to his happy good morning, two people grinned and waved and two people frowned, obviously incapable of accepting cheerfulness so early in the morning. His partner ignored him because his nose was down almost touching the autopsy report he was re-reading.

Kyle looked up, waved a yellow highlighter and said, "Morning. Just read something that you mentioned but it didn't sink in before. Our dead friend, Fred, had blue liquid cleaning residue on his skin. The handle of the knife was also soaked in the stuff. You're late. Where were you? I tried to call you last night but you weren't home."

"Sorry. Did we hear anything from Danni Thompson?" asked Alex, ignoring his partner's question.

"No. Should have detained her on Monday. But c'est la vie, cannae arrest just because we have our suspicions, can we now. She reminded me of the older sister. You've met her. Her first husband beat the crap out of her, then the second one turned out to be a drunkard so she gave up men for twenty years. She became a real estate broker and invested in commercial properties. She makes more money than you and me and a kitchen sink salesman. Getting married, the old girl will be sixty next month and she's getting married on her next birthday. Did a background check on the guy, no assault charges, money in the bank and the wife likes him."

"So, what's the point. Life ain't fair but it all turns out okay twenty-five years later. We still have to do something about Danni Thompson if she doesn't return soon, Kyle. One murder per lifetime is enough. But it may have fried her brain, seeing her mother get killed. It can cause a chemical imbalance in the brain. That's why abused kids grow up to be more depressed or aggressive than the norm. Did you know that?"

"You and the wife, where do you get this psycho babble from? She reads it in those women's magazines, Cosmo and MS magazines. Are you starting to read women's magazines?" asked Kyle.

"I'm serious. There are whole books written about this. One is called *Emotional Intelligence*. I was discussing it last night. Most well-read people have heard of it."

"Ah ha. A born-again bibliophile. Yuk! With whom, laddie, were you discussing your emotional health with?"

"Bea Prancer," said Alex turning red under Kyle's overbearing eyes and shaggy eyebrows which were going up and down like a jumper on a trampoline.

"That explains it. At Bea's house were you. She's a fine looking woman. Now I know why you're so bloody chipper. I hope you're not going to start singing and waxing poetically, metaphorically, pulling petals off the daisy," said Kyle. His eyes lit up with the humour.

"Yea, yea. Let's get going. Martine Tremblay awaits us in Hamilton. She'll be home during the day because she's not working."

As usual Alex drove, he turned off the main highway onto a country road taking the scenic route while Kyle read the week-end reports, reading outloud anything his partner should know. "Aye, here's an interesting one. I forgot we even asked for it, Marcus' idea. Send a botanist to check out our suspects' properties. This confirms it. Fred had two hydrangea plants in his backyard. They grew in the border beside the stairs leading up to deck; exactly where Maggie Nichelton said they would be. The hydrangea, along with other plants in the garden, had recently been either dead-headed or pruned."

"Yea, so what does that tell us. Only that the poison could have come from Fred's backyard. Did the plant guy check out Danni's backyard?"

"Yes, he did. Nothing. Her yard is a patch of grass five feet by six feet, three boring bushes called Mor Gold and four paving stones. The author notes that the bushes have green leaves with gold edges and are cheap, usually costing less than $6.99. Also on Danni's patio is one sixteen inch terra cotta container with two dead geraniums. When and if she comes back we must ask her if she knew Fred grew hydrangea plants and find out if she spent last Monday night with him. I suspect she did," said Kyle.

"What about Niels Wolfe? What's in his yard?"

"His girlfriend is studying landscape architecture and invited the botanist to have a tour of her backyard garden and take pictures. Here, take a look." Kyle waved a five by seven photograph under Alex's nose.

Like a duck, Alex pulled his chin in so he could glance down at the picture in front of his nose. He said, "Swamp, it looks like a swamp with shiny things floating between jungle grasses."

"Ornamental grass garden with lily pond and moving ivy sculptures. It's the girlfriend's hobby. Twenty-two kinds of grasses and four kinds of lilies with a bubbling pond and two filters. Four pages, the guy must have loved the place, but no hydrangea or any other known poisonous plant, just grasses. I wouldn't spend my hard-earned money on grass."

They pulled up to the Tremblay home just in time to see Pierre swing his leg over his bicycle seat. Alex hopped out of the car and called over the roof. "Hello Pierre."

"What are you doing here? I have to go to school," said the teenager wrinkling his forehead and dropping his bike on the ground. As the two detectives walked toward him, he stumbled backwards up the stairs.

"That's okay, we came to talk to your Mom, not you," said Kyle.

"She's sleeping, maybe you better come back this afternoon. She doesn't really like people in the house when she's alone. Why don't you come back after school?" asked Pierre with a rigid face.

Alex nodded and said, "Maybe we should come back later, we have other people to see while we're in town. You don't want us to wake your Mom up so early. Very considerate. What do you think, Detective-Sergeant Bottleman?"

"Okay, we'll come back later," said Kyle. They drove off and parked at a strip plaza around the corner. A few minutes later, Pierre zoomed past fast pedalling down the street presumably to school.

"Well, let's go see Mama Martine," said Kyle with a grin. The two detectives returned to the Tremblay house and knocked on the door several times.

"That little shit must have warned his Mom we were here but we didn't see anyone drive out of the street and there's no back alley," said Alex looking into the living room window.

"But why would she want to avoid us?" asked Kyle.

"I suspect she was working for Victorian Payroll Services. If the scam is what we think, Martine Tremblay probably worked either at home or at the odd temporary jobs in places like the police, hospitals, government offices. Her salary was paid by the government agency to the Common Sense Employment Agency. For the same person and identical hours, Victorian Payroll Services issued another invoice to a different private sector company who could claim the salary as an expense against profits. Victorian Payroll Services would charge them the cost of taxes, benefits and 20% administration fee. The T-4 slips sent to Revenue Canada from employment agencies are only required to indicate salary and benefits paid to the temporary worker by the agency. Nowhere does it state where the temps worked and governments never submit the names of temporaries hired from agencies to Revenue Canada. They only report public and civil service positions."

"Alex, you already told me this, twice," said Kyle shrugging his shoulders.

"Once it was set up, it didn't take much work, just press a few keys on the computer. You're not interested in this are you, Kyle? Every time I talk about Fred committing tax fraud you change the subject," said Alex.

"I know how the scam works. It doesn't matters. Look at this place. She isn't raking in any fat pay cheque. The eavestrough and driveway need fixing and the stucco could use a can of paint."

"Maybe Fred was blackmailing one of his regular corporate customers and they decided to kill him rather than be reported to Revenue Canada."

"No, Alex. No one gets murdered over taxes."

They walked back up the driveway, along the front of the house and looked down the side of the bungalow. "Let's check out the backyard to see if she grows hydrangea," said Alex.

"On what grounds? Sir. On what suspicious grounds do you suggest we enter and search this Canadian citizen's backyard?" asked Kyle.

"Contaminated soil. No, I think strange noises is our best defence when in a small city environment. Don't you? No, I've got a better one. The officers observed a dog foaming at the mouth and entered the property to ascertain whether it was rabid but that damn dog ran away."

"Okay, Pinocchio. I'll get the plant book so we'll know what we're looking for," said Kyle.

The shabby exterior of the house was gentrified by a well-maintained backyard with a newly turned vegetable bed, pruned rose bushes and circular perennial garden. At the back of the garden against the fence sat a pre-fab pine shed and two square bins.

“See, two compost bins, she must be a serious gardener. You have to empty one each year. Excellent. The wife wants me to do that too,” said Kyle with admiration.

“I don't see any hydrangea plants. Let's look in the compost bins and the shed.”

“We need a search warrant to look in the shed.”

“I think I just saw someone run across the yard and crawl into that bin. Look at it, it's rocking, it looks like it is going to fall over,” said Alex with a grin as he whistled *Taps* and strolled across the grass to the back fence, looked in the two large wooden slated bins, made a disgusting-smell face and shook his head.

Walking back to the car, Kyle said, “I don't think I like you this way, so cheerful. You can’t be humorous, that is my job on this team.”

>>>>>

Danni arrived back at her townhouse about the same time as the detectives were trespassing in the Tremblay's backyard. Driving home she had rehearsed the answers to questions the police might ask.

Q. **Why? Why Ms Thompson did you leave the city Monday night after I, Detective-Sergeant Bottleman, specifically told you that I wanted to question you further about your horrific past?**

A. I left because I thought my stepfather, Günther Doses, might be involved. I have since found out that he is deceased. By assisting the police, I eliminated him as a suspect which will save the taxpayers' money.

Q. **Where were you the Monday night Fred was poisoned?**

A. I was eating supper and watching the news. I cooked pasta and made Greek salad.

Q. **You are not answering the question. I asked where, not what you were doing.**

A. I had supper with Fred at his house.

Q. **Where were you the Friday night Maggie was assaulted?**

A. I was at home sleeping. It happened at midnight. You can't expect a woman whose boyfriend just died to have an alibi at midnight.

Once home in Toronto, Danni collapsed on the couch, she looked around, this was her sanctuary. When she was in Montreal, she had felt like a shopping cart careening down a hill of memories crashing, resting in a ditch just to get up and topple over again. Safety was her overstuffed flowered couch in her narrow townhouse with the doors locked. The living room was hers, clean, comfortable, painted just a shade paler than Dijon mustard. On the walls were peaceful pictures, predominantly blues and greens, depicting mountains behind tranquil lakes.

After having a bubble bath, a long afternoon nap, two cups of raspberry tea and ten chocolate-covered coconut cookies, Danni felt human and happy to be home.

She looked at the mail and the answering machine. Three days worth of messages, three days since she had run away, maybe after three days the police wouldn't want to talk to her, maybe they would leave her alone.

Reluctantly, Danni picked up a pen and pressed the pyramid shaped flashing red light on the answering machine.

- Ms Thompson, this is Detective-Sergeant Bottleman. Please call me as soon as you come home. My card is in your mail box. The phone number is on it.
- Danni, hi, this Bea. We're worried about you. Please call the minute you get back.
- Ms Thompson, this is Detective Bottleman again, please be advised that if I have not heard from you within the next twenty-four hours, a warrant could be issued to ensure your availability for questioning.
- Danni, hi, it's Maggie. Bea told the police you went to Montreal. But you don't have to worry. I don't think you poisoned Fred. Every plant you grow dies. I told the police you don't even know what a hydrangea bush looks like, do you? We both loved him. And I always wanted an older sister. It's okay if you have problems, so do I. We can run the agency together. Don't worry, just come back.

Danni stopped the tape and rewound it to replay the last message. She played it twice over muttering under her breath, "Poisoned, Fred was poisoned. No way. How?"

The next voice on the answering machine made her sit up straight.

- Hello. This is Siggy Doses. When we had coffee yesterday, I forgot that there was a box in the basement that belonged to your mother. Call me at 999-2989.
- This is Siggy Doses again. Call me there is a legal matter I would like to discuss with you.

- Lallie, this is your Uncle Siegfried calling again. This is my third call. I know you are there. Pick up the effing phone.
- You bitch, you're just like your mother, too good to talk to me. You want your mother's crap you better call me by two o'clock today or I'll burn everything. Your mother killed my brother, not the other way around or maybe it was really you, you bitch, you killed your mother. The police were here questioning me because of you. I told them insanity runs in your family.
- Call me or you'll be sorry.

Danni turned the machine off.

Evening, Thursday

The two detectives listened to the answering machine tape while Danni paced around the dining room table like an anxious animal in a dog run.

"The whole family is crazy. I hear it in his voice, he's just like his brother. Now Siggy could come and kill me because he knows my phone number, he can find out my address. Now you understand, don't you. Please arrest me, then I can go to jail." Danni stood in front of Kyle with her arms outstretched and her crossed wrists together in front of her. Hysterical tears appeared so she shut her eyes.

"Sit down, Daniella. I haven't seen you for three days. They must have been pretty rough. Invitations to arrest someone are taken seriously. Are you confessing to any specific crime?" asked Kyle. He took her arm to guide her back to the couch where he sat down next to her.

"Maybe I know ..." Danni started to say but changed her mind and instead said, "You said you were going to arrest me so do it then I won't be slaughtered in my sleep. I'm trying to explain this to you.

That man on the tape his name is Siegfried but he sounds like the stepfather, Günther." She looked at the blank faces of the two men and sank into a chair, folding double at the waist and putting her head in her hands.

"Start at the beginning," said Kyle.

While Danni told her story of going to her childhood home in Montreal, Bea arrived. Alex opened the door for her and she stood in the hallway listening to the distraught woman. At the end of her story, Danni hit the message light on the machine again and said, "Listen to him. Can't you arrest him?"

"He's a nasty piece of works. Okay, we'll look into it. I can't promise anything. Tell us about his family. When did Günther die?" asked Kyle.

"Sixteen years ago. I need a drink," said Danni. She noticed that Bea was standing in the entrance way to the living room. "When did you get here?"

"About ten minutes ago. Why don't you get the drinks and I think I have a box of chocolate and some other stuff in the trunk of the car. Back in a flash," said Bea. She ran into the room and gave Danni's knee a squeeze, then she looked at the two policemen and said, "Gentlemen, could you please help me with my groceries?"

"How much does a box of chocolate weigh?" asked an incredulous Alex. Danni looked at him and started to laugh, Bea started to giggle until they were both weeping.

>>>>>

Alex went over to Bea's house after his shift was over. She sat on the couch wrapped in a blue and white quilt reading a book called the *Tapestry Murders* by P. C. Doherty.

"Listen to this succinct line and I quote:

In the Locked Heart tavern off Pig Alley near Chick Lane, Wormwood, a professional assassin, sat quietly in a noisome corner of the taproom where the floor was soaked in urine.

That tells us so much, what era the man lived, what he does for a living, what environment he is in and what class of person he is, all in one line. Do you ever do that with a case? How would you describe our case?" asked Bea when she finished reading out loud.

"Our case, when did it become our case? I thought it was mine and Kyle's case," said Alex sitting down next to Bea. He placed his fingers on her knee but jerked his hand away because of the heat that radiated from her. "Wow! You're hot."

"Sure am." She moved Alex's hand under the quilt up her leg to her thigh. "It's a heating pad on my leg," she said with a glint in her eye. "Supper is almost ready. How's this for a synopsis?

Surrounded by opulence, the corpulent man was poisoned and disrobed, then clandestinely carried down the secret staircase to a drab office which overlooked Agatha Street, the cheapest street in Toronto."

"Sound succinct to me," said Alex. "When do we eat?" He had been looking forward to cooking with Bea which was more fun than discussing work. She showed him how to carve faces in tomatoes and they ate a few strands of spaghetti like sexy Siamese twins.

After dinner he turned to her and said in a serious voice, "Bea, listen, we'll be bringing Danni in for formal questioning at headquarters tomorrow morning, around 7:30 a.m. Circumstantial evidence points strongly to her. She has no alibi for either the night before Fred was poisoned or when Maggie was assaulted, she was having an affair with him and we found her fingerprints all over his house and the second floor office. Plus this business about her murdered mother and the belligerent uncle probably has nothing to do with Fred's poisoning. She sounds delusional. So the uncle is a pig. The legal matter is probably about Günther's estate."

"Oh give me a break, Alex, Gretchen didn't do it. I would have sensed it. Everyone who knew about the upstairs office would have fingerprints there. What about looking at Fred's business partners who were scamming the government?"

"The reality is a raging family member is usually the perpetrator. The only reason I'm telling you this is because she might need emotional support. It's totally confidential that we are picking her up. You can't tell her tonight. It was Kyle's idea that we trust you," said Alex.

Bea slid into the corner of the couch, started strumming her fingers on the end table and said, "So it was your partner, Kyle, not you, who thought the police could trust me to keep a secret for one night. He appears to be a man of empathy unlike some people I know." She leaped off the couch. "Well, goodbye, Alex, you must need your beauty rest especially since you're required to rise bright and early to fulfil your mandate of arresting innocent women in the early dawn of the new day."

"Come on, we're not arresting her yet. It was Kyle's decision to bring her in tomorrow morning. Last time we questioned her, she disappeared for almost three bloody days. If it was up to me, I would have locked her up this afternoon," he said, looking at the expression on Bea's face with dismay, then irritation. She looked like a sphinx guarding the pyramids, stately and expressionless.

"Well, it's none of my business, how you do your job. I'll see you bright and early tomorrow morning at the cop shop. Say about 7:30ish," said Bea. She handed Alex his jacket, blew him an airy-fairy kiss off her fingertips and opened the front door just to make sure he got the message that she was ushering him on his way.

So he stomped out without saying goodbye.

Chapter 15

Morning, Friday, October 24th

"Damn," said Bea. The cup of coffee toppled out of her hand, splashing the front of her camel-coloured wool skirt. She wriggled out of the skirt just before the liquid burned her. Of course, upstairs, nothing matched her blouse so she pulled on a dress, ran out the front door, turned to lock it and discovered she had forgotten her purse.

While searching for her keys; she glanced at her watch and said to herself, "It's only 6:30 in the morning. I must be crazy to be up this early. I might as well walk to the police station and get some exercise." Bea pulled on a pair of cotton socks and tennis shoes, then slammed the front door behind her.

He doesn't trust me but his partner does. Jerk! she shouted in her head. Walking was her way of thinking through her anger. Alex had made her angry but why? *I can't expect him to think the same way as me. Well, I do expect it but I shouldn't.* If a person says should or shouldn't, it means they want to control someone else's behaviour. Shouldn't be nasty, should be nice. So people should be bloody nice to each other. Why not? Alex slept with me, that means, he should trust me. *Well fine! I'm not going to trust him either.*

>>>>>

When Bea arrived at the agency, it was just after nine o'clock. Niels was busy on the phone and Maggie was telling Josie, the cleaning lady extraordinaire, that today, for sure, she could scrub both of Fred's offices.

Bea waited a few minutes before calling a meeting to explain why Danni was late. “Well, here's the story. They think she did it. I was at the police station this morning when they brought her in for questioning. She barely spoke. She was too calm, too placid, almost like she had no emotions,” said Bea her voice gaining momentum. “I was more upset than she was. She didn't want me to wait and said she has been through this before. Do you know who she reminded me of; my late father-in-law when he gave up the will to live. Detached, no strong emotions, gave the impression that he was quite capable of dealing with whatever death handed him. I don't know why I'm so ticked off, but I am.”

“Like no way. The cops are a bunch of idiots. Danni must be scared frozen.”

“It's scared stiff, Maggie,” corrected Niels.

“Her Mom was murdered. That's why she's acting so weird. I've gotta be nicer to my Mom from now on. I wish we could do something,” said Maggie.

“They don't believe her about the uncle thing either,” said Bea. “But I heard him threatening her on the answering machine. He sounds dangerous. We should find out about those nasty brothers, Siegfried and Günther Doses.”

“Maybe Pierre can help because he's, like, totally bilingual and he's coming for the weekend,” said Maggie looking at them with a questioning face.

Niels slammed his fist on the table. When he spoke the words were filled with acid overtones. “I hate the effing cops! They're imbecilic idiots! Blind, with both hands tied behind my back, I can find out who poisoned Fred. Do you know what the pigs did yesterday? They notified my bank and brokerage house that I was under investigation so they're definitely wrong about Danni. They have blinkers and less brains than horses.”

"Wow, you really hate them, eh Niels? And it makes you talk weird too, imbecilic idiots," said Maggie.

"No, I don't hate them, I despise them and I can do anything better than they can. We'll find the pigs another suspect so they'll get off Danni's back," said Niels. "But first we have to find her a good lawyer. Then, we need a list of suspects other than us. Who hated Fred? Who gains by his death not including Danni and Maggie? What secrets did Fred have? Did he know the Doses brothers?"

"Fred had lots of secrets like the Swiss bank account book, I found taped to the bottom of a teapot." said Maggie

"A Swiss bank account book?" asked Niels, his forehead unwrinkled, his anger faded and his eyes lit up with interest. "Didn't you give it to the lawyer?"

"No, it's in my knapsack. I was upset that Tony called the police on Fred and I didn't want him to get into more trouble," said Maggie. She dumped the contents of her backpack on the table.

"How can he get into trouble? Fred's dead," said Niels.

"I don't know but I loved him. I haven't told Tony or the police everything I found at Fred's house because I don't want people to think he was sleazy."

"Good girl. You don't have to tell them everything. I certainly haven't."

"Niels, was Fred sending in phony Revenue Canada T4 slips?"

"Oh, Maggie, wake up and smell the coffee beans being ground in the grinder. You can weigh on a scale everything Fred did in his life. The scale would tip toward the golden good side. Fred was wonderful to his staff and strange to his ex-wives. He loved them all and two-timed them all. He was good at business but during 1991 recession he learned how to finesse on the dark side of the tax man. But, I don't think he was ever prejudiced against a soul. He liked people and never judged anyone on anything except how hard they worked," said Niels.

"That's true. Do you remember the time he hired the bag lady who was sitting on the front steps of the agency? He took her to the walk-in clinic down the street, bought her a winter coat and boots, then sent her to a warehouse to do inventory control. I like her even though she's, like, totally weird. Mrs Funky or Doris ..." said Maggie.

"Mrs Fundy! She was here that Tuesday and I sent her out, on an assignment, the day that Fred died. She had just finished a terrible job where the work conditions were horrible," said Bea. "I was shocked."

Niels and Maggie started to laugh. "Nope," said Maggie, "the working conditions were probably okay. She's nice but delusional. She always says there were insect droppings at any job we sent her on, especially cockroaches. She has to clean her desk with Lysol or wear gloves until the cleaning is done. Once when she was here, I spilled a loaded hamburger on the reception desk. That same afternoon she came back and scrubbed my desk so the bugs wouldn't come overnight to have a snack."

"But she works hard, types accurately and gets good references if the assignment is short-term. Less than a week. Where did you send her, Bea?" asked Niels.

"I gave her a two-week assignment inputting invoices for a plumbing company. They're located in a strip plaza in Etobicoke."

"Eweeh! Slime in sewer pipes breeds mould and fungus. With each flush of the toilet, mutant cockroaches will grow and grow until they erupt though kitchen taps contaminating all those who dare to pour bacon fat down their pipes," said Niels making a gruesome face and moving his hands like a spider across the table and up around Maggie's neck. She hissed at him like a snake and he sat back down.

"Mrs. Fundy's not that bad. I like her. She usually talks to me when she comes in but I didn't see her that Tuesday. Here, I found it," said Maggie handing Niels a dark yellow bank book. "Is it real?"

He opened the bank book. His forehead puckered and his lips pursed, in concentration, as he flipped the pages of the book. While he was reading the inside of the front cover, he stood up and asked Maggie, “Can I take this to my office? I have to check something on the computer.”

Afternoon, Friday

Later that day, Maggie and Bea went to the opulent upstairs office to wait for Niels to finish working and for Pierre to arrive.

“Do you want a drink?” asked Maggie. On the tea trolley, in front of her, was a wide array of liquor and wine bottles. “I found a bartending book in the library. I'll make you a fancy drink. And then I have to tell you something really important before Niels gets here.”

“Okay,” said Bea.

“Well, I thought Josie did it and now I think Mrs. Fundy did it. But, I'm scared to tell anyone important. So you decide.”

“You think either Josie or Mrs. Fundy poisoned Fred?” asked Bea in amazement. “Why?”

“No! I don't think that they killed him. I think one of them cleaned up his body, moved it downstairs and took his clothes off so they could wash them. Then when she came back, he was dead.”

“It did cross my mind, Maggie, when I heard about the cleaning fluid on Fred's body that maybe Mrs. Fundy had gone into the office either before or after she saw me.”

“Yea, but Josie has keys too. I didn't tell the police but every Tuesday, Josie cleaned Fred's house AND the upstairs office. The day he died, guess what she was doing when I arrived at his house. Laundry. And she seemed more worried about me than upset about Fred.”

"We should tell the police about our suspicious. The women didn't hurt anyone. It would just solve one part of the puzzle."

"But, Bea, maybe they could be charged with `doing indignities to a corpse.' I once read that somewhere."

Footsteps could be heard coming up the stairs so Maggie whispered, "Promise you won't tell anyone until we talk about it some more." Bea nodded her head.

Niels appeared at the door, threw himself in a chair and started talking, "Okay. What time is this, Pierre, kid coming? I'll need him to read French stuff on the Internet."

"Pierre's leaving Hamilton right after school. He should be here by five o'clock," said Maggie.

"Fine, You better leave a note downstairs letting him know where we are," said Niels, waving the mustard coloured bank book in front of him. "To access this, I have to find the account number and when I do, we can pay a lawyer for Danni out of it. We could also hire a private investigator. After all, the funds technically belongs to the stepchildren, including you, Danni and Pierre. So give me your written permission and I'll make magic money."

"That would be awesome. So it's a really true bank account?" asked Maggie.

Niels nodded and said, "Oh yea, it's a really, really big bank account."

When Bea left the office an hour later, Niels and Pierre were huddled around the computer looking up information that originated in Quebec and travelled electronically to Zurich while Maggie was reading a print-out on the 1968 murder trial of Günther Doses.

Chapter 16

Morning, Saturday, October 25th

The morning sky was still dark when the phone rang next to Bea's bed. She rolled over to snatch the receiver before the fourth ring and said a groggy, "Hello."

"We're releasing Daniella Linda Hemming Doses Thompson in about half and hour. I thought you'd like to know," announced a male voice that sounded as if it was coming from a 1930's radio. "Oh, by the way, the Montreal police called this morning to advise us that two young men walked into headquarters late last night asking about the criminal records of the brothers, Günther and Siegfried Doses. The police there, rest assured, told them where to go." Click!

"Oh, well thanks Alex," said Bea to the dial tone buzzing in her ear. "What the hell is his problem? He just wants to know everything that I know. Which is nothing." She looked at the red glowing letters on the clock radio, 6:45 a.m.

>>>>>

While Bea was waiting, at the police station, she inquired if Detective Alex Sanderson was in the building. The clerk came back after a few minutes and said, "Sorry, he just left. Could another officer help you?"

She shook her head, walked over to one of the hard chairs in the lobby, and sat down. She thought, there must be a sadistic supplier of waiting room furniture for hospitals, doctors' offices and police stations. This nefarious company must purposely undersell the competition just to ensure that the people have uncomfortable chairs to sit on. The message the chairs sent out was; you, the public, deserve to be uncomfortable, your lower back is unimportant, you are nothing, zilch, nada.

Bea was dozing when an image of two red Porsche convertibles appeared in her mind's eye. Sidewalk painters throwing up multi-coloured palettes and stumbling over falling easels appeared behind her closed eyelids. The two cars hurtled down a narrow cobblestone street. Alex, driving with his feet, had a cowboy hat in one hand waving it like a rider on a bucking bronco. In his other hand, pointing to the sky, was a silver Colt 57 with a glittering diamond and ruby handle.

Just ahead, driving the second Porsche, was Niels dressed in an impeccable suit and wearing a golf hat embroidered with *007*. Pierre stood in the backseat holding a portable computer. The computer transformed into a machine gun ratt-tatting away, while he laughed like a hyena.

Just as an imaginary silver bullet zoomed through the air, something grabbed her shoulder waking her up. Bea leaped out of her seat and opened her eyes to see Danni standing in front of her. "Sorry, I didn't mean to startle you. Thanks for picking me up. I can't wait to get home," she said giving Bea a stiff hug. "Sorry you have to see me like this."

One day and a night in prison had metamorphasized Danni from a business woman into a sloppy hag. Her face was streaked as if washed in a puddle of stagnant muddy water. Her clothes usually impeccable looked ill-fitting and cheap because they were stretched, wrinkled and spotted with what looked like coffee.

They drove, in silence, to Danni's townhouse. While she showered, Bea ran to the grocery store to pick up the making of an Alberta breakfast: steak, eggs, potatoes, tomatoes, toast, orange juice and coffee.

They were relaxing over their second cup of coffee when Bea said, "This morning when Alex called me he mentioned that Pierre and Niels were in Montreal. They'd been to a police station and had asked about Günther Doses and his brother. I don't remember the brother's name."

"Siggy. How could you let them go? What are they planning to do there?" asked Danni. Her face more fearful than livid, turned red and blotchy with emotion.

"I don't know. Something must have come up after I left the office last night. Niels was looking for evidence that Siggy Doses or someone else might be responsible for poisoning Fred," said Bea.

"Why would Siggy poison Fred?" asked Danni.

"I don't know how exactly. When I left last night Niels was busy researching the Doses family. He found out that the house, on Bartholomew Street, is registered under your Mom and Siggy's names. Maybe when he died you should have inherited your mother's share."

"So what does that ugly house have to do with Fred? The police already told me about the registration on title. Who cares? Siggy told the police that I threatened to kill him to get the house. He even said that he always suspected that I killed my mother not his, *oh, so,* innocent brother. See how evil he is. If Niels and Pierre try anything; Siggy will fry and barbecue them for breakfast while he talks on his cell phone about the hockey play-offs," said Danni.

"Sorry, I think they're just trying to help. They should be okay. The boys are phoning us at noon. Why don't you have a nap and meet us at the agency for lunch?" asked Bea.

"Okay, thanks. I don't understand why Niels would do this. Maybe it's a game to him. He's kind of naive. I don't think Niels has ever met a violent person in his whole life. He's almost a genius but he's been spoiled and adored all his life by a gaggle of women, all those sisters, his mother and now his girlfriend, Debbie. Have you ever met them? They're Pollyannas, that's why Niels makes fun of them."

"You sound jealous that he has a family that loves and spoils him. He hasn't always had it easy, especially being Metis. He told me that he got beat up at school, then the police arrested *him* for fighting. To make matters worse, another time, the police gave Niels' paper route money to the boy who had kicked him in the stomach."

"I believe it but he's an arrogant jerk sometime, you can't deny that. Why does he care enough to go to Montreal? He must have another motive," said Danni.

"I don't know. But don't underestimate him. To Niels, this is a competition between his intelligence and the polices' collective ability. If he finds evidence that proves you innocent and Siegfried Doses or someone else guilty, Niels will be in his glory. He was furious when he heard you were brought in for questioning so he must think of you as the unjustly accused and because you are female and a friend, he may feel protective towards you," said Bea.

"Yea, we are friends. And it keeps his mind off his other problem. What's going on with the fraud investigation? Who knew Fred kept a second set of payroll records? They asked me a lot of questions about Niels involvement in Victorian Payroll Services and Victorian Investments."

"Listen, you need your rest. I have to skedaddle. We'll see you for lunch. We may be in the secret upstairs office. I guess we can stop calling it secret. Last night Niels started calling it the `war room'."

"Bea, can I ask you one more question?" asked Danni. "How was Fred poisoned? I was in Montreal when they announced the autopsy results. I don't understand how he could have been poisoned. The police wouldn't tell me. They asked me questions about Fred's garden, about the hibiscus. No, not that, some other plant that starts with the letter `H'," said Danni.

"*Hydrangea macrophylla.* My understanding is that the most lethal poison is found in the buds. The leaves and seeds of a hydrangea plant are poisonous too," said Bea. "Fred had a couple of those plants in his garden beside the stairs to the deck. Did you know that?"

"I don't remember."

"It's so bizarre. The two other things I heard while you were away was that it was icing sugar on the knife they found near his body which means that Fred did go buy goodies that Tuesday morning. Also poisonous leaves were found in the salad that had spilled under the library table."

"I can't believe Fred was poisoned. What was the plant called again?" asked Daniella.

"*Hydrangea macrophylla*. *The Toronto Star* had an article about it in the Sunday gardening column. It's interesting. The bush grows wild along the rivers of China and Japan and the word comes from the Greek, water and bowl. Some species have been in Canada for over a century but the one that killed Fred is the most common and has only been popular for about thirty years," said Bea.

>>>>>

Meanwhile back in Montreal, Niels and Pierre sat, in a rented Toyota, in front of the house on Bartholomew Street, with the sarcophagus gazing back at them. The two men looked at each other, grinned nervously and gave a high five. "Okay, let's do it," said Pierre, his forehead shining with bravado. The rest of his face didn't shine because it was covered with a short fake beard.

"You look too adventuresome. Look more depressed. Remember you're a loser trying to help your poor, suffering, abandoned mother," said Niels straightening his clip-on cowboy tie. "One more time, what's your name?"

"Elliot Doses."

"Right! What's my name?"

"Redman."

"Right! Let's go slay dragons and catch the he-devil," said Niels, pounding his chest and giving a war cry as he hopped out of the car. Pierre gazed nervously around the quiet residential street to see if anyone had heard his friend's shout.

They strolled up to the front door and rang the bell. The door was opened by a thin woman, in her late fifties, who squinted at them with tired eyes outlined in heavy blue-black eyeliner.

"Does Mr. Doses live here?" asked Pierre in a quavery voice. He peered, around the lady, down the hallway.

"Yes, he does. Who may I say is calling?"

"Elliot Trudeau, I mean Elliot Doses, Sophia and Günther's son," stammered Pierre.

"Really, I'll go get him," said the woman, then she firmly closed both the screen door and the inside door.

A few seconds later Siegfried Doses appeared. He asked, obviously impatient. "What do you want? I'm not buying anything."

"I think you're my uncle. My father was Günther Doses," blurted out Pierre. "My Mom adopted me when I was a baby and she never asked for anything from your family."

"What the hell you're talking about. My brother had no living son."

Siggy started to close the door but Niels shoved his boot into the doorway. Then he slouched against the frame and said, "Show him the baptismal certificate, Elliot. Have a look, Mr. Doses. It's legitimate. Check with Father Jonathan at Our Lady of Perpetual Hope. He signed the bottom of the certificate to show it's a true copy."

"Who are you?" asked Siggy.

"Mr. Redman, at your service," said Niels who stuck out his hand which Siggy pointedly ignored. "I came along to provide my young friend with support. I strongly recommend you listen to his story. Not listening could create negative financial consequences for you."

"Don't even think of threatening me, punk. I've been around a hell of a lot longer than you have. Come back in an hour when my wife's car is out of the driveway." Siggy Doses snatched the sheet of paper out of Pierre's hand and asked. "Did that bitch, Daniella, send you?"

Niels shook his head in the negative. Pierre also shook his head and said, "Daniella, we couldn't find her. My Mom said half this house is mine because my Dad wouldn't sign the adoption papers when he was in prison. I hate my parents, one is dead and the other one is a murderer. My adopted Mom tried to protect me but now she has terminal cancer." He threw his hands over his face and started to sob interspersed with loud burping noises.

Niels patted him on the back and turned squinty-eyed to the belligerent man standing in the doorway. "Fine, I'll take this poor young man for brunch."

"Brunch. Get outta of here. Tell the kid to quit snivelling or I'll give him something to cry about. Now go away!" He slammed the door.

They sauntered back to the car. "Don't look back," said Niels with his arm around the sobbing boy's shoulders. "It shows a lack of confidence."

"Can I talk now?" said Pierre, the moment that his bottom hit the car seat.

"Yes, you may Shakespeare, your performance was magnificent, the wailing and whining was especially masterful. He really believed that you are from the loins of his brother."

"You sounded really impressive when you said that bit about financial consequences. Just like a teacher. Now what are we going to do?" asked Pierre.

"Sustenance. Let's eat but first I have to find a bank that's open because before we match wits with the devil again, we need cash. There must be a bank open on Saturday in Montreal," said Niels as he pulled into a shopping centre. "Woo, I was right. I'll be back in about half and hour. Why don't you go buy us some grub? I'm going to lasso us some mola from over the Atlantic Ocean; then we'll call the little ladies in Toronto, pardner," said Niels.

"Ouch!" yelled Pierre, when he ripped the fake beard off his chin. He rubbed his face and leaned over to look in the car mirror and continued in a petulant tone. "That hurts. I don't think I look like I'm over thirty. That's what the baptismal certificate said."

"Details, jerks like Siggy Doses, don't know the difference. Old people and people who never had kids can't tell a seventeen year old from a thirty year old."

"Niels, you don't have kids either," said the logical Pierre.

"Irrelevant, my dear Watson. Because I'm under forty and I'm planning to have children soon. Now, listen, I'm starving. Go buy food. We can eat in the car, maybe fried chicken. You do sort of look like a teenager."

"Da! I am a teenager."

"Very funny. Here's two hundred bucks, buy a new dress shirt and dress pants. No jeans, dark wool-blend dress trousers with a crease in them. Now I gotta go to the bank," said Niels reaching into the back seat to retrieve his briefcase and laptop.

>>>>>

It was just after eleven o'clock in the morning when Bea met Maggie at the agency. Bea quickly told her about Danni's release from jail.

"They didn't charge her with anything. So what does that mean?" asked Maggie.

"It means that they don't have enough evidence to lay a charge against her," replied Bea.

"That's good, eh? Let's change the subject. What are we going to do with Martine Tremblay when she comes? She'll be here in a few minutes."

"Let's take her upstairs for the interview. One look at her face will tell us if she knows about the upstairs office."

"Shoot, I just heard the front door. You better talk to her because she doesn't like me," said Maggie. "I know, you bring her upstairs and I'll be pretend to work at the computer with my back towards the door."

A slender elegant woman stood beside the reception desk looking around when Bea walked into the lobby. She extended her hand to the woman, and said, "Hello, you must be Martine Tremblay. I'm Beatrix Prancer. Please come with me."

"Thank you," Martine said, with a faint French-Canadian accent. Without comment, she followed Bea through the agency and up the stairs.

"Shall we sit in the library," said Bea, indicating a chair beside the refectory table. "I have your résumé here but first let's get to know each other a little better. I had the pleasure of meeting your son at Mr. Waddle's funeral. Pierre is a delightful young man. You must be proud of him."

"Yes, Pierre is mine. I understand that you may have a position for me." Martine sat at attention, spine straight, eyes forward, fingers intertwined and palms together. She reminded Bea of a stone-faced soldier, sitting at a court martial table, awaiting a verdict.

"Yes, we understand that you were doing some work at home for Fred and that you've worked for the Common Sense Employment Agency off and on for quite a few years," said Bea.

"Yes, I have. My last assignment was preparing and submitting forms and invoices for companies registered with Victorian Payroll

Services. I sent everything, I was working on, to the estate's solicitor, Tony Eco. He rudely told me that my services were no longer required." Martine's voice was clipped and held a bitter tinge that she couldn't hide.

"I'm sorry to hear that. I see here that you're a bilingual legal secretary. As I said, the résumé we have on file is outdated. Did you by chance bring an updated one?"

"No, I didn't bring one. You didn't ask me when you called." She reached over and snatched the old résumé out of Bea's hand. At the same moment the phone in the middle room rang.

"Common Sense Employment Agency," Maggie said into the receiver.

"Maggie, it's Pierre Le Plume in gay Montreal drinking de bon vino in the de sunshine." His voice echoed out of the speaker phone. His exaggerated phoney French-Italian accent continued to blare into the room. "Ah, it iz cool, so cool at the Hotel La Citad..."

"Oh, no! The speaker phone is on." Maggie jabbed the button to turn it off and whispered into the receiver. "Be quiet. You weren't supposed to call until noon. Hold on. I'm taking the phone downstairs." With the receiver propped against her ear, she picked up the phone and started to walk toward the stairs. Realizing that the cord couldn't go far enough, she ran back to the desk and again inadvertently pressed the speaker phone button. This time Niels' voice boomed out across the room, "Siggy Doses is a total asshole. He called Danni a bitch. Pierre and I are going back to...."

Martine jumped up and grabbed the receiver out of Maggie's hand with such force that she disconnected it from the base. Maggie gave her a simpery smile and said, "I guess, like, your son forgot to tell you he was going to Montreal for the week-end."

"What are you doing to my son? You putain. I told him to stay away from you," screamed Martine. She picked up a chair and threw it. "Talk to my son again and I'll kill you."

Maggie dropped to the floor and rolled under the desk just as the chair hit the wall behind the desk. Martine ran around the desk, kicked Maggie full in the face, bent down and looked at her with fanatical hatred and said in a quavering ominous voice, "You tell Pierre to come home now or he will get it worse than you did." Her legs kicked under the table hitting Maggie who rolled from side to side, under the desk, turning so as to protect her face.

With a surge of adrenaline, Bea dragged Martine out from behind the desk but the madwoman slapped her across the face. Martine picked up a soap stone statue and whipped it across the room at a display shelf of shimmering Murano glass animals. As if in revenge, none of the hard animals shattered when they tumbled down onto the carpeted floor.

At the same time, Maggie could be heard on the telephone talking to the police. "Yea, it's an emergency. She's psycho. She's kicking me and throwing things. I already told you the address, 197 Agatha Street, upstairs in the Common Sense Employment Agency." She screamed from under the desk. "Police! The police are coming! I called the cops."

It was as if a glass of cold water had been thrown in her face. Martine stopped throwing books when she heard the word *Police*. She looked, for a second, like a trapped, fragile deer with nowhere to run but the muzzle of a 303 shotgun. Uncontrollable sobs shook the distressed but dangerous woman as she collapsed on the middle of the floor.

"Bea, be careful. Look at her feet. They're the feet that kicked me last week," whispered Maggie in amazement. "My Mom is going to kill me when she finds out I'm hurt again."

"Your Mom is going to kill you," said Martine. "Your poor mother. Your poor mother to have such a horrible daughter." Martine stood up and moved toward the stairs repeating over and over. "Your poor mother to have such a horrible daughter." Without looking up, she walked into the beefy arms of Detective-Sergeant Kyle Bottleman.

Following behind him were Danni and Detective Alex Sanderson who looked around the trashed room and said, “Okay, ladies, what's going on here? This place is becoming notorious and it's not even a brothel. We were on our way here when dispatch notified us that there was another 911 call from this location.”

“We were having an interview when this crazy psycho lady came up the stairs and started throwing books and things at the ... the three of us. I hid under the desk and Bea tried to restrain her but couldn't, hum, so she ran away screaming obscenities about mafia and employment agencies from outer space,” said Maggie, “and she was wearing purple pants and a bright yellow halter top. I knew she was crazy. I think she's a bag lady that eats worms.”

“A bag lady that eats worms. How, Ms. Nichelton, would you know that?” asked Alex with his notebook poised and his pen flourished.

Bea jumped in before Maggie could embellish her story further. “Maggie is really upset so she's confused. Maybe Danni can take her to the hospital.”

Kyle examined Maggie's bruised face and said, in a brusque manner, “She'll live. She can go to the hospital only after I hear the truth, not fabrications and lies. Now, Mrs. Tremblay, you are not, as we say - known to the police. So I think we should hear your side of the story first.”

“Why? She just got here. The truth is that the crazy lady looked like one of our temps and I didn't want her to get into trouble so I lied. There, I lied. I lied. I lied. I admit it.” Maggie confessed in a funereal tone. Her eyes stared at the floor and her shoulders drooped forward.

"Fine. I donnae have time for bullshit. No one was badly hurt this time. Let's discuss something else," said Kyle with a determined look in his eyes.

The clock, on the mantel, in the sitting room, struck noon. It bonged twelve time as if announcing to the four women and two men that the interrogation was to commence.

Bea, Danni and Maggie sat on the couch and Martine sat in the leather wing chair. The two detectives each took a straight-back chair from the library and placed them facing the women. Alex sat down with his black notebook and pen poised. Kyle stood behind his chair resting his two hands on the wooden frame. He looked at each woman individually, intently and silently until they squirmed like children caught stealing nickels from the bottom of their mother's purse.

"Danni, you may not even know what Niels and Pierre have been up to in Montreal. They're such bad actors that Siggy Doses might just believe their ridiculous story. You, Mrs Tremblay, I haven't figured out where you fit into this amateur sting or why you let your son participate," said Kyle.

"Let my son participate. I didn't let him do anything. Pierre told me he was visiting his grandpa's." Martine pointed and looked with accusing eyes at Maggie. "Ever since he met that woman, he never tells me anything."

"Sting?" Bea asked in an inquiring tone. "What sting?"

Danni looked at her co-workers, rolled her eyes and said, "Tell the cops what Pierre and Niels are up to. They're doing it to help me but I'm okay. The police have almost cleared me, haven't you? One of the neighbours saw me come home early on both the night before Fred died and the night Maggie was beat up. There's a neighbour that looks out from behind her curtain every time a car pulls up within view of her window."

"We're still investigating but, yes, your neighbour saw you come home on those two nights. That's not the issue. The issue is what are Niels and Pierre trying to pull-off in Montreal?" demanded Kyle looking at Maggie. She quickly lowered her eyes and stared at her folded hands.

"Tell them damn it," demanded Danni. "I told you Siggy was bad news. Why are you, two, being so obtuse? Niels and Pierre could find themselves in terrible trouble."

"We're not saying anything because we don't know what Niels has planned. The phone got disconnected seconds after they called so they didn't tell us anything," said Bea. "That's the truth." Maggie nodded in agreement.

"Let me tell you, ladies, something. Ms Thompson is absolutely correct when she told you that Siggy Doses is a dangerous man," said Kyle.

"Thank you. At last someone believes me," said Danni.

"We never didn't believe you, we just needed confirmation which we received this morning. Now if you don't mind, let me continue," said Kyle. "The Quebec police just happened to overhear a conversation between your two friends and Mr. Doses. If it weren't so bloody dangerous, it would be ridiculous," said Kyle. "Pierre pretended to be Günther Doses' late son, Elliot. He also claimed his mother was Sophia Doses."

"What! I had a baby brother," asked Danni jumping up in shock.

The detective nodded at her and continued talking, "Yes, we found not only a birth certificate for Elliot Doses but also a death certificate dated one day later. Now on with the story. Niels is pretending to be a consultant that finds the owners of old bonds and stagnant bank accounts. He has come up with a wild story about an old mortgage number being the secret code to a large Swiss bank account. In this account is money Fred and Günther hid away in the 1960s."

Bea looked at the detective with a forced smile. "Is any of it plausible? There might be a Swiss bank account."

"True, so we called Tony Eco who informed us that he had no record of a Swiss bank account but that doesn't mean much. Your late boss evidently had funds tucked away, here and there overseas, in the Cayman Island, St. Maartens and Luxembough. So, let's accept that a Swiss bank account exist. What do you think, Maggie?" asked Kyle.

A moment of heavy silence hung in the air before she looked at Bea for support, received none so blurted out, "I'm too upset to think, like, my brain is confused."

"Well, let me try to unconfuse your brain by having you ask me a question. Ask me how Fred and Günther made the money that is deposited in the alleged Swiss account." Kyle raised his palm outward toward the women as if to shush their impending speech. "Don't bother answering. I will tell you because it shows that someone, probably Niels Wolfe, has an excellent imagination. He told Siggy Doses, this morning, that Fred and Günther sold illegal birth control pills, in the early sixties, to teenage girls from a lunch truck that went from high school to high school."

Kyle raised his eyebrows and his sharp blue eyes gazed at the four women sitting in front of him. He stood ramrod-still, just his eyes moved slowly from one female face to the next female face waiting for one female to speak. Maggie, of course, lost the silence contest and said, "Maybe Niels made that part up because, like, I don't think birth control pills were illegal this century, were they?"

"Don't they teach you anything in school these days," snapped Danni. "Birth control pills were illegal and people went to jail for providing them less than forty years ago."

"I wasn't even born then. The sixties is ancient history. It's only retro so stores can sell clothes."

"Let's focus, ladies," said Kyle. "Where are Niels and Pierre staying?"

"I don't know where they are now," said Maggie. "Last night they caught a flight from the island airport to Montreal. Niels made reservations at Le Pavillion. It's a hotel near Dorval Airport. That's all I know."

"All right. Does anyone else have something they want to tell me?" asked Kyle.

""No," said Danni. "but if you know that the boys were at Siggy's house early this morning, you must know if they left there or you wouldn't be asking all these question. So are they okay?"

"Yes, your friends are fine. They were at Siggy's house twice this morning. We'd like to tell them that whatever they're planning; it is stupid and probably illegal. When do you think they will call you back?"

Suddenly, Martine sat up straight and shrieked, "I want my son back. I want this woman and that man, Niels, arrested for kidnapping Pierre. I demand it! I demand it!"

All heads turned toward Martine. Her eyes were crazed with suppressed rage and her feet were incessantly striking the coffee table. She stood up, pointed her finger at Maggie. "Her. She stole my son. Gave him money. She seduced him. Her face, it's putrid. She lied. I was trying to beat the answer out of her before you came. I was trying to get her to tell me where they took my son. Arrest her."

Kyle moved toward the agitated woman with his hand outstretched as if she was a puppy who needed a reassuring sniff before trusting him. "Ah lass, tell me about this. It sounds serious. Why don't you and I sit down and you can tell me about it." He turned to Alex and said, "Detective Sanderson, take these other women downstairs and hold them for further questioning. I'm going to take a statement from Mrs. Tremblay. She knows quite a bit about this case, don't you, dear."

Martine looked at the detective then tilted her head to the side internally debating whether to trust him. With brow furrowed in concentration, she watched the three women walk toward the door leading downstairs. "Why is he letting them walk ahead of him?" Martine asked Kyle.

"He can shoot them in the back if they run and we know where they live. Now, tell me about your troubles with Maggie Nichelton. What happened?"

As the others tip-toed down the stairs they heard Martine confess to assaulting Maggie. They stopped mid-way down to finish listening but Alex gave them a gentle shove to keep them moving. At the bottom of the stairs, the upstairs voices had faded into distant murmurs.

"Sit down ladies," said Alex.

"What am I going to tell Pierre?" asked Maggie, emitting heavy sighs of angst as if she was a bad actress acting out the final death scene in a Shakespearean tragedy.

Danni looked at her, rolled her eyes and strode out saying behind her shoulder. "This is just too much for me. I'm going to my office."

"Hey! Stop right there. Get back in here. Let's stay together. I'll tell you when you can leave," barked the detective as Maggie darted around Danni who had stopped inside the door frame.

Maggie also came to an abrupt stop with one toe behind her in a figure skater pose, and said, "I'm, like, starving. Can't we get something to eat? Then you can ask us a bunch of questions."

"Back in here, young lady. You're not going anywhere. We're waiting right here for your buddies, the infamous actors, to phone back," said Alex. He waved at the chairs indicating that they were to sit down.

"Well, the phone will only ring upstairs because we call-forwarded it there," said Maggie with a superior shrug of her shoulders.

"I'll be right back," said Alex. "You women, ladies, are irritating me. Give me a good male criminal any day. Stay here while I take the call-forward off the phone." Before walking up the stairs, he turned around and gave them a stern look. "Try not to gossip like hens in the chicken coup before the rooster comes home."

"That's so sexist. Why can't we talk to each other?" asked Danni. "I have a lot to tell them about Siggy Doses."

"Just wait till I get back. I want to hear whatever you have to say about him."

From the bottom of the stairs. Bea watched Alex climb the stairs. Three quarters of the way up, he turned around, looked down and winked at her. "Making sure I make it up to the top before you start colluding."

"I don't even know how to collude but you might like to transfer the phone to the interview room so we won't be sitting here when Martine comes downstairs. The number is 585-JOBS," said Bea to Alex's back. She heard him mutter, "She's always right. I give up."

She turned around and whispered to Maggie, "What are we going to tell him about the bank book?"

"Nothing, I gave it to Niels to spend; no strings attached. He's going to pay for Danni's lawyer and the airline tickets to Montreal and his hotel, food and car rental. If we tell, Niels will be in supreme shit. And me too because I should've given the bank book to Tony."

Danni interrupted, "Who cares about some bloody bank book? It's your money, Maggie."

"It's your money too, Danni."

"Yes, it is, isn't it. The problem is that pig, Siggy. I told you before, he'll put those guys on a spit and barbecue them for breakfast."

"Shush, whisper," said Bea. She put her finger up to her lips for silence so she could listen for returning footsteps on the staircase. "Okay, we're safe, keep talking."

"Tell the cops what the guys are up to," ordered Danni.

"We can't because Martine disconnected the phone before Niels said anything," said Bea.

"Let's talk about something else. What's really important is that Pierre's Mom just went berserko because of me. What are we going to tell him? Your Mom's rabid," said Maggie taking her forefinger, circling the side of her head and sticking her tongue out. "Ever since Fred was poisoned; bad luck has followed me like the tail on a dog."

"Oh, please, Maggie, stop being so bloody melodramatic. Pierre already knows his Mom has mental problems. He lives with her. I can't stand it when people like you, who were born with an emotional silver spoon in their mouth, make these pronouncements as if the people who have been living in hell - don't know it. Pierre is happy to be away from his Mom. He's probably having fun. Just think Niels isn't spending his own money so, I bet, they're staying at the best hotels and eating at the most expensive restaurants in Old Montreal," said Danni in exasperation.

"I wasn't born with a silver spoon in my mouth. My Mom was poor when she wasn't married."

"I said emotional silver spoon. That means that someone loved you even when you were obnoxious."

"Well, maybe," said Maggie. "I just thought of something even more important, maybe Martine poisoned Fred."

Suddenly Bea stepped away from the door and said in a louder than normal voice. "So we agree. We are telling the cops absolutely everything."

Alex came down just as she finished her sentence and the other two women had flung themselves into chairs.

"Okay, ladies. Let's go into the first interview room and we'll discuss food and last night," said Alex.

Maggie put her arm around Danni's shoulder, gave her a loud kiss on the cheek and said, "Friends."

"Okay, but act like an adult. The police are going to question us and you're making jokes. They write down everything you say and do. They have a behaviour scale that they rate you against. So just be polite and answer his question with simple sentences. Don't use any adjectives or adverbs and don't describe how you feel ever," whispered Danni in Maggie's ear. Raising her voice she continued, "The policeman said to go straight to the interview room, not take a detour."

"Thanks for reminding me. Alex, can I please see if there's pop in the fridge? I'm thirsty and you can't arrest me for being hungry," whined Maggie.

"Stop it," said Danni. She looked at Alex, her face paled, then she turned three shades of red and started to stammer. "I'm sorry. She's just being silly because she's hungry and upset about Martine kicking her in the face. She doesn't mean to be disrespectful."

"It's okay," chuckled Alex. "Come and sit down. Maybe we should order something to eat. How about a pizza? But first a statement about what happened upstairs."

"Martine hit me again. She went totally ballistic. I didn't want to tell because I didn't want her to go to jail because of me. We asked her to come down to the agency for a pretend job interview but we were really planning to question her about Victorian Payroll Services."

"We never had a chance to ask her any questions," said Bea.

Alex turned to her and harshly said, "Maggie's barely an adult but you, Bea. You're mature. Did you lose your mind? That woman, Martine, could be a killer and you went along with this little twerp's plan to lure her here with a false promise of a job. I'm really disappointed, Bea. I expected more common sense from you."

"How dare you make this personal. Don't try and make me feel guilty because if you had only asked *nicely,* I would have told you everything."

Alex opened his mouth to respond but changed his mind and turned back to Maggie. "Now tell me everything leading up to Pierre and Niels' miraculous appearance in Montreal."

>>>>>

About half an hour later, two uniformed policemen came strolling by carrying two large square cardboard boxes and a six-pack of diet-coke. They delivered the pizzas and one of them started chatting with Alex. "So your boss called. Said to be here and to go upstairs at exactly one-thirty." The policemen eyed their watches and the pizza. "Who's he got upstairs so special? He said kid gloves treatment, book her, take her to a justice of the peace at College Park and he'll arrange for her to go to Queen Street for an immediate assessment instead of jail. Must not be your ordinary crazy."

Pizza smells: spicy pepperoni, oily mozzarella, Spanish onion, fresh mushrooms filled the air of the small room when Bea opened the boxes. She offered a slice to each of the policemen who looked at Alex for permission. He nodded his head and picked up a piece himself. "Sure. Take a break, then go upstairs."

Alex closed the door after the policemen left and a few minutes later they heard muffled footsteps on the hallway carpet.

"Who's going to tell Pierre? Maybe we shouldn't tell him," said Maggie just as the door opened.

Kyle walked in and responded to her question, "Someone has to tell him. And if he's under sixteen we'll call Children's Aid."

"Tomorrow is his eighteenth birthday," said Maggie. "He's going to be really upset at me. Some birthday present."

"It wasn't your fault, lassie. Might be a good thing. She's sick. Maybe, just maybe she'll get some help. Pizza. What kind of police brutality is this, pepperoni pizza and pop." He grabbed two slices, slapped them together to make a sandwich and said on his way out, "I'll see you later."

They sat around talking and waiting for Niels and Pierre to phone back. Nothing. Around 3:30 p.m., a telephone technician arrived to install a tracing device. He said, "You all may as well go home. This machine will pick up any calls and relay them to the communications centre." The three women nodded their heads in agreement at the technician's statement.

On the way out Bea idled up beside Alex and casually said, "Coffee, in the morning, at your favourite restaurant or my kitchen."

He turned to her and smiled slightly. "Sure, eight-fifteen sharp at your place. I'll bring something. Any requests? Bagels."

"With cream cheese and lox would be nice."

While Danni, Bea and Alex walked to their respective cars in the parking lot; Maggie jaywalked across street and ran to the intersection to board a westbound streetcar. Three stops later she hopped off and trotted back to the agency.

Once there she stood reading, over and over again, the words carved in the classical stone cartouche above the main door of her building. Commercial architecture, especially banks and low-rises, constructed at the turn of the century, had ornate partial unrolled scroll stonework. In the centre of the cartouche was a large oval stone. It read: *Built - 1914 with Integrity and Charity.*

Maggie skipped into the agency. The police had once again put a yellow plastic ribbon around the door to Fred's office so she turned around, walked up to the second floor and entered the upstairs office with a shiny new key.

Chapter 17

Morning, Sunday, October 26th

At six-thirty in the morning Niels flipped open the lid of his laptop computer, connected it up to the hotel room phone and read his e-mails. He looked resentfully at the teenager who lay quietly snoring in bed. Where were sisters when you needed them? Now he was stuck telling Pierre about his mother. Niels re-read the message from Maggie, then shut the lid of the laptop with a resonant bang.

Pierre groaned, rolled over, opened open one eye and sleepily muttered, “Morning. What time is it?”

“Rise and shine time. Breakfast of the champion's time. It's the only meal you should never miss,” said Niels. He sounded like an advertisement selling processed sugar-laden cereal.

“Okay, I'm starving but I have to phone my Mom first.” Pierre sat up and stretched. “She’ll go ballistic if she finds out I'm not at my grandpa's place.”

“I have to talk to you about that. Why don't you read Maggie's e-mail while I go downstairs to order breakfast?” Niels opened his laptop and pointed at the screen. Without saying another word, he picked up the menu and walked out the front door.

When he came back into the room, Pierre stood at the window looking out over the city. The cloudless blue sky was clean, pure and unmarked.

“Hello, I'm back,” said Niels, stating the obvious. Pierre didn't answer so Niels climbed back into bed and pulled the sheet and blanket over his head. They both stayed in the same position until the room service waiter knocked on the door and rolled in a trolley with five silver-covered dishes.

Niels jumped out of bed. “Pierre, breakfast is here,” he said. “Ta da!” He lifted and clanged the lids together like cymbals. “Presenting strawberries in Devonshire cream, pancakes with pure maple syrup, eggs Benedict, butter croissants with ham and cheese omelette and fruit salad with real whipping cream. “You looked hungry.”

“Wow!” Pierre sat down. He looked anxiously at the food and the silver utensils. “Who's paying for all this?”

“De Suisse banque account is paying,” said Niels in his best German-Swiss accent.

“Okay.” When Pierre had finished eating he mumbled, “Thanks. Can I please be excused?”

“No, as a matter of fact, I need you to translate documents before we meet, Siggy, the evil one. We also have to find a good estate lawyer for Danni while we're in Montreal.”

“I have to go home to look after my Mom.”

“Listen, man, I read Maggie's e-mail; it doesn't sound like there's much you can do. Let's phone her. She can tell you what's going on.”

>>>>>

Unlike Montreal where it was clear and crisp, Toronto was overcast and grey. The first snowflake of the year hit the ground while Bea lay dozing in a comfortable semi-sleep, semi-daydream state. She was just starting to awaken and to think about getting up when there was a loud knock on the door. Once again she ran downstairs, in her nightgown, with her hair mussed. She opened the door to find Alex standing on the doorstep bundled up in a red plaid blanket coat waiting for her. She said, “Sorry, I slept in again. I must look terrible.”

“You look great. Go back to bed,” Alex suggested with a grin.

"Okay." She turned on her heels, yawned, took his hand and upstairs they went.

Later in the morning while they were preparing breakfast singing along with Sunday morning oldies and Beatle songs, the phone rang interrupting their happy duet.

"Hi Maggie. I'm glad you phoned. I was going to call you after breakfast," said Bea. "Alex is right here. He said that the guys didn't phone back last night. And Martine was booked for aggravated assault but she's not in jail. She's somewhere called the Metro Toronto Forensic Services assessment clinic at the Queen Street Mental Health Centre."

Bea propped the cordless phone under her chin, winked at Alex, and poured him another cup of coffee while she listened to Maggie talk. "Oh, really. Oh yea, he's sitting right here. Sure I can tell him that Niels phoned and that the guys are fine but they won't be back until Wednesday. And they're changing hotels so you don't know their phone number."

Suddenly, she turned her back to Alex and walked toward the back door. He followed behind her, started to tickle her, then he snatched the phone out of her hand.

"Okay, Maggie. What's going on?" asked Alex in his best policeman voice. "This isn't a game. I want you to tell me right now what those guys said." Bea listened to the one-ended conversation with trepidation. "Where did you e-mail him from last night? He's going where! No. Yes. Don't even think about it. No. I can't stop you. No, it is *not* a good idea." Alex's voice was becoming increasingly loud and dictatorial.

Bea stood in front of him waving her hands. "Let me talk to her." She repeated again in a louder voice. "Let me talk to her." He shook his head so Bea faked a grab at his crotch, plucked the phone from his hand and ran into the living room.

"Maggie dear, why don't you come over and have some breakfast. I'll make pancakes and Alex would love to have a cup of your special coffee. Okay, see you in half an hour," said Bea. She hung up the phone before he could grab it back out of her hand.

"I can't stand her coffee. I hate flavoured coffees," he said plopping down hard-enough to hear the couch springs creak, then he folded his arms across his chest and picked up a book. After a few minutes of reading, he looked at the title of the slim paperback and threw it back on the coffee table. The cover read *Menopause is Murder*, a collection of mystery and crime stories by women of a certain age.

>>>>>

Alex cleared the table of syrupy plates and cutlery as Maggie talked. His back muscles held restrained anger and each dish he picked up off the table, he dropped into the sink and washed vigorously as if he was a warrior against bacteria. The two women, intent on conversation, were also intent on appearing oblivious to his actions.

"I told Pierre everything about his Mom. I called the Queen Street hospital before I came here, then I stopped at the agency to e-mail the guys again. That's why I'm so late. She's fine but she's not allowed to have visitors because it's really a jail," said Maggie.

"You e-mailed Niels Wolfe again, did you? How convenient. You wasted my time, Kyle's time, the police technical squad's time and you wasted taxpayers' hard-earned money. I could charge you with mischief, young lady," said Alex. To hide his temper he turned away from the two women.

"I forgot that he had a hot mail address until last night when I boarded the streetcar to go home. Then a light bulb went on in my head because I remembered that Niels e-mailed the agency last time he was out-of-town. Sorry."

Making no effort to hide his sarcasm, Alex asked. "Where did you get the address from?"

"I phoned, Debbie, Niels' girlfriend. She helped me send the first message. It's easy as eating chocolate."

"Really. Where are Niels and Pierre staying?" questioned Alex.

"Uhm. They were staying at the downtown hotel on Rene Leveque Boulevard but Niels said they're going to check out this morning."

"Good, so they're coming home?"

"Not exactly. They're going to church, then for a bus tour of old Montreal this morning, just like tourists."

"Really. What else do they have planned for today?"

"Niels said he has to talk to Danni about the old house where her Mom was killed. Weird, eh," said Maggie, "Niels is, like, retentive, obsessed about this house and it's not even his. He went on and on about estates, lawyers and claims. Danni has to do this and Danni has to do that. I shouldn't tell you this because he's still mad at the police. Sorry."

"Sorry, doesn't cut it. I don't think you are, like, as dumb as you are pretending to sound," said Alex imitating Maggie. "Just give me his e-mail address?"

"I didn't bring it. It's at the agency. I told you they're not in their hotel room right now anyway. He's taking Pierre out for his birthday."

Alex left the room but came back a few minutes later swearing under his breath. "Damn, they've already checked out." He looked at Maggie angrily. "They left about half and hour ago. What were you doing? Chattering away about the guys being tourists just to keep me away from the phone. What's with you? I want to protect them, not arrest them. I repeat they should not be dealing with Siggy Doses.

He's a dangerous man, a gangster, who lives in an expensive house and wears expensive suits but is still a gangster."

Maggie looked like she was going to cry and said in a childish voice. "Niels didn't tell me where he was going because he said he doesn't trust me to keep my mouth shut. It's really your fault, you shouldn't have searched his house or humiliated him in front of Debbie or questioned his mother."

"I've had enough of you," said Alex turning his back on her. "Bea, phone Danni to see if Niels has called her yet."

She dialed the number and said, "It's busy but she lives less than ten minutes away. Let's go. She must be talking to him right now. If we hurry, we'll be able to catch them on the phone." Bea grabbed her coat and yanked on her boots.

"Okay, I'll drive," said Alex. With the portable siren on the car roof, they careened down the quiet Sunday morning streets at a hundred kilometres per hour. When they arrived at Danni's, there was no vehicle in the carport. They banged on the door. No answer.

He shook his head in exasperation as they walked away from the house. "Well, that was a waste of time. Maggie, where do you think those two renegades could be in, say, an hour?"

"Notre-Dame Basilica," said Maggie from the back seat. She put her chin on the top of the seat and smiled a wide please-forgive-me smile.

"Church? Niels never struck me as the religious type," said Alex.

"Pierre's Catholic, he's depressed. So when Niels asked me where he should take him to cheer him up, I told him, go to Notre-Dame Basilica. It's the most beautiful church in the world. I went to Old Montreal for our high school graduation trip. Are you anti-God or something?" Alex did not respond to her remark.

He dropped Bea off at home and drove off with Maggie back to the agency. Bea passed the day, relaxing. She went grocery shopping, went to the dry cleaner, picked up blown newspapers from the yard and read a book. Later in the afternoon, she listened to her phone messages. There was only one, very interesting message.

> 'Hi, it's Danni. I'm driving back to Montreal today. I spoke to Niels this morning. He's right, I have to fight for what is rightfully mine so I'm off to match wits with the deceitful Doses. Niels has a strange plan but I think it'll work. We'll probably be sending Pierre home tomorrow so don't be surprised if he shows up on your doorstep. Don't worry, revenge is mine and it makes me feel in control for the first time in a long time. Bye.'

Chapter 18

Morning, Monday, October 27th

The morose seventeen year old, standing at the window staring out at the grey snow clouds, made Niels feel guilty. Feeling guilty was not an everyday emotion for Niels and it made him irritable. Every few minutes Pierre would look up to the top of the sky as if searching high and low for the elusive Pegasus to fly by, then a few seconds later he would peer down at the miniature people walking on the street twenty stories below.

Niels didn't like silence so he asked, "Does it look like it's going to start snowing?"

"Maybe," muttered the teenager.

"Have you ever been in Quebec in the winter?"

"No."

"Should we order breakfast in or go to the coffee shop?"

Still facing the window, Pierre shrugged his shoulders up and down to indicate, I don't care.

"We can wait and eat breakfast with Danni. She'll be here soon from Ottawa." The youth gave another despondent shoulder shrug. Niels picked up his coat and said, "Fine, come if you want to or not but I'm going downstairs to the coffee shop. You knew you would have to go home eventually. What about school?"

"Hate school."

"It's none of my business but why don't you ask Maggie if you can stay with her."

"Can't."

"Why not?" asked an exasperated Niels.

"She's almost twenty-two," replied Pierre. His neck flushed and turned blood red as he rested his forehead against the window glass.

"You like Maggie, eh? Let me think about this. Why can't you stay with your grandfather?"

"He's in one of those tiny senior's apartments and he eats in a dining room with a bunch of old farts."

"I have it!" shouted Niels. "You can stay at Danni's townhouse while she's here in Montreal, that'll give you a few days by yourself."

Pierre turned around, nodded his head but didn't look Niels in the eye. Niels marched out the door and said behind himself, "You should live on your own for awhile. It's awful but some guys like it. I did it for almost a year. Hated it, but everybody should learn how to cook, clean and do laundry for themselves. I can't believe I just said that." He turned around to look at the teenager's reaction to his humour.

Pierre blurted out, "I'd like to live by myself. I don't wanna live with my Mom anymore. See." He lifted his shirt to reveal numerous faded yellow to haemorrhage red bruises. "I knew something was wrong with her, but I didn't want her to go to jail. She can't control herself."

As the boy's shirt dropped, Niels exclaimed, "I can give you a living allowance out of the Swiss bank account if you promise never to tell the authorities. It's only common sense because you have to survive." He pulled him back into the hotel room, grabbed the Gideon Bible from the top drawer of the nightstand and placed Pierre's hand on the book.

"Swear on this bible," said Niels. "Raise your right hand. Now swear outloud after me."

Pierre repeated after him. "I, Pierre Tremblay, promise to faithfully attend school until reaching the age of twenty-one. With this attendance and semi-annual proof of passing grades, a sum equal to my living expenses will be deposited in an account set up by Niels Wolfe. I hereby sign my oath in the combined blood of Niels Wolfe and Pierre Tremblay."

Under his heel Niels smashed a disposable razor blade, the dark-blue plastic shattered into sharp spiked pieces. Carefully, he picked up the exposed blade, wiped it on his shirt sleeve, and lifted Pierre's right hand. He placed the hand on the table, palm upward, then put his hand next to Pierre's. With the tip of the razor blade, he sliced first the teenager's index finger, then his own; droplets of blood welled to the surface of their fingertips and as the two men pressed their fingers together, the blood mixed sealing their oath.

>>>>>

"I just got here, Niels. What's the rush?" asked Danni in the hotel coffee shop.

"I don't want the police to trace me to this hotel. We checked out but the cops may send someone looking for us. I'll explain on the way to the bank. We have to open two bank accounts before we go to the lawyers and Pierre catches the bus back to Toronto."

"Why two accounts?" asked Danni.

"One for us and one for Pierre."

"Why does he need his own account?"

"It's a long story. Which reminds me I told him he could stay at your place while you were here."

"You told a teenage BOY he could stay at my house. You are so arrogant, Niels Wolfe. No way. No way. My home is sacred, it's my sanctuary."

"His mother is in the loony bin. He needs some downtime."

"Why can't he stay at Maggie's place? She thinks he's the cat's meow," said Danni.

"He has the hots for her," said Niels.

"So? What's he going to do for money?"

"I'm giving it to him from the Swiss account."

"What's with this bank account? Whose money is it?" asked Danni.

"It was Fred's but now it's yours, Maggie's and Pierre's."

"What about the other two stepchildren who are beneficiaries?"

"They don't count. I don't know them," said Niels.

"You are so frigging arrogant. Okay, so how much money is in this account?" asked Danni.

"Now or before I withdrew money to pay for your lawyer and our trip here. Give or take a million and a half dollars, American."

"Really, that's unbelievable. But how can you withdraw money from it? It's not your account."

"It's a numbered account. Whoever has the number, has the withdrawal power. Maggie found the bank book taped to the bottom of a tea pot and I figured Fred must have hidden the access codes too. Guess where I found them with detailed instructions on electronic deposit and withdrawal?"

"Behind the spice rack?"

"No."

"Okay, I give up. Where?"

"Inside a pair of socks. I also found some other interesting documents in an envelope under his shirts," said Niels.

"Like what?" asked Danni.

"Personal papers, all his old marriage licences, divorce decree absolutes and a few Canada Savings Bonds. Like a good boy, I left them where the police or Maggie would find them."

"What did you do with his marriage licences? Was there one for when he married my Mom?" asked Danni.

"Didn't look at them. Figured it was none of my business. We're going to open a new Swiss account under the name, The Waddle Trust. I registered the company as a charitable corporation with Fred as President, you as Vice-President and me, me, me, of course, as Treasurer. I backdated the incorporation application and took it to the registration office and told them they had made a mistake. They are so over-worked and understaffed that they back-dated the corporate registration to the day before Fred died. When we fly to Switzerland with the appropriate documentation; we control the trust. Smart, eh?"

"As long as the bank thinks Fred is alive right?" asked Danni.

"No, wrong, we're going to tell them Fred is dead."

Late afternoon, Monday

As they walked out of the legal office of Patterson, Gagnon and Gagnon, she punched Niels in the arm. "Two-hundred and twenty bucks an hour. That's atrocious," said Danni. "Also, Niels, I can speak for myself. He's going to represent my mother's estate, not you."

"Yea, but I'm going to pay him," said Niels

"Out of my portion of the inheritance."

"Well, I didn't hear you giving him any specific instructions and you needed a letter written to Siggy today. At two hundred bucks plus an hour you're allowed to set a deadline to get it done. At least I told him to do it. You just sat there like a bump on a log."

"I did not!" exclaimed Danni.

"You did too. Every time anyone says the name Günther you freeze up, that's why you need me," said Niels.

"Somehow or another. I managed to survive without you for years and years."

"So who's richer, me or you?" asked Niels.

"I never defrauded Revenue Canada," retorted Danni.

"You can be such a witch. I didn't commit tax fraud; Fred did. I invested the profits from his scheme and got an excellent return on the investment."

"Fred never gave me thousands and thousands of dollars to invest."

"I know. Maybe you should learn how to turn on the computer."

"Screw off."

>>>>>

Pretending to be a race car driver, Pierre rolled and squealed his new carry-on suitcase up and down the hotel room finally turning into the bathroom with it. "Niels," he yelled, "can I take a soap and shampoo home? There's two of everything in here."

"Yea, sure. Take 'em all. Pierre, let's get going," said Niels. "The express bus for Toronto leaves at seven-thirty. Danni's finished writing the letter giving you permission to stay at her place so you won't get arrested for breaking and entering."

The teenager came out of the bathroom and stood over her shoulder so as to read the letter she had written. "Awesome," Pierre said. "You have any videos?"

"Yes, but do you know how to use a VCR?" asked Danni.

"Da! Of course, I know how to use a VCR."

"Well, do you know how to use a gas stove?"

"Just ignore her, Pierre," said Niels with a dismissive wave of his hand. "More important. You know what your part is. Incognito, you are to be incognito. Here's the key to the upstairs office at the agency. Remember don't talk to anyone until you get my e-mail. Don't lead the police to the computer directory until Wednesday morning. The cops have to find the file with indictable evidence against Siggy by Thursday morning."

Niels stood in front of the teenager, hand inside his shirt, like Napoleon on the field of battle. Pierre stood up and saluted as his General Wolfe issued forth questions. "What's the evil file called?"

"D-A-D for Damages against Doses," answered Pierre clicking his heels and standing at attention.

"Where are the D-A-D files located?" asked Niels.

"In a directory called H-I-P," replied Pierre.

"Excellent! And what does HIP stand for?"

"Honour is Pierre's."

"And what is the password?

"W-A-W, Wolfe at Work."

Pierre and Niels emitted a war cry, raised their fists into the air and cried, "Off with his head."

"And on to the bus," said Danni as she threw them their coats and threw her arms up in the air like presidential candidate giving a speech to an auditorium. They all marched out single file.

Chapter 19

Tuesday, October 28th

Danni and Niels returned exhausted but exhilarated to their adjoining rooms. That morning they had once again checked out of their hotel. This time they moved into a charming 1800s mansion that had been renovated into a luxury guesthouse. Each room had a sleigh bed, a Jacuzzi and a sitting room in an alcove or screened porch looking down on the island that was Montreal.

They spread out the blueprints of the Doses' house on the king-size bed. "Excellent, these are excellent. I can't believe Siggy's dumbbell wife just told her builder to hand over the blueprints to her house," said Niels, as he unrolled another set of drawings.

"She's not dumb, she's just gullible," said Danni.

"Oh, Mizz Doses," said Niels, in a sugary, sweet conniving voice, "we just *love* your house. Our real estate agent gave us the wrong address. So we walked right into your backyard and peeked in the window and saw your adorable kitchen and sunroom. And my wife said to me; darling, that's the kitchen, I want. So that's why, I'm calling you, Ms Doses. First, I'm so sorry we trespassed on your property but because we did my wife and I decided after seeing your stunning kitchen to renovate ours. So, please, please tell us the name of your decorator. I would so appreciate it. Barf," Niels put his finger in his mouth as if to induce vomiting. "What a mark. She should have an scarlet 'M' tattooed on her forehead." With a fine black felt pen, he drew a circle around the main floor bathroom windows on the blueprint.

Danni walked over to look out the window. She gazed down at the St. Lawrence, and said, "Whatever happens the river keeps flowing so, Niels, you don't have to go through with the plan for me. I can just sue Siggy. It doesn't matter how long it takes."

"No." He picked up a rigid cardboard blueprint tube, swung it around like a sword and hit the bed with a hard loud wallop. "The man is a scumball! He's truly evil and he probably killed Fred."

"How could he have anything to do with the poisoning? Fred died in Toronto and Siggy lives here in Montreal. Why would he want to kill Fred? Maybe the poisoning was accidental."

"Get real! I wasn't going to tell you this because, shit, I'm chivalrous. Okay, here it is. Fred hired a private detective to look into your background and the day before he died he received a report. On it he had circled Siggy's name and wrote in capital letters, underlined twice with two exclamation marks - STILL A BASTARD!! In the margin of the page he also wrote - MUST BREAK UP WITH DANNI. TELL HER TO SUE SIGGY.

"Screw off. Where did you find the private detective's report? Pretty strange that no one else found it," said Danni.

"It was in the upstairs office mail tray. Fred must have read it the morning he died. I checked out the second floor long before the police searched it. Being chivalrous, I ripped up a report on Maggie's Mom too. Let me tell you what Fred found out."

"Stop it! I hate you. Why are you doing this to me?" Danni spit the word at him. She picked up a blueprint tube, smacked him on the shoulder with it, then chucked it against the wall. "I hate you."

"You hate me. Don't shoot the messenger. Why don't you hate that bastard, Siggy? Do you know what else he is; a child pornographer. You should see the disgusting depravity," Niels said. "Look!"

"No, I don't want to see it," she said. "You're a sadist."

"Look at it before you meet Siggy tonight. It'll motivate you. I'm not doing this because I'm pissed off at the cops. They can't touch

Siggy or they would have arrested him years ago. We can kick him where it hurts, make him bend over, financially castrate him."

"I know he's an asshole. I remember a few months before my Mom died, Siggy sat watching when Günther slapped her across the face. Siggy just calmly commented. 'Don't touch her face. It'll get you in trouble.'

"I'm sorry, Danni. Look what he's doing now. If we steal his money, we steal his power. He has four porno Web sites. Last night I found out where they originated from and more importantly where the site's membership fees were going. Surprise! Straight to Switzerland to the same bank where Fred's account is."

"That's reaching. Fred had nothing to do with that," snapped Danni.

"No, I'm not suggesting that. But Fred probably did know Siggy back in the sixties," said Niels, just as the laptop in front of him beeped a burlesque tune. He turned the screen toward Danni and pointed. It was as if his finger was commanding her to look at the small screen.

"Turn it off, that's enough. I don't need to see that filth. I especially don't want it in this beautiful room. Yuk. Turn it off. Turn it off now!" Danni gagged, stood up, grabbed her coat and said, "Screw off, I'm going shopping."

"Revenge, think avenger, you can be an avenger," Niels said to her back as she rushed out and slammed the door behind her.

Evening, Tuesday

From the front seat of the rented car, Danni said, "Okay, so the cuckold wife just drove away with a smile on her face. I hope she has a good time with her grand prize of two free tickets to the opera and supper reservations at the Café de Paris in the Ritz-Carlton."

"She's such a mark to believe that the Quebec League of Women Interior Designers forgot to give her a prize until today. Oh, and what a shame, the last day to use it is today. Like, man, sometimes I'm so brilliant it overwhelms me," said a muffled male voice from the back seat. "I just knew Siggy wouldn't go to the opera."

"Shut up, Niels. I need a knife." The light brown skin crumbled as Danni peeled off the outside layers of the onion.

"Use your nails."

"I don't have long nails."

"Use the car keys then. You're procrastinating, Danni," said Niels from his position under a blanket in the backseat of the car.

"Okay, here goes." She dropped her head onto the steering wheel so pedestrians couldn't see her holding the raw onion under her eyes. A few minutes later she walked up the sidewalk on Bartholomew Street and rang the doorbell.

"What the hell do you want?" asked Siggy when he saw who was at his door.

"I just want to talk to you about everything, the house, my brother that I didn't know existed. What's going on? I'm confused," said Danni looking at him with painful, pleading red-rimmed eyes.

Ten minutes later, Siggy and Danni drove away in his slate-grey Mercedes. Niels strolled around to the back of the house and snapped on a pair of skin-tight surgical gloves. Deck chairs were conveniently stacked up under the main floor bathroom window so he climbed on them and crawled into the window. He muttered, "Good girl." His adrenaline surged as he opened the bathroom door and called out, "Bonjour, hello. It's the telephone man. Anyone home? No. Good."

On the kitchen counter was an open bottle of red wine and two windmill-cut crystal glasses. Niels put the wine glasses up to the light, picked the one that had a trace of Danni's lipstick on the rim, rinsed it and poured himself a drink.

"Upward and onward," he said saluting himself as he moved out of the kitchen into the interior of the house. Being methodical, he searched room by room; starting with the main floor which contained the living room, kitchen, sun room and bathroom. On the second floor there were two large bedrooms and a bathroom with a Jacuzzi and wicker loveseat.

On the third floor, Niels whispered, "Bingo. Now where could Siggy have hidden the passwords." With an appraising eye, he examined the large room. Five computers, five phones and only one chair made up Siggy Doses' satanic world. Not a paper nor a pen was visible so Niels turned the phones upside down and found the password written on masking tape. "No imagination."

Click, click, click, enter were the only sounds that could be heard. An hour passed, then the next hour started to tick by. Niels squinted in concentration and his neck was thrust forward like a crane when he heard the sound of footsteps coming up the stairs. He quickly clicked the shut-down icon on the five computers, then ran to stand behind the door. A glance at his watch told him that just over two hours had passed.

Nothing. No sound. He stood still another minute, then carefully opened the door to listen and started to tiptoe down the stairs.

Flush - the sound of toilet water rushing down the pipes froze him in his tracks. The bathroom was, just to the right, at the bottom of the stairs. Niels scurried back upstairs and stood frozen behind the door. His heart beat increased three-fold as the door swung open pushing in the tip of his nose. He held his breath. Siggy Doses walked in, turned on a computer and opened a window. He looked around, then walked out again.

Siggy's footsteps faded, as he went downstairs to the main floor. Niels tip-toed to the second floor and darted like a chased rabbit into the bathroom where he hopped into the bathtub and hid behind the shower curtain. A few minutes later, he climbed out of the tub and peeked through the crack in the door just as Siggy walked up to his office.

One.

Two.

Three, four. In his head Niels counted to two hundred, then he tiptoed swiftly down the stairs, past the sarcophagus and bolted out the backdoor.

The car wasn't there. It was gone! Niels looked up and down the street. He stymied an urge to run. Instead he took a shallow breath and strolled toward the end of the street. On the corner he again looked both ways then abruptly turned right because with his peripheral vision he saw Siggy standing on his front porch.

Honk, honk. A car pulled up beside him. The passenger door opened, "Hop in, honey," said Danni in a sultry voice.

Niels jumped in and yelled, "Let's get out of here. Drive. Where the hell did you go? I almost had a heart attack when the car wasn't here."

"Sorry," said Danni, "Siggy insisted on walking me to the car. He stood on the sidewalk and watched as I drove off. It was so creepy. Are you okay?"

"I'm fine. Pull up over there. Let me drive. It helps me to relax. The mission was a success. We have a plane to catch in a few hours."

Chapter 20

Very Early Morning, Wednesday, October 29th

The morning sun hadn't risen over the eastern horizon when the plane's wheels slipped inside its massive steel and aluminum underbelly. Danni held Niels' hand and gave it a squeeze as the plane lifted off, from Mirabel Airport, for Zurich.

"We did it. We did it. He fell for it, hook, line and he's a greedy stinker," sang Danni. "It's going to work, isn't it, Niels? I'm still worried. What if the police find out you broke into Siggy's house last night and transferred all the money from Siggy's bank accounts into the Waddle Trust account? And won't the Swiss bank think it's weird that I just walk in, claim to be Fred's mistress and, oh, bye-the-way, banker dear, here's a death certificate, please freeze these accounts? Don't worry that hundreds of thousands of dollars were transferred into the account just last night."

"For the tenth time, it's a simple plan, it'll work. You, Maggie and Pierre are beneficiaries of Fred's estate and, you-three, are a majority of the stepchildren so you-three gave me permission to invest your inheritance for the greater good of society. It's ethical because I incorporated the Waddle Trust under the Charitable Corporations Act and we will use the money to do good works."

"Don't bullshit me, Niels. I wasn't talking about Fred's money in Switzerland. What about the money you stole out of Siggy's accounts while I lured him away to cry on his disgusting shoulder?" asked Danni.

"I don't give a flying fig about stealing Siggy's money and transferring it into another more worthy account. His money is contaminated and we're going to sanitize it, nobelize it. The only infinitesimal, micro-minuscule risk is that Siggy checked his bank accounts this morning, figured out what happened and hopped on a plane to follow us to Zurich. It won't happen, he's too provincial and he can't call the police because they're already investigating him," said Niels. "Think of what we have done, we have eliminated a pestilence, we have applied pest control and changed the world into a better place, for all, especially kids. We have taken control."

"I've never had total control over anything in my entire life. Bad things always happen to me. Sometimes I don't even know they're happening. Maybe you're right. This time I'm not unintentionally doing something wrong, I'm purposely doing something illegal but for a good cause. Does that makes sense?"

"Stop worrying. You're pulling the plug on a plague called Siggy Doses because as of ten o'clock this morning he's flat broke, busted. All his cheques are going to bounce. Not a penny nor a franc shall be his. And at eight-thirty-five a.m. tomorrow morning, all the money will be locked in, no one can touch it because it will be part of Fred's estate." Niels grinned and his eyes shone with anticipated triumph. "We will be like a soft breeze blowing, sweeping up what is rightfully yours. Many will benefit from a newly created philanthropic trust set up by me, Cornelius Wolfe the First." As he spoke he toasted himself by lifting a glass of orange juice into the air and bowing to it.

"Cornelis! Is Niels short for Cornelis? Maybe you should change your name to Corny Hood. Tell me again how the police are going to get Siggy?"

"Danni, for an intelligent woman, you're a pain. It'll be fine, trust me."

"It's because I'm not accustomed to conniving, lying, and tricking criminals. You're enjoying this far to much," she said, pressing the button on her seat and pushing it back.

"Give it a rest. This man deserves to be fleeced. A charity, not the frigging police or the government, deserves to receive his ill-gotten gains. And you deserve retribution. I'm right," he said.

"I know you're right, Niels. Also, why does the new account for the Waddle Trust have a name? I thought Swiss accounts were numbered accounts that didn't have names attached to them."

"It's an option to have an account by number only or, the usual way, by name and number. In 1934, the Swiss legislated that bank accounts must be locked in secrecy. This was to foil Hitler's attempt to track down the assets of German and Austrian Jews. This thoughtful policy leaves open a door for fine financial finagling."

"You've changed. You even talk different than a few days ago. I'm just nervous that the police won't arrest Siggy and he'll come after us. Well, he won't come after us personally; he'll probably hire a hit man. Tell me again how the police are going to catch him?"

"Okay, one more time with feeling. I sent Pierre the information on Siggy's dirty website names, advertisers' post office box numbers and courier waybill numbers to my e-mail address at the agency. Last night Pierre sneaked into the upstairs office and saved the files into the hard drive of the computer. Today, he will, accidentally-on-purpose, find the file while he's visiting the agency. Then he will coerce Bea into calling Alex who will, if he has more than five brain cells, immediately recognize the importance of the file and contact the RCMP who will arrest Siggy. Trust me."

Pleased with his role of being a deviant do-gooder with good planning skills, Niels lay his head down on the side of the airline seat and shut his eyes.

>>>>>

While his co-conspirators were flying over the Atlantic Ocean, Pierre walked into the agency. He hadn't spoken to a soul since

Monday evening when he said good bye to Niels and Danni at the Montreal bus station. As he walked into the waiting room, a voice startled him. “Excuse me, young man, you can't go back there without an appointment. Can I help you?”

“Hi. Is Maggie in?” asked Pierre. He looked over the reception desk at an older, stout woman. The name plate on the desk read, Mrs. H. Fundy. When he leaned toward her the smell of ammonia made his nose twitch so he moved back slightly.

“No. I'm sorry. Ms. Nichelton is not available,” said Mrs. Fundy.

“Oh. Where is she?”

“If that were your business, she would tell you herself. Wipe your feet on that mat over there and have a seat and I'll get someone to talk to you in a few minutes. Have you filled out an application form?”

Pierre looked down at the woman's wrinkled, spotty hands with dismay and shook his head in the negative. “No. I'm still in school. What about Bea? Is she here?”

“Ms. Prancer is interviewing all morning. Ms. Prancer is VERY busy today. I can make an appointment for you with someone else,” said the efficient guardian of the Common Sense Employment Agency.

He shook his head, and walked out muttering, “What an old bat. I wish she would shrink, then I would step on her.” He went up the elevator to the second floor. Using the key Niels had given him, Pierre entered the upstairs office and called Bea and Maggie's direct lines. Both phones were call-forwarded so he hung up at the third ring.

After checking to make sure the files he had saved from Niels' e-mail were sitting in the correct directory on the hard drive, he played a few computer games. Suddenly, he jumped up and ran down the narrow stairs leading to Fred's old office. The door opened about an inch, then hit something metal. Pierre pushed the door with his shoulder, kicked it with his foot and finally in frustration hit his forehead against it.

Back upstairs, he once again picked up the phone. “Hi, may I please speak to Bea Prancer?” he asked as polite as can be.

“She's interviewing at the moment,” replied Mrs. Fundy.

“Tell her it's her son, Pierre, and I had an accident.”

“Oh, dear. I'll get her right away.”

A few seconds later he heard Bea's concerned voice. “Pierre, is that you?”

“Yea, it's me.”

“What happened? Are you hurt?”

“NO, it was that lady at the front rec...”

“That's Mrs. Fundy. We've been expecting you for two days. Where are you?”

“Upstairs. That Mrs. Fundy wouldn't let me in.”

“Upstairs, where? You mean, upstairs, here,” said Bea in amazement. Pierre stamped his feet on the floor and she looked at the ceiling. “Okay. I believe you. I just heard you. Come downstairs.”

“The door going to the downstairs office doesn't open,” said Pierre. He sounded more than a little contrite, almost whiny.

“No, you have to use the elevator. You'll see why when you come downstairs. There's a wrought iron spiral staircase sitting in front of the door. Maggie is renovating. Damn, I have another interview in two minutes.”

“That's okay. I'll come down in half an hour. I can stay up here, check out the bar behind the bookcase and play computer games.”

“It's kind of early for a drink, Pierre,” said Bea chuckling. “But I'm glad you're back. We were worried about you.”

Afternoon, Wednesday

During lunch, Maggie reached over to touch Pierre's hand a couple of times just to reassure herself that he was there, safe and sound. "You can tell me," she said, "I promise I won't tell. I promise. Tell me what they're doing. Niels isn't responding to his hot mail and the police are pissed off that Danni left the province again. Tell me, tell me, please."

"I don't know anything except that I have to make the police look at the computer files in the upstairs office. I found a file that looks like illegal business records," said Pierre, wolfing down his lunch with his forehead horizontal to the table top.

"Can I look at it?" asked Maggie.

"No, only the police can look at it."

"Who decided that?"

"No one."

"It was Niels, wasn't it? Look at me, jerkface. You're lying. I can tell."

"Am not," replied Pierre catching her eye and holding it. He didn't blink and kept staring at her until she stuck out her tongue.

"Bullshit, Pierre. Something happened, didn't it or are you mad at me about your Mom?"

"No, I'm not mad at you. I don't even think about her. I should go see her, shouldn't I?"

"She hit you too so you don't owe her anything unless she apologizes and never does it again." Maggie's eyes gleamed with compassionate common sense as she took his hand and said, "Don't worry, your Mom will be okay. That Detective Kyle said she was sick and now she'll get the help she needs. Maybe just phone her."

"Okay, I'll phone her. Can't you talk about something else."

"Never fear, I have questions," said Maggie. "Is Niels still acting like an undercover agent? Where is he? What's he up to? You can trust me. I won't blab to the world."

"I can tell you what we did in Montreal but I can't tell you what they're doing right now. They wouldn't tell me their plans just in case the police questioned me."

"Oh."

"We have to get the police to look at the computer on the second floor. I promised. It's really important. Life and death. You can help me," said Pierre.

"How? Why don't you just ask Bea to call Alex?" asked Maggie.

"I already asked her. She said it wasn't appropriate and she didn't want to bother him at work and the police already checked out the agency's computers."

>>>>>

Through the plane window the city of Zurich glowed with sunshine and fall colours. The landing gear released and the plane's wheels touched down at exactly 3:14 p.m. The customs check was fast and business-like. Niels hustled Danni down the corridor, pulling her along as if she was his rolling suitcase. When she stopped to look out a window on the way to the baggage pick-up, he grabbed her arm and almost yanked it out of the socket.

"Hurry up. The bank closes at five o'clock. We only have an hour. Step one has to happen this afternoon. I have to give them an original copy of the Waddle Trust's incorporation papers today or else. The bank has to have evidence, on file, that Fred was the president," said Niels. The start of panic could be heard in his voice.

Danni ran after him as he galloped down the long wide aisle of the airport. "Niels, you look like you're going to explode. Slow down. Listen to me. You go. You go straight to the bank. I'll pick up our luggage and find us a guesthouse or hotel. Just come back to the airport. I'll wait in one of the restaurants.

With a grin, he nodded his head, turned and ran toward the nearest exit sign. Danni called after him, "Get some money exchanged at the bank so I can go shopping too."

>>>>>

Meanwhile back at the agency, over the course of the afternoon, Maggie and Pierre tried to convince Bea to call Alex. They begged her, they bugged her and they offered her bribes, including cooking her dinner and cleaning her house. When that didn't work, they tried to blackmail her by saying they would call her daughter and tell her lies. It was almost closing time when Bea exited a washroom stall to find Maggie, with sorrowful puppy dog eyes, standing waiting for her.

Bea threw her hands in the air and said, "I give up. I'll call him. What am I supposed to tell him?"

"Thank you, thank you, ask Pierre," said Maggie, giving the woman a hug and a kiss on the cheek. "You saved his life." The two women walked out of the washroom to find the teenager in discussion with Mrs. Fundy.

"I don't care for young men who lie to me," said Mrs. Fundy. "Mrs. Prancer has one daughter, not a son."

"I'm sorry, but I thought you'd never let me talk to her," said Pierre.

"Lying can become habit forming. Next time you come, explain yourself, don't just sulk and walk out. You have a nice face, it's clean."

Maggie came up behind Pierre, hugged his waist and whispered loudly in his ear. "I did it. Bea is going to phone Alex. You, like, owe me big time for snagging her as she came out of a toilet stall." He turned around and gave her a tentative, almost embarrassed, hug back.

"Okay," said Bea. "What do you want me to tell Alex?"

"Just tell him to come and meet you upstairs," said Pierre.

"He won't just come without an explanation. I have to give him a reason."

"I'm not supposed to tell you. But I will. There's evidence on the computer upstairs that will send Siggy Doses to jail forever. He sells child pornography and Niels thinks he killed Fred."

So Bea agreed to call police headquarters. Pierre's grateful face made her overcome her pride because she couldn't admit to a couple of kids that she had called Alex, at home, the two previous nights and he had not returned her calls.

"Could I please speak to Detective Sanderson?" Bea asked the police switchboard operator

The voice at the other end replied, "I'm sorry, he is out-of-town until Thursday. Can someone else help you?"

Chapter 21

Morning, Thursday, October 30th

The Swiss guesthouse was on a street of four and five-story high painted stucco buildings with beautiful muted facades. Under each window hung a flower box and under each flower box was a painting of a bird enclosed in a circular border. Danni looked over the edge of the black wrought iron balcony while she waited for Niels to bring breakfast. Tears appeared and she sighed while looking at window boxes overflowing with fall greenery, mainly ivy vines and long blooming reddish geraniums.

Hearing a knock, Danni turned around and went to open the door. Niels burst in and said, "I wish Debbie were here. She'd love the bakery."

He handed the two large paper bags to Danni who looked inside and said, "There is enough here to feed a small army. Wow, four loaves of bread, twelve buns, a flan, two dozen cookies, and six chocolate eclairs. What's in the small bag?

"Hard salami sausage, apples and bananas."

"What? No veggies."

"We can have the sausage for lunch and take the leftovers on the plane with us," said Niels as he spread the baked goods on the table. "The bank opens at eight-thirty so let's eat and run. Step two is your baby. Yesterday, I had no problemo with step one. All corporate documentation, on the Waddle Trust, is in the hands of our Swiss banker. He gave me his business card, here it is, be sure to ask for him."

>>>>>

After pigging out, the two friends walked toward the bank where the accounts were housed. Niels found a café in which to sit and wait for Danni. As she was leaving, she heard him order more pastry and another coffee.

Danni was dressed in a classically-cut navy micro-fibre suit, with a creme-coloured silk blouse designed to reassure any conservative banker that this was, truly, a respectable woman in mourning, an intelligent woman with a substantial bank account. She had smoothed her hair back into a French knot and when she walked into the bank, Danni lifted her chin up with a confident tilt.

There were only three people, in the line-up, waiting for teller service. The man, in front of her, instinctively sensing an attractive woman behind him, turned around and said, "Bonjour."

"Bonjour," replied Danni, and in French said, "I thought they spoke German here."

"Ah, this is Switzerland, I am from Lac Léman, Lake of Geneva where the dominant language is French. You are American?"

"No, Canadian."

"Ah, Canadians are always welcome because they are not so verbose or patronizingly insecure as other nationalities," said the middle-aged man.

"Well," said Danni, "thank you, I guess."

He took her arm, guided her in front of him and pointed at the next vacant teller. "That one, he speaks both excellent English and French. You go," he said, giving her a gentle push.

"Thank you," she said again.

"It is nothing," said the gracious gentleman. "But if you're in Switzerland for more than a few days you must visit the canton of Vaud and Lake Geneva. Then, maybe we will meet again." His eyes acknowledged her and he gave a sensuous bow as she walked up to the teller's cage.

The teller was not another charming Swiss man. Contempt for customers was written on his emotionless jowly face. His thinning yellow hair appeared harsh like it came in regular contact with a smelly bleach bottle. His only acknowledgement of her presence was a sharp nod and he looked, without curiosity, at the documents in her hand.

First, she laid down on the counter, Fred's death certificate and the mustard-yellow bank book Maggie had found taped to the bottom of the teapot. Clipped to the bank book was a piece of paper on which was written the account number.

Next she handed the teller a piece of writing paper. Neatly written in ballpoint pen were three lines. The first line read, The Waddle Trust and the next two lines were a series of numbers. He opened the bank book and started to speak German. She shook her head and glanced behind her but her gentleman-friend had finished his banking and left the premises so she turned to the teller and said in English, "I understand you speak English and French."

"Of course, Madam, which do you prefer?" responded the teller in precise French.

"English"

"Fine, Madam, and what can the bank do for you today?"

"This is a death certificate for Frederick Waddle," Danni stammered but continued. "I'm a co-signer on a charitable trust account and I wanted to make sure you had this." She pushed the death certificate across the counter.

The teller looked at it and nodded his head. He clicked a few buttons on the computer in front of him, blinked his eyes, and though barely discernable, pursued his lips in repressed interest. He turned to Danni and said with a flicker of respect, "Do you have a valid passport?"

"Yes, it is right here," she said. "Also I wrote down the name of the estate's lawyer on the back the paper I just gave you."

The teller nodded his head, looked gravely at Danni's passport and asked, “Were you Mr. Waddle's wife?”

“No, I wasn't. I was his fiancee. Why do you ask?

“Just curiosity. I heard that French-Canadian women are not permitted, by law, to take only their husband's surname. One more question. Do you wish to withdraw funds from either of these accounts today?”

“No, but I would like to ensure that the money in the Waddle Trust is used for charity. That was Fred's last wish.”

“Understandable. Please have a seat over there,” said the teller with a restrained smile. He pointed toward a row of chairs across the marble foyer. “I will be back presently with the manager for legacy and estates, Mr. André.”

With spine straight and shoulders pulled back Danni walked across the bank floor. Suddenly, her ankle twisted and collapsed sideways and her leg shot forward. She fell, landing hard on her bottom.

Afternoon, Thursday

“I think I could live here,” said Danni looking out of the window as the plane ascended into the air. “It's a beautiful country. From the air it looks so clean and safe. Look at that stone farmhouse with the red and blue metal roof. Oh, Niels, I hope, for once, I did the right thing. Mr. André was so helpful after I fell down in the middle of the bank floor. He even offered to drive me back to the guesthouse. It was a bit manipulative.”

“Yea, it was a lot manipulative but it worked. The bank's desire to provide excellent service went up, up when their beautiful customer fell on the floor, floor, floor. We did it. Even I can't believe you did it,” said Niels. “All of Siggy's and Fred's money is transferred into the Waddle Trust account and the bank can keep that account frozen until Fred's estate is probated."

"Over a billion dollars, that was the balance."

"The interest will pay our salary because you and I are the Waddle Trust. I wonder what Siggy did when he found out his money was all gone?" asked Niels.

"I bet he tried to withdraw cash out of a bank machine. He probably thought that the bank card was demagnetized, went into the bank and found out that his balance was zero. Then he drove home furiously, fuming, maybe thinking his wife had left with the plumber for Brazil."

"But as he drove up to his house, there, waiting with a duly-authorized warrant and handcuffs, stood the police. They should have arrested Siggy this morning."

"I hope so, Niels," said Danni laughing. "You are the best schemer in the world. Everything went according to plan this morning."

About six hours later they landed at Pearson International Airport, where Debbie and four of Niels' sisters were waiting for him. Danni watched the Wolfe family fawn over their helpful but hypocritical son and when he looked at her standing alone on the edge of the crowd of women, he said, "Come on, my sister, Katrien, will drive you home. She lives close to your place."

>>>>>

Danni inserted her key into the deadbolt lock but when she started to turn the key, the door swung open. Just like she had been taught at self-defence class, she pushed her keys between her middle and index finger, then she called out a tentative, "Hello."

With anxiety, she rushed through the living room, kitchen and out the back door into the postcard yard. While standing on the cement patio, a familiar laughing shriek could be heard coming from the second floor bedroom window.

"That little stink," said Danni. With a burst of energy, she ran through the house and up the stairs, but came to an abrupt stand still midway up at the sight of Maggie and Pierre. They were naked, romping and rolling around on her bed, giggling, laughing and hitting each other with her pillows. "You're the best," said Maggie. She grabbed Pierre by his arm and rolled him onto his back. Then she sat on his stomach, leaned over and kissed him on the forehead.

Without a word, Danni swung around, went downstairs, picked up her suitcase and rang the door bell twice. She opened the front door and shouted at the top of her lungs, "Hi, anybody home?"

Upstairs in mid-pillow attack, the two nude jack-in-the-boxes jumped off the bed and ran into the walk-in closet.

"It's Danni," whispered Maggie.

"Frig," said Pierre.

"Go get my clothes."

"What are we going to tell her?"

"Nothing, tell her you were sleeping."

"Okay," said Pierre, in an anxious voice. "Shit, she'll kill us for using her bed." The young adults started to chortle.

"Shush, yell downstairs," said Maggie. She grabbed a sheet from the upper shelf and wrapped it around Pierre. With a grin, she kissed him on the shoulder and gave him a push out of the closet.

"Hi, Daniella," yelled Pierre from the bedroom doorway. "Um, welcome back, I just worked, woke up."

"Do you want me to come up? Are you sick?" asked a smirking Danni, from the bottom of the stairs.

"No, I'm fine. Don't come up. I'll be right down. And let me carry your suitcase upstairs. I don't want you to hurt your back."

Five minutes later, Pierre carried Danni's suitcase into her bedroom. The bed was stripped and clean sheets were neatly folded and laid out as if in readiness for an expected guest. They both looked around trying not to show curiosity.

"Thank you, Pierre. I think I'll have a shower; then you can tell ..." The doorbell rang, they both started and simultaneously scooted out of the bedroom.

"I'll get it," said Pierre. He ran downstairs so fast that he tripped over his own feet and stumbled down the last three steps. When he opened the door, there, with an impish grin on her face, stood Maggie.

He silently mouthed to her, "How did you get downstairs?" Her eyes glittered with triumph when she ran to Danni and hugged her. "You're back. Welcome home. You have to tell us absolutely everything."

"I'm back," said Danni. "and you're here. So nice of you to come visit with us."

"Yes, I just came to party with Pierre," said Maggie, looking at him and starting to titter. "Celebrating the fact that we got the police to look at the computer files. We sent the files on Siggy Doses to the Crime Stoppers television show too. They won't know where the files came from because we e-mailed them from the Cyber Café."

Pierre could not keep his eyes off Maggie. As she walked into the house, he hurried behind her and pulled on her waistband.

"Stop it," she said, giving him a dirty look.

"You have dirt and dried leaves all over your back," he whispered in her ear.

"Pierre, if you have something to say, say it outloud," said Danni.

"Sorry. Where's Niels?" asked Pierre.

"He just went home," said Danni. "Why did the police only look at the information this morning? They should have found the file about Siggy's illegal activities yesterday."

"Yea, but it's okay. They must have looked at the stuff this morning because, guess what, we also sent a disk to the homicide squad last night. And we taped a note on the disk that read, "IMPORTANT EVIDENCE on A:\DAD\HIP," said Pierre.

"What?" said Danni looking at the two young people in disbelief. She picked up a paperback book and threw it at them. "Out, both of you out. Maggie, don't you have an agency to run. And you, Pierre, I want to talk to you after I unpack and have a shower."

Chapter 22

Saturday, November 1st

Front page - **The Montreal Sun**

PORNO KING ARRESTED

The police have sufficient evidence to charge Siegfried (Siggy) Doses with distribution of child pornography. Doses will appear in court Monday morning. Many people are asking why it took so long to arrest a man who allegedly sold horrific images across five continents via the Internet.

Doses has been known to the police since he started out in the 1960s selling drugs from a fleet of lunch trucks to kids at high schools in Montreal. By the early 1970s he had moved into running a restaurant that was a front for cock fights. In the 1980s he had a drug and condom mail-order business.

Over the past twenty-five years, numerous charges have been laid against Doses but he has been able to weasel out of them. This time the police say they have enough evidence to put him away until a hearse comes to pick him up. Evidence was provided by an anonymous source who called in to an Ontario television program called Crime Stoppers.

Chapter 23

Morning, Monday, November 3rd

Danni looked, with affection, at the teenage boy frying buttermilk pancakes at the gas stove. He turned around and asked, "Are you sure you don't want to eat breakfast?"

"Thanks, no. How was your supper with Niels last night?" asked Danni.

"Fun. We went to Licks and had giant hamburgers and fries. I promised him, I would go back to school this week. Can I stay here for one more night? I have to visit my Mom in that jail hospital they have her in."

"Sure, I kind of like having you around. It stops me thinking too much," said Danni. "I haven't told anyone this but I'm planning to quit my job at the agency and manage the Waddle Trust from somewhere in Switzerland. I'm also putting the townhouse up for sale this week. You're welcome to stay until I sell it."

"Wow, thanks a lot. I should stay in Hamilton to look after the house while my Mom is in the hospital. The gas and hydro bill need to be paid or the pipes might freeze," said Pierre.

"Talk to Niels and Tony Eco, between them they'll help you pay your Mom's bills even if you're not living there," said Danni.

"Yea, Niels sure is cool. He's, like, the best person, I've ever met. He helps me so much and he's so great," said Pierre.

"Don't get carried away with the hero worship thing. He's just brilliant at planning the best and the most profitable way to deal with any given situation. He's a man of contradictions, totally unexplainable. That's probably why we both like him so much. See you later. I'm going to work. I've only been gone ..." Danni stood up and burst into tears as she walked out of the room.

>>>>>

Bea, Danni, Maggie were sitting around the interview table having their morning coffee when Niels came strolling in. In his arms he balanced a stack of small cardboard boxes.

"Wow, six boxes of donuts," said Maggie. "Pig out time."

He put them on the table and said, "These are to celebrate that we, the employees of the Common Sense Employment Agency, are once again together. When did you hire Mrs Fundy as the agency's receptionist? She's out there moving the couch and vacuuming under it."

"Can you keep a secret?" asked Maggie.

Danni and Niels looked at each other, nodded and smiled a conspirator's smile that said, of course, darling, trust us. "Who would we tell that isn't sitting in this room?" asked Niels.

"I found Mrs. Fundy's résumé and it said in 1974, she worked as receptionist at a funeral home."

"So?"

"So, I just asked her if she had cleaned up Fred's body after he died."

"What did she say?"

"She said, 'Yes, of course. Right after Mrs. Prancer interviewed me, I stopped by Fred's office to say hello. He had just expired so I cleaned him up because I knew he would have appreciated it. I wanted to rinse out his clothes but I heard a peculiar voice calling through the door so I hid behind the desk.'"

"Where did she put his clothes?"

"In the garbage can in the subway."

"I had to give her a job," said Maggie. "I figured since she looked after Fred and made sure no one saw him covered in vomit and you-know-what; she deserved a job. It turns out Mrs. Fundy is like, the best receptionist. Almost better than me. To keep her happy,

I let her spray insecticide around the toilets every Friday night. It's okay because the smell is gone by the end of the week-end."

"Excellent management decision, Maggie. So did Tony Eco phone you on Friday?" asked Niels.

"No," replied Maggie.

"Well, as the treasurer of the Waddle Trust, I will give him a call. In the meantime, tell me who you would give a million dollars to; if you had that much to give away?"

"I saw a guy this morning who was so sick that he was walking with bare feet in the snow and it made me so sad because he should be in a safe place. I'd give money to whoever could help him. What about you, Danni?"

"I'd buy a manufacturing plant that produces guns and find something else for the employees to make. I hate guns," said Danni, who looked at Bea, in anticipation of her philanthropic wish.

"A million dollars. I would use the on-going interest on the capital to provide respite care for parents with handicapped adult children," said Bea.

"Wow, heavy," Niels looked at them with an air of exaltation and said to Danni, "Well, Ms Vice President, I assume we will hear from the estate's solicitor soon. I have things to do and people to phone." He stood up and slapped his hands to his side, quite unable to sit still long enough to have another coffee and donut.

Evening, Monday

As she stepped over the threshold of her townhouse, Danni called out, "Pierre, I'm home." Upstairs, she heard heavy footsteps, walking in the hallway, directly above her. "Pierre, it that you? Pierre!"

"Hi," he said, coming down the stairs hitting each step as if his legs belonged to an elephant's. In his right ear was an earphone that was attached to a CD walkman. The wires for the other earphone were wrapped around his ear like a droopy antenna. "Sorry, I didn't hear you come in."

"What's that delicious smell?" asked Danni. When she took off her coat, Pierre acting like a proper English butler took it from her with a flourish.

"Supper. I'm leaving tomorrow morning. I'm going back to Hamilton to finish the semester there then maybe I'll move to Toronto. I talked to the lawyer guy, Tony, this afternoon. I cleaned up the kitchen and made a roast, potatoes and carrots for dinner. We're having pumpkin pie for dessert. It was frozen, but smells really good."

"I'm glad, Pierre," said Danni. Spontaneously, she reached over and gave him a hug. "Can I ask how your visit with your Mom went?"

"Super weird. She apologized to me and got all soppy. After that we talked about how I had to change the filter on the furnace and cut the grass. Then an attendant told me to leave because Mom had to go to lunch."

"Sound like things went pretty well. Anyway, Jeeves, when will dinner be served?"

"Dinner will be served in half an hour, Madam," said the teenager.

"Fine, Madam will have her shower; then join you downstairs for an aperitif. After dining, I must visit the authorities, to inform them of something important." As she went upstairs, Danni turned around and said, "Thank you, Pierre. It was brave to visit your mother. You've helped me make a decision about something I've been avoiding."

When he heard the shower go on, he cranked up his music and started singing. Just as he placed the salt and pepper on the kitchen table, he looked up.

In the doorway stood a man dressed for a day on the golf course. He wore walking shorts and a neat three-button tee-shirt but instead of a golf club, he held a black revolver with a silencer aimed forward.

Pierre stared, not comprehending, but before he could reach up to remove his earphones; a bullet hit his temple, just to the right of centre. Then, a second bullet hit his chest, right through the centre, and his eighteen year old body collapsed onto the clean ceramic floor. Blood erupted from his chest and dribbled out of his mouth. A spasm of awareness and pain engulfed him as seen through his open eyes, then they closed. He was stone dead. Two minutes had elapsed.

>>>>>

With just a towel wrapped around her, Danni looked both ways and scurried out of the bathroom into her bedroom. She dried herself, stepped into clean underwear and wandered into the walk-in closet to decide what to wear. Back in her bedroom, she grabbed a pair of socks out of the dresser drawer.

Just as she started to sit down, out of the corner of her eye, she saw a large human-shaped heap under her bedspread. She poked the bed and said, "Okay Pierre. Grow up. It's not funny to jump out at women in their bedroom."

She yanked the covers down. A scream froze in her throat.

There lay Pierre, eyes dead open. She touched his lifeless cheek. He was no longer. Danni stared at the bullet hole in his temple and pushed the covers further down to look at the matching hole in his chest. A blood stain smeared his shirt and the reverse image of the stain was imprinted on the top sheet.

Danni closed the boy's eyes, then she collapsed onto the floor beside the bed. Her head touched her knees and her arms flopped down. Suddenly she jerked her hand away. She looked under the bed, pulled out a revolver and smelt the barrel.

A few seconds later, she reached up to the bedside table for the phone, but her hand couldn't find it because sitting on the table was a mouldy cardboard box. Danni stood up, looked in the box and gasped. There lying on top of a yellowing christening gown was a windmill crystal wine glass and a *My Little Golden Book.* The title read - *The Dog on Bartholomew Street.* She stoked the book and lifted the warped cardboard cover. The inscription read: 'To Lallie, the best daughter on Bartholomew St., Kisses and hugs, lots of love, Mama.'

Danni put the inscription up to her cheek, kissed it and stated in a horrific whisper, "I'm going to kill you, Siggy."

Chapter 24

Wednesday, November 5th

Front page: **The Montreal Gazette**

MURDER-SUICIDE IN THE SUBURBS

The police have said it appears to be a murder/suicide. Siegfried (Siggy) Doses, who was charged last Friday with a number of offenses including distribution of child pornography, was found fatally shot in the hallway of his Bartholomew Street home. A second male was found, in the kitchen, in a garbage can. He has been identified as Pierre Merlin Tremblay, an 18 year old drop-out from Hamilton, Ontario.

A suicide note found on Siggy Doses' computer also implicates him in the October 7th poisoning death of a Frederick Waddle in Toronto.

Once again real life proves to be more sordid than fiction. The characters in this true story were enmeshed in sex and family violence. Waddle was once married to Siggy Doses' sister-in-law, Sophia. Günther Doses, (deceased), brother of Siggy, murdered Sophia in 1968. Waddle was also once married to Pierre Tremblay's mother, Martine. Martine Tremblay was Fred Waddle's third wife and is presently in the Queen Street Centre for Mental Health undergoing a forensic assessment after assaulting Waddle's stepdaughter, Maggie Nichelton. The police would not comment on whether Siggy Doses was connected to organized crime.

>>>>>

Friday, November 7th

Page 14 - **The Montreal Gazette**

Siegfried Doses, who was well-known to the police in the Montreal area, died Tuesday, November 4, in a murder-suicide. The police have stated that they are accepting suicide as the cause of death and no further investigation will take place. However, the Montreal police will be assisting the Toronto police in their investigation of Doses' connection to the October 7th poisoning of Fred Waddle and the reasons for the murder of Pierre Tremblay. They are trying to ascertain why Tremblay was in Montreal.

A source in the RCMP, who worked closely with both the Montreal police and Interpol on investigating Siggy Doses, indicated that his suicide leaves a bad taste in everyone's mouth. It was too convenient and Siggy didn't have a suicidal personality, the source noted. It didn't give anyone their day in court, especially the officers who have been working for over a year gathering evidence to use against Doses.

Chapter 25

Morning, Saturday, November 8th

In November, warm days were few and far between as if they had used up their autumn allocation in September and October. The sun was bright in the clear sky and a not-quite-freezing breeze blew through the weeping willows and silver maple at Prospect Cemetery.

Once again the employees of the Common Sense Employment Agency were attending a funeral. Tony Eco and Maggie had arranged for poor Pierre to be buried just down the road from the mausoleum.

“I hate funerals,” said Maggie to Danni, as they walked away from the grave site. “I still don't understand why Pierre went to Montreal to see that awful jerk. If the priest wasn't right ahead of us I would say the F-word, fifty times or even worse. I hate Siggy so much that it makes me want to throw-up. Don't you hate him, Danni? I wish he didn't die then he could go to jail and everyone there could beat him up and chop his balls off.”

“Yes, I hated him but he's dead so forget about it. Life goes on. I have something that I want to tell you. I'll be leaving for Switzerland tomorrow morning.”

“You're leaving me too. Thanks a lot.”

“I'll talk to you all the time.”

“Yea, right.”

“There's phones, e-mail. You can come and stay at my house and tour Europe,” said Danni.

“I thought you loved your house and Toronto,” said Maggie. Her face was set in an expression of utter sadness.

“I have to go, love. I can't stay here. You can visit me. I promise.”

Niels who had come up behind them heard the last of their conversation and said, “Danni, you have my permission to administer the Trust from anywhere in the world. But why leave the country?”

“I just have to go,” said Danni, “and I have an invitation to visit Vaud and Lausanne. I don't want to stay here anymore.”

“Me neither,” said Maggie. “Maybe, I'll sell the agency and go back to school to become a cultural anthropologist and travel all over the world. Do you want to buy the agency, Bea? I'll sell it to you real cheap.”

“Let's talk about that some other time. Everyone seems to be moving on to something else. What about you, Niels?” asked Bea.

“I'm going to manage the assets of the Waddle Trust and I think I'll set up a new consulting company. The police are still trying to implicate me in the tax scam that Fred ran under the Victorian Payroll Services so I'm dissolving Victorian Investments because the cops will never believe that ....”

“I ONLY INVESTED THE MONEY, I DIDN'T EMBEZZLE IT,” said Maggie, Bea and Danni together like a chorus of showgirls.

“Ha, Ha,” said Niels.

“It's just a joke, Niels. We have to laugh at something and it may as well be you,” said Bea. “I met you all a short time ago but I feel like we’ll be friends forever.”

Maggie eyes overflowed and she burst out sobbing, “I was more than friends with Pierre and now he's gone.”

“Maggie, you made his last days very happy,” said Danni.

“You don't understand, I loved him.”

“Yes, I do. I heard you upstairs having fun the night I came home from Switzerland.”

“Really, you heard us. Pierre would have died if he knew. He did die but not from making love, right?”

“Maggie, believe me, his final days were happy. The last time I saw him he was singing away to himself. You have to tell me. How, in the world, did you get down to the front door so fast? I was in full view of the door when you were upstairs."

"I went into the spare bedroom, opened the window, took off the screen, and jumped onto the roof of the carport that you share with your neighbour. Then I climbed down the tree in their yard and ran around to your front door and knocked. I bet you were surprised." For the first time that day, she smiled just a bit.

"That's amazing. Did you ever re-lock the window or put the screen back?"

"No, I didn't go back upstairs. Later, when I told Pierre he laughed so much he doubled over and pretended to fall on the floor. That's how I'm going to remember him, laughing," said Maggie.

Suddenly she grabbed Danni's hand because walking directly toward them was Martine Tremblay. Maggie shut her eyes, hoping the bereaved mother would ignore her but the woman walked right up to her. Martine stood in-front of Maggie who opened her eyes and blurted out, "I loved Pierre so I cried all night. I'm so sorry."

"I'm sorry too," said Martine. With that she turned around and started to walk away. Abruptly, she stopped, turned, looked directly at Danni and said, "You're shrinking."

Chapter 26

Sunday, November 16th

It was a week after the funeral and Bea handed Alex a glass of warm mulled wine. He heaved a heavy sigh and complained, "I don't have a choice in this. I've been ordered off the investigation. As of today there is no investigation. The Staff Superintendent said, 'that, with limited resources in the homicide department, your time is better spent on active cases.' The only reason the Waddle investigation is not continuing is because of money. My counterpart in Montreal has been told the same thing. Cease and desist the investigation."

"Maybe it's better we don't know the whole story. Maybe we'll never know everything. Maybe it doesn't matter," said Bea.

"Bullshit, I'm willing to believe that Siggy shot Pierre and himself. The bullets came from the same untraceable gun. But why would he poison Fred? Siggy was a gangster. If he wanted to assassinate Fred he would have hired a hit man or run a truck over him. How many men poison people with pretty pink flowers?"

"When you explain it that way, it does seem pretty far fetched."

"There is a lot the police don't know. However, we do know that Siggy's money disappeared the same week he was arrested. That same week that Danni and Niels were in Zurich. Gee, what a coincidence they were visiting a Swiss bank. But I'm not allowed to investigate. They told me to leave up to the Suits who don't give a damn."

"Didn't you question some of the people involved?" asked Bea, as she poured more wine and looked, with concern, at Alex's frustrated face.

"Couldn't interview your friend, Danni, because she's left the country. Remember, I saw her at Pierre's funeral and told her, we had questions for her. But, lo and behold, now she's gone for good. Do you think that Kyle or the department would let me fly to Switzerland to interview her? Fat chance. And we have no grounds to extradite her. She was probably the last person to see Pierre alive. And Niels, he came in for questioning with two lawyers and an accountant. It was useless."

"Pierre's death was a shock to all of us. Danni wanted a fresh start away from bad memories and after all, the Waddle Trust was discovered in Zurich. I got a postcard from her on Friday. It looks peaceful and beautiful there. What did Niels say at his interview?" asked Bea.

"That he went to Switzerland to freeze the Waddle Trust account because as treasurer of the corporation it was his fiduciary duty to give both verbal and written instructions to the bank. Verbal manure, that's what he shovels. It just sounds intelligent."

"Did you ask him about poor Pierre?"

"Yea. It was bothering Niels too. When we asked him questions about Pierre, the bullshit stopped. He said there was absolutely no reason for Pierre to go to Montreal. He was happy, had a case of puppy-love for Maggie and was planning to go back to school in Hamilton. I'm sure Niels was telling the truth about Pierre," said Alex. "What really pisses me off is that I'm not allowed to investigate how Pierre got to Montreal. He didn't drive because he didn't know how and he didn't take the bus or train. It's almost as if Siggy's death was the final chapter, but the preceding chapter is missing."

Epilogue

Thirty years later, October 7

My dearest Bea and Alex,

Maggie, her husband and two younger children were visiting in August. I won't see my adopted family all together again for the I have terminal liver cancer. Bea, I can see you running out, to the garden, to fetch Alex so you can read the bad news together.

I am leaving my farmhouse to Danny, my namesake. He is continuing his studies at the Technical School of Berne and will stay with me for the last few weeks that I have left here on earth.

You must be surprised to receive such an antiquated form of communication, a hand-written letter. It seems an appropriate vehicle for a confession and words just flow from the ballpoint pen I bought a few months ago.

By the time you read this you have probably been to my funeral. As you know I instructed my executors to pay for your travel and hotel expenses and a little extra to relax at a good spa in St Moritz. You may as well have a vacation while you are in Europe. Especially you, Alex, hope you enjoyed yourself because this letter will make your blood boil.

Thirty years ago today, Fred took his last breath. It was Tuesday morning, October 7th. I loved him very much.

Now for the point of this letter, it is a confession. I accidentally poisoned Fred but I purposely murdered Siggy Doses. Here is my statement written down in blue ink on white paper. The handwriting is irrefutably mine. I own the hands that wrote this letter, that did the deeds, that killed the men.

Not a day passes that I don't think of Fred. He was the kindest man I had ever met. Every day I regret the mishap, the sequence of events that led to his poisoning.

I was mixing a salad on the wooden edge of the deck just as the sun was setting. Fred came up behind me, kissed me on the back of my neck and I dropped the bowl. Its contents tumbled right on top of the two hydrangea bushes that had been pruned that day. In the dusk, I felt around and picked everything up: poisonous seeds and poisonous leaves, lettuce, cucumbers and tomatoes and threw them back into the bowl. I waltzed into the kitchen dumped everything into a colander and ran water over it. After cleaning the deadly mixture, I threw in a can of Spanish olives, crumbled a block of feta cheese and poured garlic olive oil and balsamic vinegar dressing over it. Then I tossed it with a flourish, made a radish into a tiny rose and served it to the man I loved.

I didn't eat any because I'd had a caesar salad for lunch. I remember saying to Fred, 'I'll become a rabbit if I eat lettuce two time in one day.' Fred loved salad. I found out later, that the police found a spilled container with lettuce, tomatoes and hydrangea leaves under the library table which meant Fred took my left-over salad to the office the next morning. He must have eaten it with his donuts for breakfast.

Why didn't I confess? It was inadvertent, unintentional, truly accidental. Panic attacks were hitting me every time the police questioned me and I froze inside. After all these years even now just writing about being questioned makes me anxious.

On with the story, I only found out how Fred had been poisoned when I came back from Montreal. It took me a long, long time to figure out that I had done it.

That Detective Kyle Bottleman - he was the biggest danger. If I had spoken to him, I would have thrown myself into his emphatic arms and told him the truth. But never again did he sit down across from me or look at me with those piercing blue Highland eyes so he never made me feel the necessity to confess. Give him this letter, tell him justice was done. Thirty years of loneliness and remorse were my daily punishment.

That is the end of confession one.

Confession two is more complicated but causes me no distress. I didn't and don't feel even an iota or a smidgen of remorse for slaying Siggy Doses. When I assassinated him, I was completely aware of my actions. It was a virtuous revenge for:

1. my mother,
2. dear sweet Pierre who never had a chance to grow up,
3. vulnerable children everywhere, and
4. me.

It was a cathartic experience. I felt like David slaying Goliath. The nightmares about my mother's murder stopped after Siggy, the devil, was eliminated. You knew about the child pornography and drugs he sold but what you don't know is that he killed Pierre in my sanctuary, my house.

I found Pierre with a bullet hole in the centre of his innocent forehead and another in the centre of his pubescent, almost hairless chest. He didn't have a chance, he was Siggy's message to me. Left bleeding in my bed.

So do you know what I did?

I made a cup of tea, cleaned the blood from the kitchen floor and planned my retaliation. I didn't call Niels because he didn't deserve the guilt.

It was just common sense - death-neutral. Tit for tat, that is how I saw it. If Fred and Pierre couldn't be alive then why should that bastard, Siggy, walk the earth.

Well, enough justification, I should continue with the confession.

How? I pulled two black plastic garbage bags over Pierre's body, one over his feet and one over his head, then I tied a belt around his waist. I tried to lift him up but he was too heavy so I fetched my outdoor garbage can and slid Pierre, feet first, into it. Very practical those heavy duty garbage cans. The one I owned was made of sturdy plastic with two handles, two wheels, and a snap-lock lid.

I rolled him down the hallway, bumped the garbage can down the stairs and out to the back of my car. Then I heaved it up with Superman-like strength into the trunk and with bungee cords held the lid in place. It's true what they say about absolute desperation giving a person a surge of adrenaline.

I was compelled.

I drove all night to Montreal.

Arrived just after two in the morning so I checked into a roadside motel.

When the cathedral bells rang at eight o'clock that morning, I watched his skinny wife stroll to the bus stop. A short time later, the children, of Bartholomew Street, left for school and the few remaining adults drove off to work or shopping. When the street was quiet, I backed the car into the driveway.

Ding, dong went the door bell. Siggy answered it. His eyes narrowed with rage when he saw me standing on his doorstep. I had remembered that the RCMP might have a listening device in Siggy' house so I handed him a note. It read, 'Help me, I found Pierre dead so I brought him here.' Then I pretended to faint so he instinctively stepped forward to catch me. But luckily, I had the assassin's gun behind my back and the first shot hit him in the crotch.

He folded over like a peanut butter sandwich, a perfect example of poetic justice and toppled over onto his side. When Siggy tried to